Faith smiled softly and placed her hands flat on the table. Dylan was blown away when he felt himself moving, rising slowly in the air until he was lying flat on his back ten feet over the table.

"Impressive," Dylan said. But then Faith felt a sharp pain in the side of her neck, and suddenly Dylan was free-falling. He should have landed on the table, sending the balls and the blocks and the cups flying everywhere. But instead he only fell until he was an inch away from landing, then hovered in the air, turned over, and sat himself back down.

"You might not be ready for something as heavy as me," he said. "I've got a huge head."

PATRICK CARMAN

PULSE

KATHERINE TEGEN BOOKS
An Imprint of HarperCollins Publishers

Katherine Tegen Books is an imprint of HarperCollins Publishers.

Pulse
Copyright © 2013 by Patrick Carman
www.epicreads.com

Library of Congress Cataloging-in-Publication Data
Carman, Patrick.
Pulse / Patrick Carman. — 1st ed.
    p.   cm.
Summary: In the year 2051, when most Americans live in one of two
gigantic, modern States, Faith Daniels, part of a dwindling group that
lives between, learns that she has unusual abilities that could help when
the inevitable war begins.
ISBN 978-0-06-208577-1 (pbk.)
[1. Science fiction. 2. Psychic ability—Fiction. 3. Technology—
Fiction. 4. High schools—Fiction. 5. Schools—Fiction.] I. Title.
PZ7.C21694Pul 2013   2012026745
[Fic]—dc23

Typography by Joel Tippie
19 20   PC/LSCH   10 9 8 7 6 5 4
❖
First paperback edition, 2014

People will give up their freedom
for safety from a certain kind of threat.
—A.Q.

Contents

part one

OLD
PARK
HILL

Chapter 1

Here We Are

Faith Daniels was sleeping soundly when several things in her room began to move. She was a tall girl with long limbs that extended beyond the bed into the cool air of her bedroom. The first object to move was her blanket; it slowly covered her foot, which had wriggled its way free in the night. A dark hallway lay beyond her open door, and though no one was there, the door swung slowly closed. It made a soft sound, and Faith stirred but did not wake. A dark shadow fell over the bed, blocking the faint moonlight through the window.

On her nightstand, Faith's standard-issue Tablet was thin, with a glossy surface the size of a sheet of typing paper. As she slept, its sleek form rose quietly up in the air and drifted over her body. It stopped abruptly over her face, then its movements became more jarring—sharp tilts back and forth—as it descended toward the sleeping girl, as if it were an animal sizing her up. Faith's soft breath left a foggy mark on the glass.

And still she did not stir.

The Tablet flew with violent, lightning speed around the room. It stopped inches from the bedroom window, rotated, and faced the darkness outside. The screen turned on, and Faith Daniels kicked her foot free of the covers. She was not a girl who liked warm toes in the dead of night.

Faith had a password like everyone else, but whatever ghostly presence had made the Tablet move also had the power to unlock its contents. For the next hour something searched the Tablet. It looked at the songs Faith had chosen, the stories, the TV shows and movies, the words she'd written.

At 2:11 a.m. the Tablet turned off.

It returned to its home at the side of Faith's bed.

The door to her room opened once more, just a little.

The blankets were left alone.

There was movement outside the window, quiet and careful.

A phantom or something else had found what it had come for and was gone in a flash.

On the first day of school at Old Park Hill, Faith walked past what was once an open-air mall. She turned in toward the rubble and made her way through a modern ruin of concrete and exposed rebar. It was not a place Faith had ever known as a destination for buying things. All her purchases were made on her Tablet, which sat snuggly in her back pocket. She pulled it out and held it by its bottom right corner and its top left corner with her thumbs and fingers. Applying slight pressure, she heard a familiar *snap* and pulled the Tablet on opposing ends, feeling it stretch like taffy. The Tablet snapped again, a much larger size now, rigid again and ready for some real input. Faith tapped away as she stood there, reading through a message from her mom, looking at her schedule for the day, and sending out a note to a friend. When she had purchased several shows she wanted to consume as she navigated her day, she snapped the Tablet back to its smaller size and returned it to her pocket.

For Faith, the very idea of shopping was contained in the digital world, where everything felt like the air she breathed: at once her own and everyone else's, too. Songs, movies, shows, books—these were the things she paid for; *this* was shopping. These things were in her cloud of knowing. And there were jeans and tight T-shirts and makeup, just as there had always been—but real items were very expensive, and buying them was rare.

There were, it seemed to Faith, empty spaces everywhere, made emptier still by what they were filled *with*: a shameful regret; the scorching, un-American scent of failure. People had simply started moving away, most of them to one of the two States, and they weren't coming back. This, Faith had long ago decided, suited her just fine. There was a striking aloneness in the leftover city, a vast openness that agreed with her personality. She liked the idea of being one of a few, not one of too many. And yet it did feel haunted at times, like the soul of something invisible was in the air all around her. Like something was trying to fill the empty space.

There were many other reasons for the fallen city around her, reasons adults talked about all the time that were not interesting to Faith. She had no nostalgia for a time before when the world was different, for she had no memory of those things. This was her time, her world; and for all its desolation, Faith Daniels loved it. She was not interested in how the world had come to be as it was or when it had changed. She was not interested in moving to one of the States, where a hundred million people lived on top of one another. She was interested in her Tablet, her music, her art, her height. Boys.

Faith liked to sit on the steps of what was once an Old Navy, as she did now, and buy a song. Songs were cheap; a single Coin paid for dozens of them. Faith had thousands of songs already. They made her feel things, and feeling was something she liked very much. And it always felt somehow right to make her purchases as she sat in the shadow of retail wreckage all around her. She had sat in the very same spot fifteen days before and purchased something expensive, something she'd saved a lot of Coin for. It was the shipping that cleaned her out. The distance between her and the nearest State, where what she wanted was manufactured, was so great, it was difficult to connect.

Ninety-six Coin for the jeans she was wearing, the jeans that were long enough for her exceptionally long legs.

When she'd purchased her song and it was playing in her ears, Faith stood in her fifteen-day-old jeans and walked past a vacant store—Macy's, the sign said—then turned sharply and walked out of the empty parking lot. Her old school, a mile in the opposite direction, had closed a month earlier as enrollment slipped below a hundred. She'd moved schools three times already in the past two years, so she was used to it; but this was the first time she'd been part of a merge between two dying schools so close to each other. Faith had also relocated twice from cities farther away, where the emptiness had pushed her family out. Her parents always stayed where they were as long as they could, but the end result was the same: they moved closer to the Western State, its shadow growing larger.

She forced herself to forget even the names of dead schools, the friends she'd lost, the feeling of not knowing who would be missing from one day to the next. This was her reality: things changed, people vanished, everything got smaller and emptier. And one day, when no one else remained, she, too, would be forced to join the State; and her way of life would come to a close. The end was near enough; she could almost reach out and touch it. This created in her not sadness, but a reckless sense of having to fit very much inside of a little time.

She could make out the school now, up on the hill, staring down at her through an early-morning mist that clung to the trees. She felt the tightness of her jeans and smiled at the prospect of more, not fewer, boys, because falling in love was high on her list of things having to get done in the space of a little time.

"When are we getting that car again? This has *got* to stop."

Liz Brinn was coming down the sidewalk, alternately staring at Faith and at her Tablet, which was in its pocket size. She held it in one hand, tapping out a message on the small screen with her thumb.

"Unless you've got about a million Coin hidden in your Tablet, I think we're on foot for the rest of our lives," Faith said. "It's not so bad. Beautiful day. And you should look up when you're walking."

Liz, who was a full head shorter than Faith, looked up from her Tablet and glanced behind her. "It was a long way over here, longer than the last place we went to school."

"Maybe you should get a bike," Faith suggested. Liz and Faith had been inseparable ever since Liz's boyfriend, Noah, had vanished into the Western State. His departure devastated Liz, left her confused and fragile. After Noah it was just the two of them—Faith and Liz—holding on to each other and not letting go. As they watched more and more people leave, they'd renewed a promise: *We see this through until the end, and we don't let anyone else in. Too risky, too painful. Better to gut it out and hold on to each other.* Looking at Liz, there in front of a new school full of people who would soon be leaving, Faith wondered if the day would come when she'd find herself without her only friend.

"You and me to the end, like we talked about," Liz

said, but then she smiled a sly smile and raised her dark eyebrows. "Maybe we'll find you a short-term boyfriend, just for fun."

Faith felt a rush of anticipation. She'd recently been obsessing over the idea of a boyfriend, something that had eluded her for a little too long. She was sure this was because she was tall and lanky like a stork, and no boy wanted to date a girl taller than he was. There was also the unfortunate matter of slim pickings: so few boys tall enough to count.

Liz leaned back and looked at Faith's butt.

"Nice jeans, that's going to help. Got any Coin left or did they clean you out?"

"Cleaned me out," Faith admitted.

"It was worth it," Liz said, and then she slapped Faith on the butt and laughed loudly enough to draw the attention of the principal, who was standing at the main door glad-handing new students as they went inside. Faith and Liz stopped in front of the sprawling high school campus. It had been built in 1975, which made it seventy-six years old, but it didn't look a day under a hundred. There was a billboard at the top of a paint-chipped white pole with a message:

WELCOME, NEW STUDENTS.
WE'RE GLAD YOU'RE HERE.

Liz looked at the billboard, shaking her head. "I bet they are."

They waved weakly as a few of the students from their old school entered the main building. The other students looked shell-shocked at the prospect of starting at a new school, including the fact that it would involve shaking the cold, clammy hand of the principal. When Faith arrived at the door, she got her first look at Mr. Reichert and was immediately concerned. His skin had the pale texture of someone who had been ravaged by acne as a teenager. He cut his own hair or had hired a lawn maintenance supervisor to do it for him. It sat like a black dome over his egg-shaped head, straight and speckled with dandruff. He smiled hugely with the bleached white teeth he was clearly proud of showing.

"Welcome, girls, we're glad you're here," he said. He held the door open with his dandruff-speckled shoulder as he reached out his hand. Liz looked at Faith like she'd just smelled a glass of possibly sour milk. Faith nodded and smiled, then brushed past Mr. Reichert without saying anything or touching his clammy hand.

"Stay to the right, down the hall," he said, flashing that smile again. "You'll find your way. And don't go past any of the barriers; some places are closed."

Liz slid through the doorway before Mr. Reichert could hold out his hand, and the two girls were mercifully inside their new school. It was quieter than Faith had hoped, soft echoes from distant places bouncing off the long corridors heading off in three directions.

"Here we are," said Faith, suddenly unsure about the tightness of her jeans and the specter of a new school.

"Yeah," said Liz nervously. "Here we are."

Old Park Hill was constructed and managed under the assumption that 2,000 students would pack its halls on a normal day. And there was a time when this had been true. Back in the 2010s the school had even been *over*populated for a while. But now the student body had dwindled to 80 students, down from 140 the year before. Faith's previous school had been getting even smaller; at last count there had been 53. Old Park Hill, being the slightly less run down of the two, was now the proud host to all 133 students from both schools.

As Faith parted ways with Liz and began the search for her first classroom, she became aware of the almost complete lack of adult supervision. Budgets being what they were—nearly zero according to some estimates— the student-teacher-administrator ratio had gotten even worse. When there had been 2,000 students, there had been about 75 teachers. Now there were only 133 students, and a couple of teachers would have to suffice.

And they'd need to double as the principal and vice principal.

One hundred and thirty-three students.

Two staff.

And one overworked janitor.

That was what high school was like at Old Park Hill in the year 2051.

Faith glanced down the hallway, searching for help finding her class, and saw a redheaded girl surrounded by guys. She had the white complexion of a fish's underbelly, which made her green eyes look like shiny marbles about to pop out of her head. Faith knew this girl, Amy, from her old school. Faith wondered what the guys always saw in Amy; it must have been her curvy figure that attracted them.

"Hey, Amy!" Faith yelled down a long, nearly empty corridor. Amy turned at the sound of her name, her red hair moving softly like flames in a campfire. "Help me find English 300, will you?" None of the guys Amy was standing with had gone to Faith's old school, but Amy had never been one to waste any time building a coalition of boys starving for her attention. The moment Amy saw Faith coming, she took the arm of one of them and dragged him into a classroom.

"Such a *tool*," Faith whispered. Amy was the other person besides Liz who remained in Faith's life from the old days. She still played a lot of junior high drama games, and when it came to guys, Amy was a terror.

Faith showed up late to her first class with Miss Newhouse, who made up one half of the teaching staff. Miss Newhouse hardly paid attention to anyone in the room, and this was the other reason why so few teachers were present at Old Park Hill.

They weren't really needed.

It was often hard for Faith to imagine it any other way, so completely did her Tablet assume the role of teacher, counselor, and truant officer. The teachers didn't teach. They babysat. The Tablet did all the real work. Lectures were streamed in from the best teachers in each of the two States, who were given multimillion-dollar contracts and fancy cars and big houses for being not only experts in their field, but outrageously talented at teaching the material they knew. The local teachers at Old Park Hill wouldn't even administer tests. They were there to make sure no one got hurt, contain the drug use, stop fights from breaking out, and keep the lights on.

Faith sat down at her desk and reached for her Tablet. "Who do you have for English lit?" said a voice behind her. "I've got Rollins. Oh, my God, he's insane. *So* good. If he weren't teaching Shakespeare, he'd be a comic genius, no joke. Who do you have again?"

Faith turned around in her seat and saw a short, geeky-looking kid. "I haven't said," Faith whispered, and then turned back around as her own lecture started (not Rollins, but Buford, who was also amazing, but widely known as "not funny"). She put on her headphones and began listening while a red keypad was projected onto the flat surface of the desk in front of her. She was able to take notes on the lightboard and insert them on a time line running along the side of the lecture, where she would also be able to reference the material later. This was how she took quizzes and tests as well, and asked questions when she needed to. Teachers had between a thousand and ten thousand aides, depending on how many students were taking their classes. If a student had a question, he could type it in twenty-four hours a day and usually get an answer within five minutes. The Tablet delivered study halls, test prep units, and instantaneous feedback on homework. The only thing it didn't provide was microwavable snacks, and there was a rumor floating around that a future version would even do that.

A message appeared along the bottom of Faith's screen, which surprised her. Usually when a lecture began, her Tablet automatically locked out all incoming messages.

I see you got Buford. He's pretty good. Rollins is
better. What's your name again?

Faith looked around the classroom, filled with
thirty other students. Another message appeared on her
screen.

Behind you :)

Faith slowly turned around and smiled painfully.
Then she turned back to her Tablet, rolling her eyes
as soon as she could without being seen by the crown
prince of dorks.

Perfect, Faith thought as she listened to Buford dis-
sect the meaning of *Henry the Fifth. I'm here ten minutes,
and I pick up a stalker. And a hacker.*

Faith typed out a terse message and tapped SEND.

How did you activate messaging during a
lecture? And I'm busy.

There was a pause of about four seconds.

Easy! There's a back door in version 25.
It takes about an hour to code for each Tablet,

but once you're in, you can com with anyone
during lectures. It's a two-way door when I open
it. Cool, right? Didn't you hear about it?

No, Faith thought, *I don't troll the online nerd threads.*
Faith tried to listen to Buford until another message
scrolled across her screen.

I'm Hawk. And you are?

Faith ignored Hawk and went back to work, tapping out notations and tagging them to the screen with
her finger. She tapped the corner of the screen on the
Tablet, and a menu appeared, from which she chose a
drawing stylus. A square of soft light appeared on her
desk next to the lightboard, and she began drawing the
outline of a face. She was very good at faces and usually
only needed to get a really good look at people once in
order to draw them.

She looked around the room for a subject, taking in
the new students, and her eyes landed on a guy in the
back row. He wore skater shoes, skinny jeans, and a
tight V-neck T-shirt. His hair was thick and black, and
to her surprise, he was writing. With a pen. In a note-
book. He seemed to be ignoring his Tablet.

She sent a message to Hawk and began drawing with her finger.

Who's the caveman in the back row?

A moment later, Hawk answered.

Dylan Gilmore. He doesn't talk too much.
At least not to me. Also, he's an a-hole.

Faith stole one more glance. The profile of his face and upper body revealed a strong chin and muscular arms. *Please be tall,* Faith caught herself thinking. Whatever he was working on, he was really into it. And his head was moving up and down. It looked to her like he was listening to music, not to a lecture. But that wasn't possible. The Tablet wouldn't let him do that during a lecture.

There were three more messages from Hawk before the lecture came to an end. When it did, Faith turned in her chair.

"Please don't do that while I'm in the middle of a class. Buford is tough, and Shakespeare is confusing."

"No problem, I can chill. *Suuuuper*chill. What was your name again?"

Faith rolled her eyes and got up to leave, but then she thought better of the idea and turned back. She could have worse things than a friend who was really bright and knew how to hack into a Tablet.

"It's Faith. And no more messages during class, okay?"

"Totally, yeah. Got it. Faith."

It dawned on her then that Hawk was probably a lot younger than she was. They were glomming the classes together more and more, because there didn't seem to be a good reason not to. Faith was a junior, and by the looks of this little guy, he was probably a freshman.

"How old are you?" Faith asked as they walked out of the classroom.

"Seventeen. Okay sixteen. I mean, I'll be sixteen in practically no time."

There was a long pause in which Hawk decided she was going to find out soon enough.

"I'm thirteen."

"Are you sure you're not nine? You look like you're nine."

"Ouch," Hawk said, holding his heart. "That one stung."

Faith punched him on the arm. A low punch was required to miss the side of his head.

"Just kidding. You look at least eleven."

"Really? Thanks!"

They laughed as they entered the corridor and looked both ways. Faith could imagine what it had been like when there were 2,000 students and 75 teachers. The energy must have been amazing. As it was, the place felt like a morgue. A few bodies moving between doors, a very low hum of voices.

"I wonder how long they'll keep this place open," Faith asked.

"Hard to say," Hawk answered, making a note on his Tablet, which he had snapped to small and held in his delicate palm. "But I'll see what I can find out."

They were about to part when two tall figures arrived, entering the corridor from the far end of the building. At first Faith only saw their silhouettes against a bright window behind them. There was a confidence in these walking shadows that seemed out of place at Old Park Hill. As they came closer, Faith realized it was a guy and a girl, and that they were at least her own age.

"Who . . . ," Faith started to ask, but Hawk was already on it. "Wade and Clara Quinn," Hawk said, leaning in a little close to catch the scent of Faith's perfume while he thought she was distracted. "Believe it or not, they're in the Field Games, representing the outside. They're scary smart, too. Also a-holes."

Faith was starting to think Hawk thought everyone at Old Park Hill was an a-hole. But she didn't mention it, because Wade Quinn was staring at her. His sister had peeled off, but Wade's eyes were locked on Faith. It was like there was no one else in the world. The closer he got, the better looking he was, until he was standing right next to her and she was doing something she rarely ever did. Faith Daniels, five feet eleven, was looking *way* up at a boy.

"How tall are you?" she said without even thinking. It just tumbled out of her mouth unexpectedly.

Wade smiled, blond hair falling down around blue eyes.

"Tall enough," he said. "I'm Wade."

"Hey, Wade. How's it going?" Hawk asked.

Wade didn't look at Hawk or answer his question, but he nodded at him, never taking his eyes off Faith. They were having a *moment*, both of them instantly attracted to each other. Their eyes kept making contact, then dashing quickly to the floor or a locker. Wade loved tall girls, the taller the better, and he liked the way Faith's hair fell over one bright eye like she was toying with him. For Faith, it was Wade's light-blue eyes and the curl of his lips. She could imagine staring into that face for hours just for the pleasure of looking at it.

"Cool," said Hawk, like he and Wade were having a conversation they clearly were not having. "I'm good. I'm really good. This is Faith. She's new."

Wade's sister, the other half of the Twins, arrived beside him. She was almost as tall as he was, and gorgeous. She had surprisingly short hair that focused gawkers on her athletic, chiseled face. And her long, lean body offered plenty of curves, too.

"Holy shit, you're tall," said Faith. It was rare for her to encounter a girl this much taller than she was. Clara Quinn had to be six feet two.

"Thank you," Clara said, studying Faith from top to bottom. "I think."

She nudged Wade on the shoulder to get him moving, and the two of them continued down the nearly empty corridor. Wade turned back.

"Nice pants."

And then he was gone around a corner.

Hawk glanced behind Faith, checking out the pants.

"Those are definitely nice. Did you order them from the Western State? I can get things a lot cheaper from the Eastern State. I know; it doesn't make any sense, right? Which is why it makes sense."

"Yeah, okay, I'll see you later then."

Faith started walking away in a love-crush daze,

searching for her next class, and Hawk called after her.

"Be careful, Faith. The Twins are pretty intense. Better to stay off their radar."

But it was too late for Faith Daniels.

She'd only been at Old Park Hill for two hours, and she'd already fallen under Wade Quinn's spell.

Chapter 2

Grade School Break-in

Faith lived in Bridgeport Commons, which at one time had been an upscale place to raise a family. There were hundreds of houses and complexes surrounding a man-made lake in the middle, and Faith lived in one of the narrow, three-story units at the edge of a tree-lined side-walk. The development included paths for running and walking, a pool, and even a grade school at the far end where all the little kids could get an education safely without venturing very far into the world outside. If she walked out of Bridgeport Commons and took a left, the mall where Faith had sat and purchased a song was only ten minutes away.

By the time Faith was born, Bridgeport Commons had been mostly vacated. A man lived alone at the end of the block, but otherwise the twelve-unit building Faith called home was empty. She didn't know for sure, because she hadn't grown up there, but she had a sense that the neighborhood had once been home to a thousand or more people. Now there were maybe a dozen, scattered around the lake, unwilling to move to the Western State until they were forced inside for good. The ones who remained were mostly cleanup crew, preparing new space for the ever-expanding Western State. But for the most part, the people who remained outside the Western State did so at their own peril. They were off grid, on their own, living day-to-day on what they could find. Food was scarce, and medical services were nonexistent. The idea was not to force people into the States, but to wear them down. Sooner or later almost everyone gave up, and then the State system would swoop in and take anyone who wanted right into the comforting arms of modern living.

The lake had been taken over by about a million weird-looking black birds with oversized web feet and white beaks. They were like prehistoric animals, slow and not very smart, barely able to fly. Once when Faith was six, she'd watched as a black car drove into the neighborhood and one of the birds had run, flapping its lame wings, across the street. The bird was two feet off the ground and moving fast when the car hit it with its grille. Faith never forgot the sound it made, a terrible *thunk*, and the way the bird flopped forward in slow motion, landing on the pavement like a bag of sand. She had been surprised to see the car keep going around the corner and out of sight.

Faith was thinking of the strange, dead bird as she walked along the lakefront with Liz, the two of them holding hands as they sometimes did. It was Liz who had first taken Faith's hand on one of their walks at night, and it had felt tingly and dangerous that first time. Faith didn't know for certain why they kept doing it, but she thought it was because they were both afraid. Afraid of being alone, of leaving, of waking up one day and finding that the hand they were reaching out for was no longer there. And also, there didn't seem to be any reason not to hold hands. No one was watching. No one knew. Faith wished that wasn't true, but it was.

"It feels empty tonight," Liz said. "More so than usual."

Faith knew Liz was nervous. She would talk about Noah endlessly, but it terrified her to think that Faith might find someone, might fall away from her and never return. She pulled Liz closer, bumping shoulders, and Liz smiled up at her.

"I don't think he likes me. Why would he?" Faith asked. A week had passed, and while Hawk had become like a shadow stuck to her side, Wade Quinn had been elusive.

"Of course he likes you," Liz said, pulling playfully on Faith's hand. "You're skinny and tall and blond, and you've got some boobs on you. He's just nervous is all."

"I'm glad you're not being superficial about this," said Faith sarcastically. "I wouldn't want him liking me for my brain."

"He's sixteen. I'm pretty sure he's not thinking about your brain."

Faith shrugged it off, but she smiled, too. She had seen Wade in the halls and had even caught him look-ing at her. And he'd messaged her a totally lame but very cute drawing of a flower after seeing her wear a yellow T-shirt with a single white daisy on the front, a daisy Faith had painted onto the shirt herself. There had been a short series of Tablet messages during the week. She hadn't said anything to Liz about the mes-sages, and as they came to the edge of the lake where the grade school playground sat, she thought of what they'd said.

Wade: Where do I land on a scale of 1 to 10?

Faith: A solid 8, 2 if you're drawing daisies. What about me?

Wade: **Eleven.**

It had gone quiet after that, and she wasn't about to turbo anything. Better to wait him out than to dive in and scare him off.

Liz let go of Faith's hand when she saw the swings, and they both started running. Only one swing was attached on both sides, and they had long made a game of racing as soon as their feet left the path and touched the grass. The first one there rode, the second one pushed. They were evenly matched and often arrived together, each of them grabbing a chain on either side of the swing and arguing over who would swing and who would not.

"You go ahead," Liz offered, even though she'd arrived first. "I feel like pushing tonight."

Faith climbed aboard, leaning back and staring into the starry night. Liz put one hand on each side of Faith's hips and pulled Faith close, then slowly pushed her away and let go, her hands empty in the cool evening air.

"How much longer do you think we can stay out here?" Liz asked, knowing it was a touchy subject.

"I don't know. A long time, I think."

Faith's long hair bunched up around her face as she swung back and felt Liz's hands on her back, pushing her away.

"I'm not so sure," Liz said. She looked off into the darkness in the direction of the Western State, which waited for them a hundred miles away.

If Liz could have seen Faith's expression, she would have known that Faith didn't want to talk about leaving. She never wanted to talk about leaving. The Western State would let them stay as long as they wanted. But it wouldn't do anything to help anyone on the outside. Help from the States had long since vanished.

"Do you ever wonder what it would be like if we went there?" Liz asked.

"It's not up to us. If our parents want to go, we're going. But I don't think they'll want to leave for a long time."

Faith's Tablet buzzed in her back pocket, and she took it out, holding on to the chain with one hand while glancing at a familiar message from her mom.

Don't stay out too late;
you know how your dad gets.

Faith was not close to her parents; none of the kids who remained were. They mostly interacted with their parents through their Tablets—little messages sent back and forth—and stayed to themselves. Faith didn't know if this was how it had always been; but it was what she knew, and it felt normal.

"Did you see the posting today?" Liz asked, stopping the swing.

"Yeah, I saw it. There's no way it can be that good." They started walking again, moving toward the grade school.

Postings were video messages that arrived on all the Tablets carried by people outside the States. For Faith and Liz, their messages came from the Western State, because they lived in the western half of the country. It was a little bit like getting a note from heaven; and every time you got one, there was another glorious feature, and more friends and family were already there having the time of their lives while you were stuck on a farm in Oklahoma watching the corn grow.

"But what if it is?" Liz asked. She pulled out her Tablet as she walked, which Faith wished she wouldn't do. "What if they really do have all the things they say they do? Sometimes it feels like our parents are just plain stupid."

Faith didn't answer, because she didn't agree and she didn't want to get into an argument. The posting had talked about new features, features you couldn't get unless you went there. That's what the postings were always about. Never about anything wrong with the State, only about how amazing it was. Mostly the State announced things like zero unemployment; zero crime; sources of synthetic-food, which tasted better than anything grown next to a forgotten lake full of brainless, flightless birds; the massive entertainment domes with a million things to do; the sporting events; the clean water and endless opportunities; everyone living to a hundred, some to one fifty.

"I don't know; it always sounds so final, like heaven, but in a bad way," Faith said.

Liz laughed.

"Have a little faith, Faith. Maybe it is like heaven, and we're the last of the unlucky, idiot holdouts."

"Maybe," Faith muttered. She was going to say something else, but she came up short. She could hear movement off to her left in the darkness that sounded larger than a flightless bird.

"Who's there?" Liz yelled, and she grabbed Faith's hand again. Liz thought about running, because the one thing about the outside that really bothered her, the thing that always made her think twice about the idea of going to the State, was the Drifters. She'd never seen them, but she'd heard about them. Bands of people, like gypsies, rolling through empty spaces, picking up strays.

"Maybe we should go back to your place and lock the door," said Liz. "We could listen to some music, watch some shows."

"We've got weapons!" Faith yelled into the night. "Better move along, find someplace else to go. Beat it!"

There was movement again, and Liz practically jumped into Faith's arms as she dropped her Tablet in the grass. A figure began moving toward them, hunching low, the glow of a Tablet leading the way.

"Run!" Liz yelled, leaving her Tablet in the grass as she started pulling Faith back toward the lake.

"Hey, Faith, it's me," a small, nervous voice said.

When Faith heard the voice, she realized that it wasn't an adult who was hunching low—it was just a short boy. "Hawk?"

"Yeah, totally. It's just me! Nothing to worry about. You're fine."

"You little urchin!" Liz said. "You scared me half to death!"

Hawk crouched down and picked up the abandoned Tablet, now in its large configuration, and held it out like a peace offering. Liz finally let go of Faith's hand and grabbed her Tablet, holding it over her head, ready to clobber Hawk.

"Liz, don't—he's harmless. Just calm down."

"You two a thing or what?" Hawk asked.

"What? Are you insane?!" Faith yelled. She glanced at Liz, who looked doe-eyed and confused but didn't say anything.

"Whew! Okay, cool," Hawk said. "You guys are just hand-holders. I get it; that's cool."

Hawk reached over and took Faith's hand, gawking like an idiot; and Faith was so dumbstruck that she just stood there, shaking her head at Liz.

"Harmless. He's like a frog."

Faith had to use her other hand to remove Hawk's grip of steel.

"What are you doing out here, Hawk? How did you even know where we were?"

"Easy! Once we're connected I can tap into your location. You'd have to leave your Tablet at home in order to lose me, and who does that? Nobody! Pretty cool, right? If you're in trouble, I'll know how to find you. Like if you fall into the lake."

Hawk pointed out into the darkness, the glow of light from his Tablet illuminating his nervous expression. "Sorry, you guys. Really, I messed up."

He looked like an injured puppy with his mop of brown hair, and both girls lost any interest in beating him up or chasing him off.

"Do me a favor and stop hacking into my stuff, will you?" Faith asked.

"But what if you're in trouble?" Hawk asked. "And how will I get you more jeans for three Coin?"

Liz stepped up and shoved Hawk hard on the

shoulder. "No way."

Hawk shoved Liz right back, nearly hitting her in the chest. "Yes way!"

"Watch the hand placement, Romeo," Liz said. "And can you get me three-Coin jeans?"

"Sure I can, but you'll have to let me hack into your Tablet first. And bonus! We can chat during lectures."

"You're right; he's harmless," Liz said to Faith. "And weird."

Faith wanted to get to their destination and started backpedaling. She smiled as she thought of the clothes and makeup Hawk was probably going to be able to get for her for next to nothing.

"Come on, Liz, let's let Hawk in on our little secret. It's the least we can do."

Liz started walking, and Hawk fell in line with her, measuring her height against his own and smelling the air around her head when she wasn't looking.

"What are you, like, ten?" Liz asked.

"Thirteen," Hawk said. "I'm small for my age. But my brain is huge."

"I bet."

They walked toward the grade school, laughing and listening as Hawk explained in complicated, incoherent detail how he had hacked into the State shopping system and gotten the pants massively discounted and shipped for free.

Even if Hawk had not been filling the air with his chirpy voice, none of them would have heard the figure dressed in black moving along the trees nearby, taking in every word.

Chapter 3

Great Story, Bro. Tell It Again.

The grade school at Bridgeport Commons had been closed for many years. The building was crawling with green ivy that covered the walls, the windows, the doors, and the roof with a thick carpet of tangled leaves. Faith and Liz went to the grade school because it was the kind of place the States didn't have: a secret place with treasures inside. On the darkest side of the school there was a broken window covered with plywood. They'd long since pulled away the thick ivy and used a hammer to pry a small, square piece of wood away from the opening. They crawled through and, once inside, made their way through the empty cafeteria.

"Now we go it alone," Faith said, glancing at Hawk, who looked shattered at the idea of being left behind by the two older girls.

"Not you, silly," Liz said, taking hold of his Tablet and trying to slide it free from his hand. He'd snapped it into its small size, using its screen as a flashlight. "We don't take our Tablets any farther than this. It sort of ruins the experience."

For Hawk, the idea of being without his Tablet even for a few seconds went beyond his reasoning.

"I can't go anywhere without my Tablet. I don't do that."

"It's not alive," Liz coaxed, gently tugging on the edge of the gleaming instrument. "It's not like a pet or a brother or a girl. It's just a Tablet. You can live without it for a little while."

Hawk looked at the Tablet and the girl, but he was not convinced. He pulled the Tablet closer, and to his astonishment, the girl came with it. She was not letting go. Liz leaned down, her lips inches from Hawk's, and he could smell her grape bubblegum breath.

"Give me the Tablet," Liz whispered, and Hawk nearly fainted. "Come on, you can do it. Let it go."

Faith was having a hard time keeping a straight face and turned away, taking her Tablet out of her pocket and setting it on a cafeteria table with Liz's. She stole a glance at the screen, searching for a message from Wade. No message—and she felt a little sting in her heart.

"Here," Liz said.

Faith turned to face her friend. Liz was holding out Hawk's Tablet, which she had finally managed to pry loose. Hawk was holding Liz's hand.

"We struck a bargain," Liz explained, trying to downplay any meaning in the arrangement. "My hand for the Tablet. I'll survive."

Faith laughed and set Hawk's Tablet on the table. She could tell that Liz was actually fine with the circumstances. The keeper of Tablets was also a hopeless hand-holder. It was a comfort, even from a geeky freshman who wouldn't shut up.

"I can't believe I'm doing this. Do you realize I haven't been this far away from my Tablet since before I was born? They put it in my crib on day one! I feel like I lost a limb."

"One step at a time. It will get easier," Faith said, then turned in the darkness, running her hand along the slick tile wall.

"I love this school," Liz said dreamily. "It's like they all just got up and walked away and didn't look back. It's beautiful and strange and lonely, you know?"

For once Hawk didn't answer. He was staring back

in the direction of his Tablet, thinking about bolting for the cafeteria.

"Here we are, my favorite place on Earth," Faith said, inviting them in like a magician's assistant. "Oh, wait! Forgot the lights. Don't go anywhere."

Faith ran back in the direction from which they'd come, and Hawk tried to follow her. But Liz had a strong grip, and that grape bubblegum breath and those dark curls of hair draped across the sides of her face.

"Steady now," she said. "She'll be right back."

And she was. The dancing beam of a flashlight arrived quickly, and Faith handed out two more. All three of them, wielding old flashlights of their own, stepped inside the room and looked around.

"I bet they don't have one of these at either of the States," Faith said. She looked down at Hawk. "Have you ever seen one before?"

Hawk let go of Liz's hand and pointed his flashlight every which way. "I've heard of them, but I've never seen one. It smells funny in here."

"That's the scent of books," Faith said, taking in a big breath through her nose. "I love it. Come on, I'll show you around."

They were standing in a grade school library that had been abandoned but left undisturbed. Faith arrived at the far corner of the room and put her hand on a row of tall, skinny picture books. The feeling of their slick spines against her fingers as they passed by, like little speed bumps, made her heart beat faster.

"Once everyone had a Tablet, no one wanted these anymore. But there's something different about holding them in your hands."

Hawk was scanning a line of picture books with his flashlight, reading the titles.

"These are in the data cloud; everyone has access to them. I've read them all. It's crazy that people used to have to lug these things around. What a hassle."

Liz had peeled off along the wall of books and pulled out a stack. She flopped down in an orange beanbag, and small bits of white Styrofoam shot up in the air through a hole in one side.

"I always forget about that before I sit down," she said. "One of these days I'm going to be sitting on an empty bag. That's gonna hurt."

Hawk still couldn't believe he was in a dark space with two older girls. He eyed Faith's long legs and Liz's dark hair as it spilled over the beanbag chair. He wished he could kiss one of them but knew that would be tricky.

Ignorant of Hawk's desires, Faith held out a book and said, "*The Sneetches* are different in print. This will change your life."

Hawk leaned back on his heels. He'd never touched a book before. He kept thinking about all the people who had touched the book, all those snotty little hands who'd also played by the lake outside. The book had a musty odor to it, like nothing he'd ever smelled before; and this, too, bothered him. He was used to the cleanness of his Tablet, the glass surface, the brushed metal casing, and the billion things inside, all vibrant and new.

"It's not really my thing," Hawk said, backing away from the book a step or two like Faith were holding a live badger.

"Suit yourself, but I'm telling you, it's not the same. And it won't hurt you."

Faith set the book back on the shelf and took two others—*Green Eggs and Ham* and *Oh, the Places You'll Go!*—and walked to the old librarian's desk.

"She likes to feel like she's in charge," Liz joked from the beanbag.

Faith sat down at the desk and opened to the first page of *Green Eggs and Ham*, holding her flashlight so the faded colors punched up in the darkness. And then she smiled a special sort of smile, a contented one, a smile that Hawk saw in the light bouncing off the pages. She was touching one of the pages, tracing the lines of the drawings with her finger, lost in a way he didn't understand. She retrieved a piece of paper and a pencil from the librarian's desk and began drawing the picture from the book.

It was the smile more than anything else that got Hawk to touch a real book for the first time in his life. That and the fact that he ached for his Tablet, and he thought maybe *The Sneetches* would help him forget about how badly he felt. He did love the strange creatures with stars on their round bellies.

"Dr. Seuss," he said, "don't fail me now."

There were no more beanbags, so he sat cross-legged on the floor and opened the book. He had never turned real pages before, but it was sort of like turning pages on his Tablet, only he had to admit, it felt very different. The pages were heavy, and he liked the way they brushed against his skin as he moved them and landed on the first page of the story. It was, he would recall much later, impossible not to touch the image. If he had done this on his Tablet, something would have happened, and that was the biggest shock. Tablets reacted to *everything*. If they were touched, they did something. When he touched a Sneetch on his Tablet, words were spoken, lessons and commands emerged, and he was expected to *interact*. But the book just sat there, and for this Hawk loved it. His index finger traced the line of the picture of the Sneetch. He felt the roughness of the paper—nothing like the slick glass of the Tablet. He felt the yellow color of Sneetches' fur like he'd never felt yellow before. It got under his skin.

Fifteen minutes later, after having been lost entirely in the story, Hawk heard a voice.

"Told you. It's not the same, right?"

Faith was pointing her flashlight in Hawk's direction, which felt blinding and harsh as he looked up. It woke him from what felt like a dream he'd fallen into; a dream with green stars and furry, yellow creatures and bright-blue water. Forever after, Hawk would never forget the words of that book, or the feeling of holding the story in his hands. He retold the whole story of the book out loud, all the way from the creation of the first star-bellied Sneetch to the very last page. "This book is about us," he concluded, looking off in the direction of where the Western State awaited them. "All of them in there, the few of us out here. It's timeless."

Liz stretched her arms over her head and let the book in her lap flop shut, yawning loudly. "Great story, bro. Tell it again."

Hawk didn't catch Liz's sarcasm. He was a tad slow when it came to pretty, older girls and their senses of humor, so he went on about the parallel between their own lives and that of the Sneetches until Liz rolled her eyes and he realized he'd already said too much.

"What are you reading?" Hawk asked her.

Liz looked at the cover of the book and ran her finger along the smooth illustration of a monster sitting on the shore where a small boat was arriving.

"*Where the Wild Things Are*. It makes me forget about everything else. It's like the rest of the world just falls away."

Suddenly, a sound echoed down the long corridor and made its way into the library.

Faith slowly shut her copy of *Green Eggs and Ham*. In all the times they'd been there, no one had ever followed them. And now it had happened twice in one night. It scared her, but it also made her protective. Who would come into this special place besides her and the people she showed? What were they doing here?

Drifters.

The word squirmed itself into her brain, and she was suddenly imagining a mysterious group of people living in one of the classrooms in the abandoned school.

"Shut off your lights," Faith whispered, and they all did. The library turned especially dark in an instant.

"What if they see the Tablets?" Hawk said nervously. "It's the first thing they'll take."

Faith and Liz were thinking the same thing, but they didn't say so. It would only upset Hawk even more.

Maybe it had been a mistake leaving them behind like they had. They waited a while longer, but there was only silence; and they began to wonder if they'd heard anything to begin with. Maybe it had been their imaginations.

"This has been really cool and all," Hawk said. "But I think I'm ready to get my Tablet back. And I should probably go home before my mom starts messaging me, wondering where I am."

Faith lived in the neighborhood, but Liz didn't. Her house was a fifteen-minute walk away, on the other side of the abandoned mall. Neither of them had any idea where Hawk lived.

They decided not to turn the flashlights back on unless they had to. Their eyes had adjusted to the dim light, and they quietly padded along the slick floor of the corridor. When they came to the cafeteria door and found no one, they all felt sure it had only been the wind through the opening. They kept thinking that, laughing nervously, until they arrived at the table and they were staring at two, not three, Tablets.

Hawk's was no longer there.

"Uh-oh," Liz said.

Hawk didn't say anything. For once he was speechless. His emotions got the better of him, and his breath started to come in waves as he picked up the note that had been left behind. It was written on a small piece of tattered paper that had been torn off what had once been a full sheet.

Get used to living without it.

"I'm sorry, Hawk," Faith said. "This is all my fault. I'm really, really sorry."

"Sorry won't get it back!" Hawk yelled. He was pacing back and forth like a caged animal. He moved his hands in phantom swipes on a Tablet he no longer had, and then he began to run. He was at the window before Faith and Liz could catch him, and by the time they got outside, Hawk was far enough away that they could barely see his silhouette moving fast along the distant tree line.

"Hawk!" Faith called out. "It's okay, we'll find it! We will!"

"God, this is terrible," Liz said. "Who would have taken his Tablet? It doesn't make any sense."

They both felt uneasy about staying in the school any longer. It was too confined now, like someone could nail the plywood over the entry and seal them in for good. Faith went through the opening first, then Liz; and when the cool night air hit them in the faces, they felt a little bit better. They walked in silence, hoping the

Tablet had satisfied whoever had followed them.

"You know what," Liz concluded as they came to the fork in the path where they would normally part ways. "This is going to be good for him. He's too attached to that thing. I bet he'll even thank us later."

Faith wasn't so sure. They walked around the lake, and Faith thought of messaging Hawk to see if he was okay. But of course she couldn't. He didn't have a Tablet. And then her Tablet vibrated. A message was there, one she hadn't expected but had been hoping for. Wade Quinn was back.

Come see me tomorrow, gym,
watch me high-jump?

"Um, it's Wade," Faith told Liz. There was an awkward pause as they kept walking, and then Liz stopped.

"Go ahead, you know you want to."

Liz stepped away, and their hands pulled apart like something snapping in half.

"I think I'll go on home," Liz said, and before Faith could stop her, Liz was a shadow disappearing into the darkness. Faith knew better than to try to change Liz's mind when she got this way. She tapped out a message and felt her spirits lift a little. Hawk would have a new Tablet before he could hardly grow to miss the old one;

she was sure of it. And Liz would come around. It was all going to be fine; she just had to keep telling herself that. She took a deep breath and hit SEND on her message to Wade.

I hope you jump better than you draw daisies.
What time should I be there?

Faith continued along the path that skirted the lake, a nervous energy in her steps as she thought of who or what she might encounter. It had been a weird night in more ways than one, and she just wanted to get home and lock the door behind her.

As she came around the final turn that would lead to her house, she saw a familiar park bench. She'd sat on it many times, drawing the lake and the birds on the pond with her finger on her Tablet. Something on the bench was fluttering softly on the breeze, though it was too heavy to be blown away entirely. Its edge lifted and fell as she arrived at the bench and realized what it was: her drawing of *Green Eggs and Ham*, the drawing she'd done at the librarian's desk in the library. The bottom third of the paper was missing. *Get used to living without it.*

Faith's hand was shaking as she ran for her front door.

How was it possible?

How had someone gotten the sheet of paper with her drawing on it, torn off the bottom, and left the note for Hawk? And all while they were still in the library?

An hour later, in another part of town, Hawk was lying in his bedroom, a small lamp over his left shoulder. There was something in his hands, but it wasn't his Tablet. It was a little wider and taller than that, but not much. It had fit perfectly in the backpack he carried around everywhere. The pack wasn't designed to carry much— two straps over his shoulders, a thin sheath of foam around an oblong pouch against his narrow back.

He turned the pages of *The Sneetches* ever so slowly, and as he felt the coarse paper on his skin, he started to breathe a little easier.

Chapter 4

Wire Code

It took Faith a long time to get to sleep that night, and even when she did fall asleep, it was more like a half wakefulness. She kept having dreams of things moving in her room. She dreamed the glass of water on her night-stand had tipped over; but instead of the water spilling onto the floor, it hung in the air and blew apart into a million droplets, then danced above her bed. Some of the droplets touched her lips, and she tasted the water with her tongue. It was cool and sweet, like spring, and she smiled in her dream. The drops came together again, returned to the glass, and the dream ended.

In time someone would tell Faith Daniels the truth, but not yet.

She wasn't ready to know, but one day she would be told.

What happened in her room was not a dream.

Faith and Liz both awoke to the same message from Hawk on their Tablets and simultaneously realized they'd allowed a new person into their tiny, private circle.

And he's back! How you guys doing? Miss me?
Let's do some hand-holding, ladies!

It was no longer just the two of them; it was the three of them. Hawk's Tablet was back, and he was becoming a fixture in their lives. Faith and Liz didn't talk about it, this idea that they'd let someone in; but they both knew it had happened. It was like they were afraid to bring it up for fear that the other one would disapprove. The little guy was definitely growing on them.

By 8:00 a.m., when Liz met Faith at the front of the school, they'd both been messaging Hawk for an hour.

"This is getting a little strange, right?" Liz said.

"More than a little. I'd say it's getting creepy. How

does a Tablet just vanish and then reappear? Who does that?"

Faith was thinking the same thing about the drawing she'd done, but she didn't know how to tell Liz about it, at least not yet.

"It was just *there*, too," Liz repeated what Faith already knew. "Right next to his bed, like it had never left his side. Means someone was in his house. Now *that's* creepy."

"Maybe someone figured out he's hacking, and they want Hawk to do the same for them? He might have gotten himself in trouble."

"And us with him," Liz reminded Faith. "We're the one's wearing the jeans, remember?"

That wasn't quite true. They weren't actually wearing them, because they hadn't been shipped yet, but Faith understood what Liz was saying. They needed to get with Hawk and talk this whole thing through. She wasn't sure nearly free jeans were worth the risk of real trouble.

Miss Newhouse was on high alert in the morning lecture sessions, pacing the room like a vampire hunting for a victim. There was a rumor floating around the school that someone was peddling a Wire Code, which had been a problem at Faith's other schools and was something she'd hoped wouldn't make the leap to Old

Park Hill. Wire Codes required a complicated hack that usually only worked for a few days before it was discovered and patched by programmers at the State.

Wire Codes, Faith knew, were nothing to mess around with. They revealed things on Tablets in ways that were not allowed. They showed things people weren't supposed to see. Staring into a Tablet where a Wire Code had been entered set the mind on fire; and once you were exposed, turning away didn't matter. You'd done the equivalent of taking the hit or injected the needle. The Wire Code was in you. Its electronic rewiring of your brain had infected you. In the four or five hours that followed, a Wire Code provided a heightened sense of reality. Colors burned brighter, flavors intensified, feelings of happiness amplified tenfold.

Faith had never tried a Wire Code, though she'd had opportunities at all her old schools. There was usually at least one floating around every few weeks on campus, and most of the students found out about them. They were made up of a sequence of numbers and letters, and they were always passed around in a very specific way. Like the drugs of the past, Wire Codes had their own culture of delivery systems and symbols. Marijuana had its joint, acid its tab, cocaine its pocket-sized cylinder tube. In the early days of Wire Codes the people who made them wrote them out on paper, but it was risky. Handwriting recognition had seen huge advances with the advent of the Tablets. Writing a number or a letter was like a fingerprint that could be traced. And Wire Codes were never passed from Tablet to Tablet, based on the widely held belief that the States were out there intercepting every questionable transmission. Somewhere in the very early days of Wire Codes, the method for delivery was chosen, and it just stuck: plastic beads on a chain or a string. Sometimes the chain of letters and numbers was short, sometimes long; but it was always strung in a loop with a series of cheap plastic beads, like a charm bracelet for a little kid.

The Wire Code alert meant Faith couldn't talk to Hawk while her lectures were going on, which was probably for the best, because she was falling behind in Buford's advanced English and she really needed to focus. Unfortunately, there was something else on her mind, something bigger and more exciting, and it was making Buford sound like a lawn mower as he deconstructed *Henry V*'s secondary characters. Her meet up with Wade was at noon, and no matter how hard she tried, Faith could think of little else as Miss Newhouse made her way around the room for the third time. She had a hawkish nose and dark eyes, she was thin like a pencil, and she leaned over sitting students with a frown on her face.

Faith looked toward the back of the classroom as Miss Newhouse stopped in front of Dylan Gilmore. Newhouse leaned down, putting both hands on Dylan's desk, and Faith slid one of her earphones off so she could hear what they were saying. One ear was filled with Buford's weed-whacker–buzz voice; the other zeroed in on the far corner of the room, where Dylan was slumped in his chair.

"Empty your pockets," Miss Newhouse said.

"Why would I do that?" Dylan had a whispery voice, low and heavy.

"Because there's a Wire Code in this school, and I'm looking for it."

"And you think I know something about that because . . . ?"

"Empty the pockets," Newhouse said.

There was a pause, and Faith could sense Dylan sitting up straighter, putting his face right up in Miss Newhouse's grille.

"Miss Newhouse, can I offer you a mint? You could use one."

Faith laughed, catching herself too late, and quickly put the headphone back on her ear. She couldn't hear anything outside the bubble of Professor Buford as she stared at her Tablet, watching him speak. Her heart was racing, but she didn't dare look back and give herself away. There was a tapping on her shoulder, and Faith jumped, making a sound she couldn't hear. When she looked up, Miss Newhouse was standing over her, motioning her to remove her headphones. She reached across Faith's desk and paused the lecture as Faith caught a glimpse of Dylan in the corner. He had stood and pulled his pockets all the way out, where they lay against his pants like little white ghosts. Of course there was no Wire Code, no string of plastic beads, each bead with a number or a letter. On inspection, his pockets had proven very empty.

"Are you having trouble focusing today?" Miss Newhouse asked Faith. "I can move you to a private room if it would help, though we don't encourage it. Isolation doesn't tend to improve results."

"I'm fine, just a little tickle in my throat is all."

Faith coughed for good measure, and Miss Newhouse, looking unconvinced, told her to get back to work.

"Yes, ma'am. No problem. Working," Faith said, then she put her headphones back on and tapped the screen on her Tablet before Miss Newhouse could object.

She moved off, signaling Dylan to sit down and stalking other students; and Faith stole one more glance at the back of the room, where Dylan was looking bored and aloof. He pushed his pockets in, shrugging his powerful shoulders as he sat down.

Cute, Faith thought. She allowed herself to linger on his big eyes and dark brows for a moment longer, hoping he wouldn't look up. *Too bad he's trouble.*

Faith couldn't decide whether or not to take Liz with her to the gym in order to watch Wade be amazing and gorgeous or not, but the dilemma answered itself when she couldn't find her in the lunchroom. Faith chewed on one of her nails, a habit she'd put out of its misery on nine fingers. The pinkie on her right hand was taking all the damage that had once been spread across ten fingers, but it was holding up. It was a tough little pinkie, only bleeding a little when Faith was extremely nervous and chewed right down to the skin.

"Sorry, little buddy," she said as she arrived at the gym. "Way to take one for the team. You done good."

Talking to herself helped; but when she entered the gym, she found someone she didn't expect, and her nerves went back into high gear.

Dylan Gilmore was shooting baskets, and Wade was nowhere to be found. The gym was empty and full of echoes as Dylan bounced a ratty leather ball. He'd shed his shirt and wore only jeans, skate shoes, and a necklace.

"Excuse me," Faith stammered from across the open

space where she stood at the door. "Isn't there supposed to be some sort of jumping going on in here?"

Dylan shot from the far end of the baseline and missed everything, then stared at the floor and shook his head.

"I would have made that. You distracted me."

"Try again. I'll be quiet this time."

Dylan faced her from across the gym and smiled, which was the first time she'd seen him looking even remotely happy. It was a nice smile. She wondered how tall he was up close.

Faith didn't have much time to stare, because Dylan seemed to be done playing basketball. He picked up his T-shirt and put it on, then took up his Tablet in one hand and put it in his back pocket. He ran his hand through his thick black hair and started walking toward the far door.

"Nice talking to you," Faith said under her breath. She wanted to believe Dylan was a good guy; but he seemed so aloof, and Hawk had said he was trouble. For some reason she yelled a question across the gym, but it came out more like an accusation. "You're not making Wire Codes, are you?"

Dylan stopped in his tracks but didn't turn around. He looked down at his shoes again, which were black and scuffed on the brushed leather.

"Not my thing," he said, turning to face her. "Tried it once, that was enough."

Faith was thinking that using wasn't any better than manufacturing when it came to drugs just as the sounds of Wade and Clara Quinn's voices echoed into the gym. They were entering from the far door, where a standoff between Wade and Dylan quickly ensued. Wade was taller, but Dylan was bigger, more solid.

"Still trying jump shots?" Wade asked. "Why bother when there are easier ways to get the job done?"

Wade was around Dylan in a flash, picking up the basketball and dribbling between his legs and around his back. Clara Quinn watched and smiled with her arms crossed at her chest as Wade darted for the basket and leaped, slam dunking the ball with ease.

"Whoa," said Faith.

"He doesn't jump as high as it seems," Dylan said as he moved toward the door. "It's all smoke and mirrors."

"He's just showing off," Clara Quinn said.

"Same Wade, different day," Dylan added. Even from across the gym Faith could see that Clara Quinn was into Dylan Gilmore. She couldn't take her eyes off him, and it was pretty obvious that she was enjoying the fact that Dylan was willing to stand his ground against her brother.

Dylan turned and put his hands out, calling for the

ball. Wade laughed, then threw the basketball like a pitcher, firing it like a hundred-mile-an-hour fastball at Dylan's head. Dylan caught it without difficulty and stared at the hoop Wade had just dunked on. It was way farther than a three-point shot; but Dylan sized it up, let fly a jumper, and hit nothing but net.

"I'll take a three over a dunk every time. Power only gets you so far."

Wade was surprised by the make but undeterred in his obvious dislike of Dylan.

"Gym's closed for practice, loser."

Dylan brushed past Clara, and she leaned toward him; but he didn't stop as he made his way out of the gym through the far doors. Faith found the display of competition exhilarating and hoped it was for her bene-fit. She was about to walk onto the hardwood floor when Mr. Reichert, who apparently did triple duty as the prin-cipal, a teacher, and the Field Games coach, came into the gym behind Faith and scared her half to death.

"Hi, kiddo, how's Old Park Hill treating you?"

Faith jumped nearly as high as Wade Quinn and made an unfortunate, high-pitched sound that sent Clara Quinn into a fit of annoying laughter.

"Be nice, Clara. Faith's still getting used to the place. Let's let her believe we're a friendly bunch for a little longer."

Mr. Reichert pulled on a janitor-style ring of keys attached to his belt and began unlocking a storage area. "How about you help me get this set up while they warm up, Faith? What do you say?"

"Yeah, make yourself useful," Clara yelled from across the gym where she was in the middle of a weird-looking yoga stretch. "We could use a team manager, someone to pick up the wet towels and fill my water bottle. Can you handle that?"

"Pay no attention to her," Mr. Reichert whispered. "Her bark is worse than her bite. She's harmless."

Faith had to rely on the principal for backup, because Wade had not come to her rescue. He was laser focused on warming up, acting like he hadn't even heard what Clara had said. Faith's Tablet vibrated in her back pocket, and she knew Liz was probably trying to find her. Or maybe it was her mother. She ignored it and began helping Mr. Reichert roll out the high-jump pits and set up the bar. A few minutes later, the Quinns were standing at the ready, and the bar was set at six feet.

"So Wade is jumping first then?" Faith asked, excited to see him fly through the air.

"No," Mr. Reichert explained. "Clara will go first. She'll only take a few jumps though. Today is her throwing day, outside. Now *that's* something to see.

You'd swear a shot put weighs about as much as a cue ball in this girl's hand. And don't even get me started on the javelin."

"And the hammer," Clara said, inserting herself into the conversation from where she stood about twenty-five feet away. "That thing is wicked cool. Nothing on Earth like throwing the hammer."

She went suddenly quiet and closed her eyes, taking a bottomless breath that ended in a trance-like moan. And then she was moving with long, languid strides. When Clara turned sharply at the bar and jumped, it was like she'd gone into slow motion and weighed about four ounces. Six feet was nothing. The bar was cleared by at least six inches.

A split second later Clara was off the mat and walking out of the gym shaking her head.

"My head's not in it today, feels off."

Faith was left to wonder how high Clara would have jumped if her head *was* in the game.

"I'm going out to throw; don't follow me."

"How high can she go?" Faith asked as Mr. Reichert motioned for her to get on one end of the height adjustment for the bar while he stayed on the other.

"Hard telling. She's only been at it for about a month. I'm guessing she could hit seven and a half feet if she gets focused."

The Field Games were the most important competitive events in the modern world. Everyone knew
what the really big records were and who held them.
Faith was nearly sure the woman's world record stood
at seven feet, four inches, which had been achieved on
a windless day in the Eastern State by a German athlete
four or five years before. As Faith watched Mr. Reichert
move his end of the bar higher and higher, she realized
that Clara Quinn, a high school junior living outside
the States, might become the next world record holder
in the high jump.

"What's she doing hanging out at Old Park Hill high
school? It doesn't make any sense. She'd be a celebrity
on the inside." Faith was trying to get her end of the bar
level with Mr. Reichert's as she talked. It was way over
her head.

"Maybe she's hiding out," Wade said with a tone
of seriousness Faith hadn't expected. "Maybe we both
are."

"Let me help you there," Mr. Reichert said, coming
to Faith's side to finish the job of setting the bar for
Wade. "And they're not really hiding out, just staying
under the radar, if you will."

"Whatever you say, boss."

Faith wanted to ask where Wade and Clara had
come from and how long they'd been at Old Park Hill,

but she was preoccupied by the new height of the bar, which had been set.

"How high is that?" she asked, standing under the bar and staring up at it. She was tall at five feet eleven, but the bar looked like it was about two feet over her head.

"Eight feet," Mr. Reichert said. "It's a good warm-up height for a full run-through."

"*Warm*-up?" Faith asked. "Eight feet is a *warm*-up?"

"Do me a favor and don't move," Mr. Reichert said.

Faith was standing at the middle of the bar staring at the pit, so she didn't realize Wade was already heading for the bar until it was too late. She was staring up to the ceiling of the gym when she heard a tiny *pop*, like the sound of a tennis shoe tapping lightly on the wood floor. She saw his long, lithe body glide into view in the shape of an arc. He was so high over her head—it was like he'd launched from a hidden trampoline she hadn't seen. The world record, if she remembered right, was only four inches higher than Wade had just cleared on a practice jump.

When Wade sat up in the pit, his hair was a gorgeous mess, and a generous smile appeared on his face. Faith could only think of one thing to say.

"You've got to be kidding me."

Wade winked and pushed himself up off the mat.

Their shoulders brushed as he went by. Faith wished she could touch his face and maybe kiss him. But she let him pass without committing a reckless act of love in front of the principal.

"Raise it," Wade said as he returned to his starting spot.

"Let's take it up four," Mr. Reichert said, which would put Wade at the world record height if he cleared it. Faith thought they should be recording it and said so, but Mr. Reichert brushed the idea off as he set his side of the bar.

"Better there's no evidence on a Tablet just yet. We want to surprise them when the time comes. More dramatic."

When the bar was set, Faith moved quickly out of the way. She wanted to see the entire thing for herself this time. Wade took a huge breath as his twin sister had done. He made the same mumbling sound at the bottom of the breath, and then he was on the move. He was like a gazelle, precisely measured in every movement. When he reached the bar, there was an explosion of silent power that vaulted him higher than Faith thought was possible. He cleared the bar with 99 percent of his body until the very edge of his heel nicked the bar and knocked it down.

"Damn it!" he yelled, pushing himself off the mat

without looking in Faith's direction. "Set it up again."

He tried three more times, each time missing by the slightest margin and growing angrier with every attempt.

"It's okay, Wade," Faith said encouragingly. "It's eight feet, four inches and you're basically clearing it. It's incredible!"

"How about you stick to drawing daisies and let me worry about this. Think you could do that?"

The comment stung, but Faith was strong willed, always had been. She'd lost a lot of friends over the past few years, and she wasn't about to let Wade Quinn talk to her that way. He was turning out to be everything she hated about hot guys. She walked out of the gym, but Mr. Reichert followed her. He knew how Wade and Clara could be: coldly focused on becoming the greatest athletes the world had ever seen. It was time to put on the principal hat and make sure the new student wasn't totally devastated.

"Don't take it too hard," he began as he caught up to Faith in the corridor. "He's very intense about the training. So is his sister. It sort of comes with the territory. Ever hear of a guy named Tiger Woods? Best golfer in the world like fifty years ago. Amazing. He wouldn't even sign autographs for little kids most of the time. Just head down, marching from hole to hole, dominating the course. Then he lost his focus, and the whole thing went to hell."

Faith felt a little better. Mr. Reichert with the pale, cratered skin and the awful haircut was turning out to be an okay guy.

"Come back in an hour," Mr. Reichert said. "I promise he'll be a different person. He's frustrated because he knows he can clear it. Don't be so hard on him."

"I never give guys like that a second chance," Faith said, walking away and thinking about the grade school, hoping she and Liz and Hawk would be going there that night. "Tell him I said so."

But Faith had to admit that she *was* thinking about it. If she could have seen what was happening in the gym while they were having this conversation, it might have changed her mind. Or more likely it would have *blown* her mind. Wade had put the bar back in place and taken up his starting position again, and this time he didn't bother with the formality of preparing his mind for the approach. He just went for it.

He cleared the bar by a foot and a half in a way that looked like he wasn't even trying. Standing on the mat afterward, Wade knocked the bar off the holders and watched it fall to the floor. There was a long pause and then a voice from the far end of the gym.

"Be careful."

Clara was back, leaning against one of the double doors that led outside to the throwing area. "She's not worth it."

Wade fell back down on the pit and stared at the ceiling. He wasn't so sure Clara was right about Faith Daniels.

Maybe she *was* worth it.

Chapter 5

I'm Just Here to See the Monkeys and Eat the Candy

Whole sections of Old Park Hill had been shut down because the place was about ten times bigger than it needed to be for the insignificant number of students attending class every day. There were long corridors around every corner that were lined with nothing but locked doors and empty lockers, places where people could sneak away and do things high schools weren't designed for. One of these corridors was of special use to Wade Quinn. He'd made some modifications, mostly out of boredom; but three days after he'd blown it in the gym with Faith, he thought it might be the kind of place she'd like.

Faith, Liz, and Hawk were standing in one of the few operational hallways. Before Wade walked up uninvited, they'd been talking about the new, cheap jeans that had shipped thanks to Hawk's Tablet wizardry. All three of them ignored Wade for about ten seconds. Under normal circumstances that would have been plenty of time for Wade to get the message and take off, but unfortunately, the annoying Amy was walking toward them. Amy was a popularity queen who drove Wade half insane with her need for attention; and as she passed by, Wade leaned hard into the circle of Faith, Liz, and Hawk, searching for refuge.

"Hey, guys. How's it going?" Wade put a hip into Hawk's elbow (Hawk was that much shorter) and gained full admittance into the circle. "I need to talk to Faith for a minute."

No one moved or spoke.

"*Alone*, if you don't mind," Wade added, glaring down at Liz like she was gum stuck on his shoe.

"Wade Quinn, are you avoiding me?"

Amy had a sugary, high-pitched voice, but the guys thought she was a knockout. Whenever she came around, Hawk started mumbling like a half-wit and shuffled in her direction. Amy had zero patience for dweebs and morons. After a one-syllable comment—*Ew*—she started backing away like Hawk were a leper reaching out toward her with a zombie-like hand. When Garrett Miller walked by, she locked arms with him and looked back sadly like Wade Quinn, the coolest guy in school, had fallen in with the wrong crowd.

"What do you want, Wade?" Faith asked indifferently as she leaned closer to Liz. "We're kind of busy here."

Wade started to speak, but the first thing that came into his mind was an insult, and he was trying very hard not to mess this up a second time.

"There's something I'd like to show you. It's in one of the closed wings, very cool. Will you come with me?"

Faith was melting inside. Wade was wearing a white tee, jeans, and Vans. His dark eyes locked on hers, and she let her gaze drift down to his lips. "Trust me, you're going to like it. And no one's going to find out. I go there all the time."

"Cool, I'll go," Hawk said with his usual flair for the dramatic. "What is it? No, let me guess. You have live snakes down there? Or a monkey. I bet he's got a monkey!"

Wade stared at Hawk like he was the dumbest kid he'd ever seen.

"It's not a monkey."

"Maybe it's an alligator," Liz said, egging Hawk on.

"Alligator? Cool!"

"It's not an exotic animal. And besides, you're not invited."

"Oh."

Liz put an arm around Hawk, which perked him right up.

"I say we all go. If you've got a monkey down there, I want to see it."

"I told you it's not a monkey! It's not anything like that."

"You got candy down there?" Liz teased. "Is it like Candy Land?"

"Aw yes!" Hawk laughed. He was pumped.

Wade looked at Faith and hoped this wasn't going to keep going in the direction in which it was headed. "You've got weird friends, you know that?"

"So I've been told," she agreed.

"Then you'll go with me, just the two of us? I'm telling you, you're going to love it."

"No thanks," Faith said, and began walking away.

Wade Quinn was nearly at the end of his patience, but not quite. He really liked Faith, especially because she played hard to get.

"Okay, your friends can come. In fact, I want them to. You guys wanna go see the monkey? And the candy?"

Hawk smiled from ear to ear.

"Holy shit, there is a monkey!"

"And candy!" Liz added.

Faith was laughing when she turned around, and she found it unstoppably charming that Wade was, too.

By the time she returned to the group, he was already out of her doghouse.

Hawk knew better than most that the Quinns were not people you messed around with. He'd tried to warn Faith to steer clear, but it was too late, and his joking around hadn't pissed off Wade the way he'd hoped it would. She'd flown in too close, and once that happened with Wade, it was usually impossible to break free of his gravitational pull. He and Clara both let go when they wanted to, often at the cruelest moment, and it was never pretty. Hawk had seen them do it to people before, and none of them were still going to school at Old Park Hill. It was why he'd gone along with the idea of a little adventure to begin with, why he'd acted like such a dork. Some people hid behind jokes or sports or good looks, but Hawk played the role of zany geek because it was easy. He was small, with wild hair and a high-pitched voice. Slipping into the head-idiot roll was both simple and effective. And it came to him naturally, because somewhere deep down inside, he *was* this goofy person; but he was also so much more. His intelligence was off the charts, way beyond what anyone who knew him understood. The mere fact that he'd been able to procure and ship clothing to his female friends for next to nothing was an epic intellectual victory; subverting the Tablet and the State that controlled it had been the equivalent of breaking into Fort Knox. For Hawk, it had been reasonably easy: three days of hard-core hacking and a lot of sugary snacks and it was done. Had the officials in either of the States known what Hawk could do—and how quickly he'd done it—the whole system would have gone on high alert.

What a lot of people didn't understand about Hawk was that he paid attention to everything, missed nothing, and had a photographic memory. He was doing just that—paying very close attention—as they left the main building walking two by two.

"Can't believe it's already getting dark," Liz said. She was walking next to Hawk, her hands stuffed into the pockets of her hoodie, staring at the back of Wade's head like she was trying to make it explode. "Don't they have security out here at night?"

"Are you kidding? We're lucky we've got two teachers during daylight. There's no one else; don't worry so much." Wade put an arm around Faith's shoulder and leaned in as they walked, an act that irritated Liz even more.

"I'm not worried. I was just asking."

"And I'm telling you, there's no one." Wade stopped and turned to face Liz and Hawk. "When was the last time you took a really good look around? This is the last open school in the city. I've been moved three times in the last year alone, and you probably have been, too. There are fewer than a hundred of us, fewer every week. Most of them are only at this school because their parents are crazy. You get that, right? It's the crazies and the cleanup crew. I don't even know why they bother to lock this place up. There's no point. No one is here!"

There was a smoldering moment of silence from Liz, but when she spoke, there was fire in her voice.

"Then why are *you* here?"

She'd had about enough of Wade Quinn and couldn't believe what a condescending jerk he was, which made it all the more startling when Faith came to his defense.

"Chill out, Liz. He's got a plan; it's just kind of secret is all."

"What the hell does *that* mean?"

"It means lay off, okay? Things aren't always exactly as they seem."

Liz moved closer to Faith, took her hand, and pulled her a few steps away from Wade and Hawk. This left Hawk in the towering shadow of a much older, bigger guy.

"What's up, bro?"

Wade cracked a half smile but didn't answer. He stood there wondering why it was that he couldn't help but put his foot in his mouth every time he met a girl he actually liked, and hoped that the whispering going on between Liz and Faith wasn't going to lead to the usual: him losing the respect of a girl he liked before things even got started.

"Please, Faith, let's don't do this. Let's just go to the grade school. You can draw and I'll read."

"It's okay, Liz. And you do worry a lot."

What Faith really wanted to say was that Liz had gotten awfully clingy lately. And that she'd always been supportive when Liz was chasing after a boy. And why was she being such a total freak right about now? But she didn't say any of those things.

"I don't think he's good for you. I think he's dangerous."

Faith wanted to scream. Liz had become so needy, with the hand-holding and the moodiness. It was suffocating.

"You don't have to come along. I'm fine."

"But I'm not. I need you," Liz pleaded. She was starting to cry, her voice shaking with frustration and panic. "I can't keep going without you. Not out here."

She'd tried to be quiet, but in the end Liz had laid her soul bare in front of two boys. Faith had let it come to this. It was her fault.

"Go on home," Faith said. "And take Hawk with you. Let's just talk later tonight. It's going to be okay."

Liz let go of Faith's hand, felt the soft fingers sliding away. She backed up until she was standing alone, staring coldly at Wade.

"If you break her heart, I'll find a way to ruin your life."

"Look, I'm sorry, okay? My mistake."

"Do you believe this guy?" Liz asked, looking to Hawk for support. "Now he's all nice like he wasn't a total monster five minutes ago."

Wade didn't say anything, but he did look at Hawk, trying to size up where he stood.

"I'm just here to see the monkeys," Hawk said. "And eat the candy. But I'm thinking, Third wheel here, not ideal." He moved toward Liz ever so slightly. "You two go on ahead; we'll catch you next time."

Hawk was too smart to put himself on the wrong side of a complicated situation, but it made him very nervous sending Faith into a locked section of the school with no backup. He felt helpless as Liz began pulling him down the sidewalk.

"And, news flash," Liz said bitterly. "Calling our parents crazy just makes you a bigger asshole."

"Whatever you say," Wade answered back. Liz had pretty much leveled him, and he wanted out of the situation as fast as possible. He put an arm around Faith, pulled her tightly to his side, and started walking.

"You okay?" he asked.

"Yeah, I'm good. She's been going through a rough time. It's been a little exhausting."

Faith felt the sting of grief as she threw her best friend under a bus, but the truth was, she really did feel like she was suffocating. She loved Liz more than anyone else she knew, but she also needed some space. She just wanted to cut loose for one night, then everything would be fine. She and Liz would work things out; they always did.

Old Park Hill had four quadrants connected by long corridors. Only one of them, which also housed the gym, was in use, and even that one had a lot of locked doors. The other three buildings were loosely connected by a series of covered walkways that zigzagged through the grounds outside. It was fall, the days getting shorter; and though it was only four thirty when they entered one of the locked buildings, there was a chill in the air and the sun had moved behind the trees.

"Are you sure no one will find us out here?" Faith asked. She was thinking of the custodian, an old guy who never talked to anyone as he walked around, stooped over his rolling cart of cleaning supplies. He had struck Faith as slightly unhinged, like he might be hiding a shotgun inside the garbage can he pushed around.

"Nothing to mop up out here. No one cares about these old buildings. They're like coffins."

Faith didn't like the sound of that. Wade flashed a key so Faith could see it, and after a final look behind him to make sure no one was watching, he unlocked the door and held it open. Faith had a moment of regret and thought seriously about going in search of Liz and Hawk. It surprised her how much she was growing to like the three of them together. It didn't seem right, being here with Wade and the two of them without her.

"Come on, you're going to like it. Promise."

Wade's eyes told her that whatever lay hidden inside, it would be at least slightly and possibly *very* dangerous. He tugged on her hand as he stepped through the doorway, and her resolve melted away. When the door clicked shut behind her she jumped, startled and afraid; and Wade pulled her even closer than before, his strong arm wrapped around her shoulder.

Like the grade school, there was no power in this building. Soft, golden light came in through the dusty windows and bounced off glossy linoleum floors. There were shadows everywhere. Faith leaned harder into Wade and tucked in under his arm, where it felt warm and safe.

"I like it here. Cozy."

Wade flashed his confident smile, then pulled away

until they were holding hands and he was turning sharply down a long, narrow corridor. It was one of those school passageways that seemed to go on forever, running the entire length of the building. Faith imagined it humming with hundreds of students talking about the latest gossip, opening and shutting lockers, going through the normal motions of a day.

"It's sad, kind of. Don't you think?" Faith asked as they quickened their pace up the long hallway. "There used to be so many people in here. Now it's just empty. It feels lonely."

"I don't know; to me it's a reminder of how stupid our parents were. They were dead wrong about a billion things. I don't know why they make us come here at all. I mean, seriously, what's the point? We get everything we need from the Tablets. World-class education, all the help we need. This place is a reminder of what doesn't work; that's all it is."

Faith didn't quite agree, though she saw his point.

"I think it would have been a lot of fun to walk these halls with hundreds of other people. You're a glass half-empty kind of person. I'm going to cure you of that."

Wade laughed at Faith's determination to see the bright side of a plan that had been doomed from the start, and it was all he could do not to keep up the debate.

They'd come close enough to the far end of the hall for Faith to see something sitting on the floor in the murky light. She couldn't tell what it was until they'd arrived right next to it.

"Where'd you get that thing?"

"I built it!" Wade said, sounding more excited than Faith had ever heard him before.

"Why?" Faith asked.

Wade pointed down the endless hallway.

"Because I wanted to put this exceptionally empty hall to some good use."

A four-wheeled contraption that could be laughingly called a go-cart sat on the floor. There were wheels and axles and two makeshift seats to sit on, one behind the other. The steering wheel was two sizes too big for the rest of the cart and looked like it had been pulled off a 1950s pickup truck. There was clearly nothing to propel the object down the hall. No engine or pedals. As silly as this thing was, Faith was oddly excited to get inside and ride.

"How many girls have you brought in here to ride in your jalopy?"

Wade presented her with his most smoldering look, and before he could answer, Faith was laughing. The truth was, she didn't really want him to address the question. "You push; I'll go first," she said, hoping her willingness to play along would impress him. Maybe he had brought other girls here; but for this one moment, he was all hers, and she was determined to make the most of it.

"Hang on a second; I need to prepare it for launch."

"Launch?"

Wade didn't answer, but as he went to work, Faith began to realize how the cart really worked. She watched as Wade attached two long bungee cords, one to each side. The other ends of the cords were tied to doorknobs on either side of the hallway.

"You can't be serious."

"Done it a hundred times and only crashed twice," Wade said as he pulled off his shoes and threw them in a metal box welded to the frame. He took out a set of tennis shoes and quickly slipped them on, then began pushing the cart from the front end.

"Glued Velcro to the bottom of these babies. Pretty cool, right?"

Faith was thinking that if Liz were here, they'd both be debating who was the bigger geek: Hawk or Wade. He'd installed a strip of Velcro tape down the middle of the floor so he wouldn't slide around, and with each step he took, Faith could hear his shoes ripping away. She was terrified he'd let go and the cart would careen out of control, running her over and killing her in the process. There was nowhere to hide, so instead she ran and jumped over the cord on one side and watched as she stood pinned against the back of the hallway.

"Wade, I don't think I'm going to do this. I just don't see it happening."

He was getting close to the wall, and Faith was having a hard time not focusing on how powerful he was. He was really leaning into the effort, the muscles in his legs and arms tightening with every step he took. When he reached the wall, there was a clicking sound, and he let go.

"Don't!" Faith yelled as he stood there, hands on his hips, catching his breath. She expected the cart to blow right over him and break his legs; but it stayed firm, the cords at its sides as tight as a high wire. Wade leaned down and plucked the cord like a guitar string, and a murky, echoing sound filled the hall.

"No worries, she's locked and loaded."

"You're crazy if you think I'm getting in that thing."

"Suit yourself. But you don't know what you're missing."

Wade jumped over the cord on the right side and took out his Tablet, snapping it from small to large. There were windows high up on the back wall, and as Wade walked toward Faith, the golden light moved across his face. He turned and gazed down the long, darkened hallway, then tapped something into his Tablet. A long line of tiny lights lit up along each side, which made the corridor look like a runway for an airplane.

"You really know how to impress a girl," Faith said. As goofy and dangerous as it all was, it was also pretty romantic.

"I do try," Wade offered. "And I promise, it's totally safe. Fast, but safe. I've had thirty-seven crash-free launches in a row."

Faith found herself short of breath. Was she really considering this madness? She imagined one of the wheels falling off, the way it would feel when she hit the first locker. She would die in a hallway go-cart accident. It would take weeks for them to find her dead body; and when they did, they'd all say what an idiot she was. But then she imagined Wade sitting in the front seat, her arms wrapped around him like the two of them were on a motorcycle riding into the sunset, and she lost all hope of ever getting out of the building without first being flung down the tunnel of love.

"This is *so Titanic*," Faith said as she settled into the backseat. "You know, that scene in the old movie where they sit in the car and fog up the windows?"

"Too bad we don't have any windows. I'll work on that."

Faith imagined all the broken glass in a high-speed

crash and thought better of the idea.

"It's okay; I like the open air. Keep it this way."

Wade Quinn sat in front of her, and she realized how wide and strong his back was. Tall people were misleading that way. It was easy to focus on their height and forget about how much it took to fill in the endless space along their spines.

"You're going to want to hold on for this," Wade said, inviting her to wrap her arms all the way around his chest and hold on. Her hands were shaking so badly it was embarrassing, but she couldn't stop. The crazy energy of the moment was pulsing through every part of her. Wade fished around under his shirt, trying to get a hold of something; but Faith had closed her eyes and leaned the side of her face into his wide back. She didn't see when he pulled out a necklace on a thin gold chain. She didn't see as he looked at the plastic beads strung on the chain and typed the code into his Tablet. The Wire Code would only work once, Wade knew, and later he would take off the beads and melt them down over a flame so they couldn't be traced back to him.

"Listen, Faith. I know you're nervous and all. This will make it easier, and a lot more fun."

Faith didn't have any idea what Wade was talking about, but she lifted her head, feeling his blond hair slide across her face. He leaned to one side and looked at her, holding his Tablet where she could see.

"What's that?" she asked; but before she could get an answer, Faith Daniels was looking into Wade's Tablet, consuming her first Wire Code. The screen was jittery and filled with strange light. Her consciousness shifted; all her senses were heightened. She could smell Wade's cologne full but distant; she could taste his lips and feel her tongue sliding along his slick teeth. Were they kissing? She thought they were, but then the cart was moving, and her senses burst awake with colors and light. They were careening down the narrow hallway at forty miles per hour. Faith was in love with this moment, out of control and not caring, pulling Wade close, her hands around his chest as he laughed loudly and happily. She lifted her head off Wade's back and tried to peer around his shoulder. It looked like they had left the ground, but that couldn't be right. If she was flying then she was flying; that was fine with her. She took Wade's head in her hands, spun his face around, and kissed him. The wind tangled their hair together, and she let her hand slip down to his neck.

"Hold that thought," Wade said, pulling away and smiling as he quickly turned forward. There was a sharp movement to one side like they'd nearly crashed into a wall, and Faith laughed, reeling back in her seat and holding on to Wade with one hand as if he were a bull she was riding into a rodeo ring. Wade applied some brake, and the cart slowed, then stopped ten feet shy of the concrete wall at the end of the corridor.

"Let's do it again!" Faith yelled. It was all she wanted in the world. She wanted to be shot down an empty hallway on bungee cords and kiss until the sun went down, but that dream was not to be. "Don't move, Faith," Wade said. "No matter what happens, stay right where you are. Understand?"

Wade was whispering to her, staring her in the face like all hell was about to break loose. It scared her, so she leaned in and kissed him again, searching for something to take away the terror that was welling up in her mind. The terror came from a sound they both heard. It was a known sound in the outside world, a sound designed to make people cut a path for the approaching menace.

Ping. Ping. Ping.

You could always hear the Drifters coming. They didn't want to encounter anyone they didn't need to and preferred to be left alone. It was part of their code, their cultish reasoning. They would never succumb to the States, no matter the cost, and this had turned them secretive about their business. They reminded Faith of the Hell's Angels, an old motorcycle gang she'd read about that had long since vanished off the face of the earth. The State hadn't exactly banned weapons on the outside, but the only weapons that remained were left-overs from an earlier, more violent age. And Faith had the feeling they dressed as they did not only to hide weapons, but also to send a message: *We are here to stay. We're not going inside the State. Ever.* They traveled in packs of ten or twenty, lived off the land, were thought to be violent and dangerous.

Ping. Ping. Ping.

Faith heard the sound again. She understood what it was: someone in the group was tapping a Coin against an empty tin can. But in her current condition, the sound had a bottomless echo that lurched closer like a demon. The fun and games had passed; the Wire Code had turned dark and menacing.

She would later try to remember what had happened and conclude that she had entered into some kind of twisted nightmare. She saw them appear in the corridor from behind a door, where they must have been staying as they passed through the area. It was scary to think they'd settled in on school grounds, but it made some sense. No one would have thought to look for Drifters at a high school. Faith remembered the tattered eagle emblazoned on their long trench coats, their tangled hair, the sawed-off shotgun barrels pointing at the floor. Those were their trademarks.

There was a lot of screaming in the hallway, but if she had been in her right mind, she would have understood that the screams had been mostly her own. She screamed because the Drifters were being thrown down the hallway like rag dolls. They were bouncing off lockers and breaking through the square sections of glass in doorways. Her senses zeroed in on one Drifter who appeared to be a woman. She was slamming into one wall of lockers, then she was slamming into the lockers on the other side of the hallway with lightning speed; back and forth, faster and faster, her body destroyed before Faith's eyes.

Three hours later she awoke from a deep sleep in her own bed. She was breathing heavily, a bead of sweat running down her exposed collarbone. Something moved in the room; but it was dark, and she couldn't see what it was. Faith felt a deep sadness welling up inside her, but she couldn't understand why. The last thing she could remember about the events of that night was the exposed forearm of a man, a Drifter fallen and silent on the cold floor in front of her. And on that arm, looking up at her, was the tattered eagle on the branch, the tattooed symbol of the Drifters. It was the image of a powerful bird lost in a broken world, ever defiant against a coming evil.

She felt the tears running down her cheeks and cried

silently. After a time, so heavy and tired, she floated back into a deep sleep and didn't wake again until the next morning.

If Faith had turned to her right and looked out her window, she would have seen that someone was watching her, wondering why she was so sad, hoping there was enough time to make things right.

Chapter 6

How Do You Say Good-bye?

Liz's obsessive hand-holding started after Noah left for the Western State. She had always been an unusually tactile sort of person. She loved the way things felt in her hands more than the way things tasted or smelled or looked. Smelling a rose, for Liz, was nothing compared to the sheer bliss of removing one of its bloodred petals and rubbing its velvety surface between her thumb and finger. To taste an apple was fine; but to feel its cool, slick skin against the side of her face as it glided back and forth, that was the really sweet part of an apple for Liz Brinn.

Before meeting Noah she had long since made her

dating decisions based on the way the other person felt in her hands. She would succumb to an invitation to go for a walk or watch a movie and find herself wondering from the very beginning what it would feel like to run her hand along the knuckles of the fresh, new hand that had arrived in her hemisphere.

"I read palms," Liz would say within ten minutes of meeting a guy. "I'm really good at it. Wanna see?"

She had come to find this lie particularly useful given her curiosities, if not devastating for her reputation. By sophomore year she was jokingly referred to as a mystical witch creature from the Black Forest who could transform into a unicorn, a sphinx, or a boy-eating monster.

It was inevitable that her long search would finally lead to Noah Logan, who was in possession of a pair of hands that were softer than a baby's bottom. Liz couldn't stop touching Noah's hands morning, noon, and night. It was his best feature; but he also had touchable, wispy brown hair and a striking smile. She'd wander the halls of school, searching for those hands so she could feel them soft against her skin. Sometimes when they kissed, he touched the exposed part of her lower back with his fingers, and she would shiver, delighted at the electric energy he produced. He had the dreamiest sleepy eyes, always asking her to his room, where she could feel his touch all over her body as much as she wanted.

Noah had a gentle personality that matched the hands, something Liz found unbelievably attractive. Everything about Noah was tender, from the way he touched her to all the words that he spoke. She was so completely head over heels for this boy that it nearly killed her when he was suddenly gone. It was like a violent storm had blown through and carried Noah up into the sky and far away. He simply vanished one day. That was the way it happened when people went to one of the States. It was like they'd never existed to begin with, and it usually happened without warning.

His departure, so sudden and final, broke something inside of Liz Brinn. She wasn't the same after he left. She was fragile, the softness she loved having turned against her in the end. Faith was the only friend who remained, and Liz needed her to fill the emotional emptiness. And so they held hands a lot. Once or twice Liz's feelings had gotten confused, and she wondered if what she'd really wanted all along was the softness of another girl; but it always passed like a soft breeze. She liked boys; this much she was sure of. She simply liked them best if they were soft, and there would never be another boy who could measure up to Noah Logan in that department. "Why do you think he didn't say good-bye?" Liz had asked Faith many times, often while they walked aimlessly.

"Maybe he didn't want to say anything that might hurt you. He was funny that way. It wasn't in him to hurt people."

This made sense to Liz; but it revealed a possible cowardice in the person she had chosen, and this bothered her.

"I think it was just sudden. He didn't have time to tell me or he would have."

"You're right. It happens that way if the parents decide to go. First they shut down the Tablets, then the white van arrives."

Unmarked white vans with no windows drove around the outside day and night. They were drones—no one drove them—powered by solar cells atop their roofs, ever waiting for someone to summon them. All a person had to do was contact one of the States, say they were ready to leave the outside world, and wait. A white van would arrive, sometimes within minutes, to whisk them away to a new life.

White vans were easy to spot but eerily quiet because they were all electric. Liz had nearly been killed once when she'd walked in front of one while staring at her Tablet. The van swerved and missed Liz, but it ran over the Tablet. Four hours later the Tablet had repaired itself, or been "reengineered." That was one of the amazing things about Tablets. Not only could they stretch and snap into different sizes, they could regenerate. Like a cut finger, a broken Tablet could heal itself. Hawk had said it best: "It's a simple matter of biomechanics and technology converging. What's not to understand?"

Liz held on to Faith's view of things, that the white van had found Noah's family so fast there had been no time for good-byes, because any other version of events was too heartbreaking to bear. And it really did go down that way sometimes. Liz had seen it happen more than once. At first she thought it was terrible the way her friends would leave without a word, not even a final farewell in the form of a Tablet message. It wasn't until this had happened twice that her mother told her not to worry.

"This is the way it works, Lizzy. There's a lot of talk about leaving or staying, but when the decision is made and a family makes that call, the Tablets get shut off. A few minutes later they're picked up. It's exciting, sort of. And they're not gone forever. They've only moved away. Remember that."

Liz seized on this important piece of information as well. It was one of the most persuasive reasons to leave the old world behind: Noah was inside the Western

State, waiting for her. And not just Noah; *everyone* was in there having the time of their lives, and they were *communicating* about it. They had Tablets, but they were tied into the G12, a network no one on the outside had access to. She had a fantasy that Noah was sending out distress signals, trying to find her, waiting for her impending arrival like his life depended on it.

Seeing Faith talk to someone like Wade Quinn made Liz wonder how long it would be before her best friend had her heart broken. How long did Faith think someone like Wade was going to last outside? What was he even doing out here so late in the game? Liz knew, better than anyone, that it wouldn't be long. Once Wade went to the Field Games in the Western State, he'd never come back. It was a virtual guarantee. What was Faith thinking getting into a relationship with a guy like that? He was a short-timer with only one thing on his mind.

At least when Wade Quinn was gone and Faith's heart was smashed into pieces, there would be an empty hand for Liz to hold on to. By then, Liz promised herself, she wouldn't need Faith's comfort nearly as much. She would get stronger, less needy. The tables would be turned. Maybe Liz would offer her hand, maybe she wouldn't.

Liz wore a rubber band on her wrist; and taking it between the thumb and index finger of her other hand, she pulled it four or five inches away, feeling it dig into her skin on the palm side of her wrist. When she let go, it snapped, stinging almost enough to make her wince. She was happy to feel the pain against her skin, and she realized with some regret that she wasn't feeling much of anything inside anymore. She sat on the curb at the mall, staring at the empty buildings and wondering what would become of her.

She didn't have to wait long for an answer.

Her Tablet vibrated, and Liz took it out of her pack, touching the perfectly slick screen. A message had arrived from her mother.

Come home. We need to talk.

The screen on Liz's Tablet went black. She swiped her finger across the surface four or five times, but there was nothing. She was confused but not alarmed, turning the Tablet over in her hands, trying to shake it awake.

"I really have to stop dropping this thing," she mumbled. But then, turning it over and seeing her dim reflection in the glass, she understood. Her Tablet was dead. It wasn't broken. It had been turned off.

She'd wondered for a long time what it would be like when this happened, a light going out in her life.

"Looks like I won't be seeing you in class tomorrow."

Liz wheeled around and stood up, backing away from a voice she wasn't completely sure she recognized. Night was gathering around her, and the streetlights had long since stopped working, which made it hard to be completely sure of who it was walking slowly toward her.

"Dylan? Dylan Gilmore? Is that you?"

"None other," he said, stopping five or so feet away and stuffing his hands into his jean pockets. "Tablet's dead, huh?"

Liz unconsciously glanced at her Tablet, which felt unexpectedly useless in her hand. Why was she even holding on to it? Unlike Hawk and so many other people, she had actually hated her Tablet from the start. The fact that someone else controlled it, so much so that they could turn it off completely whenever they chose, deeply angered her. Even though its glass screen was the one thing in her life that was as smooth as Noah's skin, she couldn't stand to look at it anymore. Liz swung around and faced the empty Old Navy store, then threw the Tablet like it were a tomahawk. It hit the cement wall and fell to the pavement below, scratched but unbroken.

"You have to hit them really hard or they won't break," Dylan said.

"Believe me, I don't need any help in that department."

Liz, who had damaged her Tablet plenty of times over the years, was not about to let a virtual stranger tell her how to do this. She walked to the Tablet, picked it up, and began banging it against the wall. It didn't take long to bloody her knuckles on the white, painted surface of the Old Navy store, a little longer to hear the screen of her Tablet crack. She dropped the Tablet on the sidewalk and started stomping on it.

"I think it's dead now," Dylan said, cautiously taking a step closer to her. She didn't appear to hear him as she continued stomping on the Tablet over and over. It wasn't until he touched her on the shoulder and she tried to bat his hand away that she finally gave up.

"Why are you here?!" she yelled. "Just leave me alone."

Dylan backed off, watching Liz like he'd stumbled upon a stray dog that might react in any number of ways.

"It's cool. I was walking through on my way to somewhere else, thought you looked a little lost, that's all."

"Bullshit."

Dylan Gilmore stopped backpedaling as Liz went on. "What's your deal anyway? You walk around looking all silent and smoldering, don't talk to anyone. And then you just turn up for no reason right when my parents decide to leave? It's creepy."

"I'm sorry you feel that way."

Liz waited about two seconds to see if Dylan was going to say anything else; and when he didn't, she decided he wasn't worth her time.

"I gotta go," she said. "Nice knowing you."

"No good-bye for Faith or Hawk?"

Liz was ready to snap. It felt like she was being accused of ditching her friends by someone who had no right getting into her business.

"You don't know me. *Or* them! You don't know *anything*. Just stay out of it."

Dylan ran a hand through his black hair and stared at his skate shoes, two habits that seemed to help him make up his mind about things when he wasn't sure what to do. When he looked up and saw that Liz had already begun walking away, he thought it might be too late.

"If you want me to give them a message, I'll do that for you. I don't mind."

Liz stopped in her tracks but didn't turn around. Was she so heartless that she'd leave without saying a word, like so many of her friends had done? Hawk was new; it was expected that he wouldn't necessarily hear from her. But Faith, that was something else. They'd been through so much together.

"I've had to do this, too," Dylan said. "More than once. I know how hard it is to come up with the right words to say."

The offer was tempting, but she barely knew Dylan Gilmore. She'd been at Old Park Hill for only a few weeks, and he'd said maybe two words in all that time. It didn't feel right sending a message through someone she didn't trust. What if he got it all wrong? And besides, it was too personal. She'd want to say she loved them, would miss them terribly, wished she could stay. She wasn't about to say those things to a guy she didn't know.

"If you see them, tell them I'll be waiting on the other side, and I hope they don't forget me. Tell them I'm sorry. I didn't get to choose this."

Dylan didn't speak for a long moment. He wanted to give her space in case there was more.

"That it?"

"Yeah, that's it. Now do me a favor and leave me alone."

Liz started walking away without a second glance. She wished Dylan would leave, but she could feel him still staring at her even before he spoke.

"When you get to the State, be on the lookout for a

message; will you at least do that much for me?"

"I don't even know you, so no, I won't."

"The message won't be from me. It'll be from someone else."

Whatever game Dylan was playing had finally sent Liz over the edge. She turned around to let him have it. She was already halfway into the first blistering sentence before she realized that Dylan Gilmore was gone. It was like he'd never been there to begin with.

"And don't come back!" Liz yelled. She began to sob and kicked her broken Tablet down the sidewalk in frustration. She looked off in the direction of the gym and wondered if she had time to run and find Faith so she could take back everything she'd said.

A white van pulled up silently behind her, and the side door opened with a whisper, inviting her inside. Liz wiped the tears from her eyes and thought about running. She took one last look in the direction of the school and gave in to the inevitable.

Chapter 7

Business as Usual

When Faith sat up in bed, it felt like she'd polished off two bottles of ancient wine the night before without any help from her fellow partygoers. She held her head in her hands and tried to remember what could have possibly made her feel this way. She'd only gotten wasted once in her entire life, more than a year ago, and that had been enough to convince her that partying wasn't her thing. It had begun at a friend's house before a rare dance put on by one of the schools she used to attend. The friend, Tess, had whipped together some sort of crazy concoction that tasted like orange juice but packed a punch big enough to level a rhino in two cups or less. Faith had guzzled down three large cups before she knew what she was doing, and all at once she'd gone buzzy in the head. An hour later she had been throwing up all over the dance floor.

It had been a total flame out, and for that she was thankful. If she'd slowly experimented with partying, she would probably still be using whatever she could find to dull the pain she felt from one day to the next. Instead, she'd had such a bad experience that one time, she'd never gone back.

"What happened to me last night?" she asked out loud. When she stood, Faith felt an immediate need to throw up and ran to the bathroom. A half hour later she was standing in the shower, turning up the heat every thirty seconds until the room filled with steam. The sound of a message arriving on her Tablet pinged into the soupy air, and she knew it was time to get moving. She'd pieced together what could be remembered and found herself in an angry mood. She remembered a fight with Liz, walking away with Wade, something about a car and the feel of Wade's chest against her palms. And Drifters. She remembered Drifters.

The Tablet pinged again—more messages—and Faith turned off the shower. Leaning down to dry her legs made her head pound, so she pulled on her old fleece robe and sat heavily on her bed.

Her Tablet was lying next to her. She picked it up and started reading through the messages. The first one was from her mom, reminding her to visit the distribution center for their monthly ration of cheese and flour. Faith messaged her back—okay, I won't forget— and fished a pair of socks out of her drawer. It was easier to put them on sitting down than standing up, and the shower had made her feel a little more human again. The second message was like a repeat of the first, but this time it was from her dad. They liked to double down on reminders.

The next message was from Hawk, and it got her moving even faster.

Standing outside your door; didn't want to wake you. How are you holding up?

Maybe Hawk knew more than she did and could tell her what had happened the night before. She typed out a message—be right down, give me five—and finished getting ready, combing her wet hair into a ponytail and applying the most basic makeup she could get away with. She slid on the new pair of jeans Hawk had basically stolen from the Eastern State and felt better still. They fit perfectly. She could already imagine how they'd turn Wade's head at school.

Thinking of Wade got her thinking of Liz, and her memory began to spark on a moment standing outside the school. She couldn't quite remember what was said, but there was a pit in her stomach that told her she'd chosen Wade over Liz, and it had not gone well. As she walked downstairs, she did something very Liz-like, messaging her while she went.

How you doing? We okay? I miss you. Let's talk.

She shook her head at how random and stupid it all sounded, but hit SEND anyway, then opened the front door. Hawk was sitting on the tiny front porch cross-legged, typing furiously into his Tablet.

"We're going to be late for sure," Hawk said, standing up so fast it made Faith feel woozy just watching him. "Should we say we were attacked by zombies and go make something cheesy in your kitchen?"

"I'm thinking kitchen," Faith said, realizing how hungry she was. She gestured to her new jeans, and Hawk nodded approvingly.

"Perfect fit. Good thing, because I don't think they're returnable."

"How about I pay you in eggs?"

"Deal."

As they walked toward the kitchen, Faith wished

Liz was there with them. It wasn't the same without her, and she hadn't messaged back yet. Faith set her Tablet on the kitchen table and got the eggs out of the fridge. There were four left for the week, but she was fine sharing them.

"So listen," Hawk said. He was more fidgety than usual, picking up the salt and pepper shakers and setting them back down again, spinning them around on the flat wood surface. "I'm not sure how you want to handle this. I mean, I don't want to get all sad on you. Sucks though. Really, really sucks."

Faith felt a nervous chill run from her head to her toes and leaned over the sink, sure she was going to vomit.

"You okay? You don't look so good."

"I'm fine. Just a little tired is all. Late night."

What had she done? She must have gotten wasted with Wade or maybe after they parted and gone and made a total ass of herself. She wished more than anything that she could just remember.

Her Tablet pinged with a message, which only made her more anxious. It would be from Liz, telling her what a loser she was. It was going to take some work to sort this all out, and she wasn't sure she had the strength to do it. All she really wanted to do was take three aspirins and go back to bed. She picked up one of the four eggs and considered its surface, which made her think of Liz and her obsession with the way things felt. The egg was cold and smooth in her hand. It was oddly comforting against the softness of her palm. She used her free hand to slide her Tablet closer on the kitchen counter, spinning it right side up so she could see who the message was from. There was a long pause, a fragile silence in which the birds could be heard singing outside the open window. The egg slipped out of Faith's hand and hit the floor, and she felt the clear liquid splash her new jeans.

Faith looked up at Hawk and finally understood why he was acting so strange.

"She's gone."

An uncomfortable silence followed before Hawk blurted out, "I thought you knew. I'm sorry." He didn't know how to keep going. He wasn't all that good in social situations involving girls in tight jeans anyway. So he said the only other thing that came to mind and hoped it was enough. "Sucks, right?"

Faith couldn't believe the message on her Tablet. She'd been so sure there would be time to make things right with Liz, to talk it all out and get back to where they were. To hold hands and walk to the grade school and read real books. The response to her message told her none of that was going to happen.

Elizabeth Brinn has been moved to the Western
State. User account deactivated.

"She didn't contact you?" Hawk asked, because he
didn't know what else to say.

"No, she didn't," Faith said.

And then she turned to the sink and threw up.

Hawk was having some problems of his own, but he knew
it wasn't the right moment to bring it up with Faith.
He'd only known her for a few weeks, and yet he could
tell she was coming apart at the seams. Any idiot could
see that much.

His Tablet had turned up missing three more times
since that first night at the grade school. Each time he
would have sworn it was right next to him, only to look
over and see that it had vanished into thin air. Each
time it was gone a little longer, pushing the limits of his
fragile psyche. Either he was slowly losing his mind—a
real possibility—or someone was messing with him. He
could only think of one person to confront about it, and
so he left Faith and found Wade Quinn.

"Look, little man, I don't know what you're talking about.
Sounds to me like you've been doing more than just
baking the goods."

Wade was a dick; there were no two ways about it as far as Hawk was concerned. But the guy had access to a ton of Coin. He always had a lot of cash in his Tablet account, and he was always happy to spend it.

"Seriously, are you messing with me?" Hawk asked. "Because I'm not lowering my price again. Wire Codes are tricky. Plus I could get in real trouble, man, like huge."

It was not Hawk's proudest moment, groveling in front of Wade Quinn, who also happened to be his only customer. "Just tell me—are you taking my Tablet or not?"

Wade smiled as he looked up from the bench on which he was sitting. Clara was sitting next to him, smug as usual, not saying a word.

"I think you're paranoid. Most drug dealers are."

"I'm not a drug dealer. That's a low blow. You're making me do this, remember?"

"Well, I'm not taking your Tablet. Why would I even do that? I hate carrying one of them around, let alone two."

"I don't believe you. You're pissed off because I bought stuff for your girlfriend. Dude, she's totally out of my league. I'm not even in her universe. Just do me a favor and leave my Tablet alone, okay? It's nerve-racking enough making this stuff for you all the time."

"You're spending Coin on gifts for girls?" Clara

asked. Hawk considered Clara the highest-ranking a-hole in the entire world. He couldn't stand how condescending she was.

"Actually, it's none of your business what I spend my Coin on. And while we're at it, I'm not making any more Wire Codes for you guys. I'm done."

Hawk was a hell of a hacker. He hadn't paid for pants and shirts for Faith and Liz; he'd programmed around that little problem. All the money he'd ever made was stacked up in Coin in different online accounts. He was loaded, but he was also tiny and generally afraid of large people, one of whom had gotten up off the bench.

"I think you should keep making Wire Codes when I'm willing to pay for them," Wade said. "It's in your best interest."

"I'm not doing that."

"Wanna bet?" Wade was standing about two inches from Hawk, staring down at him from an alarming height advantage.

"Yeah, I wanna bet," Hawk said. He had an ace up his sleeve and decided it was time to play it. "I saw Faith this morning. You know, your *girlfriend*? She's not too much into the party scene. Looked to me like someone the morning after their first Wire Code. Why do you suppose that is?"

"Is this urchin trying to blackmail you?" Clara

asked. She was genuinely surprised.

"All I know is, the day after, for a first timer, there's not much memory to go on. Very fragmented. I'm guessing you'd rather she didn't know you slipped her a Wire Code without her agreeing to it. Anything else happen you don't want her to know about?"

Wade's hands were shaking. Hawk thought Wade could probably crush every bone in his body using nothing but his pinkie, but he didn't back down.

"Stop messing with my stuff, that's all I'm asking," Hawk said. He was so sure that the Quinns were taking his Tablet in order to get him to lower the price of Wire Codes, he was willing to risk a punch in the face.

"That's going to be real easy, because I already told you; I'm not taking your Tablet. All the same, I think I need some new insurance of my own. Keep Faith out of this. There's no reason for her to know; we were just having a little fun. You keep your mouth shut, and I'll do the same. A lot of people around here would like to know who makes the Wire Codes at this school. I think I know who that might be."

"I know, too," Clara said, assuming they'd gotten the upper hand.

"You're forgetting an important detail. It's common with drug addicts, so you shouldn't feel bad. I know who *takes* them," Hawk said. "I keep a record of every transaction. Not just when they're purchased, but when they're *used*. And on what Tablet."

He was scared to death. He had just told a huge lie; and furthermore, he'd made a monster blunder. If he'd had those kinds of records, there would be only one place to keep them. On his Tablet! He'd just given the Quinns one more reason to keep taking it, and the next time he might not get it back until it was too late. All he had going for him was Faith Daniels. The only thing that mattered now was how much Wade liked her.

Wade shook his head and smiled, backing away from Hawk. He lurched forward with a fist that stopped just shy of Hawk's face, but Hawk didn't flinch, not even an inch.

"Business as usual then," Wade said.

Hawk could hardly breathe, but he was able to get the words out before he turned around and walked away. "Business as usual."

Chapter 8

You Moved Me

Once Hawk was gone, Faith took her Tablet to bed and lay down, flipping through images she'd drawn when she should have been studying. She used a stylus to draw the really intricate ones: drawings of landscapes and portraits of friends. She'd drawn Liz sitting in front of the rubble at the old mall, holding out her hand toward the open space, searching for someone to grab hold of. There was a tab at the top of the screen, and Faith tapped it. A photograph expanded on the screen, taking up most of the real estate in the top right corner. The photo was a mirror image of the drawing: Liz sitting on the bench, holding out her empty hand toward the camera, her eyes searching for something beyond what Faith could see. Faith's eyes filled with tears, and her vision went blurry.

You can't be gone. I need you here, with me. What am I going to do without you?

Faith knew it was morbid emotional suicide to look at the picture, knew it would hurt like hell to wallow in the pain she felt. But she couldn't help herself. She was all alone in the world. She'd lost her only real friend.

Flipping through digital pages with her finger, Faith arrived at a blank screen and picked up the stylus. What she really wanted, the thing she deeply wished for at that moment, was a pencil. During moments of deep sadness she sometimes found it comforting to use pre-Tablet instruments of expression. She thought she heard just that—a pencil—rolling toward her on the desk with that very distinct sound a rolling pencil makes, each of its six sides clanging as it went. The sound stopped as quickly as it had started, and she chalked it up to a mushy hangover head she still couldn't shake.

Sometimes, in her more nostalgic moments, Faith would covet the feeling of lead moving on paper. She knew it was extravagant and useless, because whenever she wrote on paper, it inevitably got lost or destroyed. It was a rare drawing or note that Faith had produced with a pencil that had not been misplaced or abandoned in one of her many moves. In the world in which she'd grown up, she had been taught from an early age that everything she needed was kept on her Tablet. Even if she lost the Tablet, it wouldn't matter, because everything she had ever created was stored in the cloud. It never crossed her mind, in a serious way, to write or draw anything important on something as transient as a piece of actual paper. In any case, the urge to stay in bed was much stronger than the pull of a pencil so far away on the desk, so she never made it out from under the blanket.

Faith began to draw on the screen with her stylus, slowly at first and then with a kind of furious, angry speed that produced a harsh but brilliant drawing. There was no doubting an artistic ability that blossomed most powerfully during times of grief. There had been a lot of grief lately, and her work had turned darker and more mature. It was sad, really, that the world had to turn so dark in order to bring out her true talent.

When she was done, she tucked her Tablet under her pillow and closed her eyes, hoping to fall away into a dream so she could forget. Her body curled up into a ball as she turned on her side, pulling the covers up close to her face. But sleep wouldn't come. She chewed on the nail next to her pinkie finger—a major failure, because she'd managed to leave it alone for a long time—and quickly ruined what had been a smooth curve against the tip of her ring finger.

There was a sound from the desk across the room, almost silent, like it hadn't wanted to be heard. The sound reminded her of something, but she couldn't put her finger on what it was, perhaps because she hadn't heard the sound very many times. Was she sleeping but didn't know it? Faith bit down on her fingernail, peeling away a piece dangerously close to the skin. It hurt, but at least it was something other than the heavy weight in her chest, that distinct feeling of a broken heart nowhere near mending.

"Hawk?" Faith whispered, but there was no answer. She lifted her head, expecting to see him, glad about the thought of it. She wasn't close to him, not really, but at least he was a person she knew. She watched as a pencil and a white note card fell to the floor and landed on the soft carpet like they'd been suspended in midair and suddenly dropped all at once. The pencil hit first, bouncing once and then lying like a dead animal on the plush, gray carpet. The note card fluttered slightly, catching on the air beneath it, then shot down like an airplane crashing into the ground. It was blank, that much she could see as she blinked three or four times, making sure she was fully awake. It was at that moment she realized what the mysterious sound had been. It was the sound of a pencil writing on paper, the melancholy sound she'd been too lazy to get up and create with her own hand.

She looked at the window to her room, where she'd pulled the blinds half shut, but there was no wind coming in.

Well, she thought, *there's no hope now.* A nap was out of the question. She was wide-awake and nursing a bad headache, but she sat up anyway. Curious about the pencil, she walked over and picked it up, examining it like a scientist, and concluded that, yes, it had simply rolled off the desk for some unknown reason. She picked up the white note card as well, staring at its blank surface. When she went to place it back where it had come from, she turned it over absentmindedly and saw that the note card hadn't only fallen to the floor; it had also been written on.

You moved me.

"What the hell?" Faith said, holding the pencil like a weapon she might need if a Drifter jumped out of her closet. But there was no one; the room and the house that surrounded it were empty.

You moved me? Faith thought as she returned to the comfort of the bed and tried to piece everything together. There was something calming about pulling the blanket up close, like it might magically serve as a shield against the dangerous world outside. She was clearly out of her mind. She'd taken something—Wade, he'd *given* her something without her consent. That had to be what was causing the twisted dream in which she was trapped. Whatever strange things had occurred last night, they were still happening now. Her mind was playing tricks on her. She'd written those words in her sleep and moved the pencil. She was hallucinating; that was the answer. It was the *only* answer.

But Faith couldn't shake the thought that she'd wanted the pencil and the note card, wished she could hold them, and thought she'd heard the pencil rolling toward her for an instant. She shut her eyes tightly and tried to forget, but the words kept coming in waves.

You moved me. You moved me. You moved me!

Faith had only sat in the chair she was in one other time. What she was about to have done was going to hurt, she knew. Maybe, down deep, that was *why* she was going to do it; but she told herself that wasn't true. She only did this on very special, very sad occasions. She knew the tattoo would help. It would hurt a lot, and that would drain some of the pain out of her. It would give her a reminder so she'd never forget. It would be the beginning of the loneliness going away, and a beginning meant there could be an end waiting somewhere off in the distance.

"You sure this is what you want?" the artist asked. Her arms were covered in tattoos, brightly colored and beautiful. Vines of tattooed green ivy ran up the sides of her neck, crawling onto her cheeks and disappearing into her long hair.

"Yeah, just don't make it very big. My parents will kill me if they find out."

"I know all about parents, kiddo. No problem there. But this is going to hurt more than the last time. You really went off on this thing."

Her name was Glory, at least that was what she called herself, and she was fairly mesmerized by the drawing Faith had made. The lines were aggressive and cruel, but they added up to a severe beauty Glory half wished she could have tattooed on her own skin. The thick, muddy lines would be hell to pay for Faith. Glory had seen grown men cry laying down that kind of ink.

"Same place, other side," Faith said as she nodded her resolve to have it done. "Put it up as high as you can, like two inches wide, so it's hidden."

Glory nodded and took out her Tablet. Faith held her own Tablet, and the transaction began; first the drawing was transferred from Tablet to Tablet, then the

Coin to pay for the procedure. It made a large dent in her account, and Faith rolled onto her side in the chair, closing her eyes as Glory prepared the needles and ink.

"Totally black, like last time?" Glory asked, wishing she could put down some color.

"Yeah, black as you can make it."

Glory shook her head almost imperceptibly. She'd learned to push down her feelings at times like this, but seeing this damaged creature curled up on the long chair like a baby brought back some bad memories. Faith pulled her long blond hair into a fist and tucked it under her neck like a pillow. It was thick and just a little bit wavy, and long enough to cover up what Glory was about to do.

Faith felt the sting of the needle touching the tender skin at her hairline but didn't move. She absorbed it like a sponge and settled in for the long haul. She curled harder into a ball, touching the other side of her neck where another tattoo lay hidden.

"You know," Glory said over the electric hum of the tools she used. "We go together like salt and pepper, you and me. Faith and Glory. Like we were fated to find each other."

"Sure, I guess." Faith was still nursing a headache, but it was rapidly going away in the shadow of the fire on her neck.

"Might make a pretty tattoo—Faith and Glory—all swirly and nice."

Faith could see the image clearly. She was already drawing it out in her mind, but it wasn't swirly and nice. The word *Glory* was surrounded in bright-green ivy, *Faith* was tangled in barbed wire. And for once there was color—red—bleeding in lines off Faith's name.

When it was over, Glory offered to show it to Faith using two mirrors, one in front and one behind; but Faith didn't want to look at it until at least a little bit of the gross swelling had gone down. It would be days before it would calm down for good, and she had a feeling she wouldn't have the strength to look at it until it stopped hurting. She'd nurse the pain, imagine the image; and when finally she did look at it, her pain would be smaller.

"Thank you, Glory. I don't think I'll be back."

"Never say never. These things are addicting." Glory held out her arms, in part to show off all the tattoos that covered her skin, but also to invite Faith into an embrace. Faith didn't put out her arms; she just moved a step closer and let Glory enfold her.

"Faith and Glory," she said. "You remember that. We're bound for both you and me."

Faith wasn't so sure, but she liked the way Glory's dark skin smelled sweet and gentle, the way her embrace was firm but soft.

An hour later Faith was back home, standing in her bathroom. She was staring into a mirror and holding a smaller one in her hand, thinking about looking. She was not thinking of the new tattoo but the old one, an image she only allowed herself to look at once in a while. It had been a month or more since she'd let herself look there; and for some unknown reason, she began this exercise by lifting the wrong side of her hair. Was it an accident, or did she really want to see the work Glory had done and hadn't been able to help herself? Either way, once she'd started to see the new tattoo, she couldn't stop. Faith pulled her hair all the way up and saw the damaged, swollen skin. Tattoos never looked good on the first day. They looked more like the result of an inky, self-inflicted cutting session. But the image was there, and it brought her to tears all over again. It was a pair of holding hands, the wrists disappearing up into her blond hair. The lines were fierce, but the result was powerful, like two people who would never let go of each other. And Glory had been unable to help herself. She'd added a tiny thread of green ivy wrapped around the wrists. She'd added a small presence of hope in a composition of grief, like a white dove against an endless black sky.

"Thank you, Glory," Faith whispered, because she

liked it. It made her feel better.

Faith took a deep breath and let her waves of hair fall against her shoulder. She looked at her Tablet and remembered that she was supposed to go and get the cheese and the flour, because that's what her parents had told her to do.

Or had they?

As Faith pulled her long hair into a knot behind her head and turned slightly in the mirror, she let herself hold the truth completely. She'd set those messages to come in herself, the reminders from her parents, which had originally been sent months and months before. Faith had copied them and put them on a rotation. And for a stinging moment every day or two, the alerts would appear like her mom and her dad had both reminded her to get the cheese and get the flour, to get home after dark. A split second later she would understand it wasn't really them. But the brief moment before that was like the electric hum of a tattoo needle marking her soul.

She took a good long look at the image on the side of her neck. It was small and well hidden, tucked secretly against the line of her hair, opposite the new tattoo she'd just gotten. There was a branch of a tree in winter, leafless and cracked. On the branch sat a tattered eagle, staring off into the distance like it would fight on and on no matter the cost. It would never relent.

Faith's parents were gone. They'd been gone awhile. And they weren't dead or somehow taken to one of the States without her. They weren't off running a long and important errand only to return at some time in the future they'd agreed on.

No, Faith's parents weren't coming back.

Her parents were Drifters.

PART TWO

FIELD
GAMES

Chapter 9

Adrift in Skinny Jeans

Field reports traveled to Meredith through a complicated series of hacked Tablets, verbal communications, and carriers. More often than not, the news was not good. She had come to recognize the steady flow of depressing information as a normal part of her day, but the latest report was different. It possessed a weight with the power to change everything.

Ten Drifters were dead. Eleven had gone in; only one had come out.

Every war she'd ever known about had started this way. Up until a certain point, there was always a way out if both sides were willing to negotiate. But certain special events were designed with war in mind. They were orchestrated to send a clear message. There was always one side that pushed the other into an understanding about how things had changed. There would be no more posturing. The enemy had gotten the party started, whether she liked it or not. Meredith was one of the few people who knew a war had just begun. She knew the plans being made in secret and the extent to which the world was about to change. It was information she had kept safe at all cost.

"All but one?" Meredith asked. She was sitting in a vast, empty space, an undisclosed location known only to her most trusted carriers. The location was closer to Old Park Hill than she was comfortable with, but circumstances being what they were, there wasn't much she could do about it. She had to be close to the front line, if not standing right on top of it. How else could she keep her finger on the most important developments taking place?

"It would seem they walked into a trap," Clooger said. He was a huge man, bearded and dreadlocked. What little could be seen of his pale skin was scarred in multiple places, like he'd boxed a thousand rounds and been cut open too many times to count. His skin was the color of milk, in part because he never went outside unless it was dark. Very few Drifters did. He held a sawed-off shotgun at his side, half hidden under a long trench coat.

"Tell me everything you know," Meredith said.

Clooger cleared his throat as if he were about to give a field report to a commanding officer, but when he began to speak, it was more natural than that. He'd long since grown weary of military formality.

"I sent a team to the abandoned building at Old Park Hill just as you asked. Eight men, three woman."

"And they holed up in one of the rooms, as I ordered?"

Clooger nodded. "They stayed quiet, well hidden. We received one message on the first night—everything was fine—and then nothing."

Meredith had sent the group to watch, not to fight. "I told them to quietly observe from an empty building. How did most of them end up dead?"

She knew this wasn't entirely true. She'd heard, from someone Clooger knew nothing about, that there had been activity in the building of potentially high importance.

"I debriefed the survivor about two hours ago. James, a low-level, just recruited last month. I'd say he was rethinking his decision. He escaped out a window before the trouble started."

There had been some important people in the group, but James had not been one of them. He was of little use to her and certainly was not allowed to know where she was stationed.

"That's unfortunate," she said, her mind already on other things. She had always been a calculating thinker, and she was smart enough to realize that the massacre was inevitable. She'd known it would come to this and, more importantly, that there would be many more casualties before it was over.

She looked into Clooger's battered face, thinking of the various Tablet networks she had control over. "Use G10; keep everyone calm. Let's not end up with a revolt on our hands."

"I'll do my best."

"And be careful about your business. Our situation is fragile."

As Clooger turned and stepped away, Meredith stared at the tattered eagle on the back of his trench coat. She wondered how many weapons he was carrying and of what kind. There was no way of knowing how many pockets lay hidden inside his coat, but she knew from experience that Clooger was a master of many war crafts. He knew a hundred different ways to kill a man and had the tools to accomplish them all.

"It wasn't my fault. It just . . . *happened*. It got crazy is all."

Wade Quinn was in an empty classroom staring

into his Tablet. The only other person within earshot was Clara, who stood by the door watching for anyone who might walk down the long, empty corridor. She loved nothing more than seeing her brother in hot water, and this situation was boiling over a gas flame. She was all too happy to throw some grease on the fire.

"He was with a girl," Clara said, loving every second of where this was going. "I told him not to, but you know Wade. He can't keep his hands off the ladies."

Wade took his eyes off his Tablet long enough to shoot his sister a cold stare, but it didn't last long. A hand slammed down onto an unseen desk in the video feed. When Wade looked back, the face in the Tablet was not pleased.

"I told you both to control yourselves, and you didn't."

"Hey, whoa," Clara said, moving over in front of the Tablet feed. "I had nothing to do with this. It was all Sasquatch here. This is on him."

"Shut up, Clara."

The command came from a female voice neither Wade nor Clara could see. She was on the other end of the Tablet feed, standing off camera. It was a voice they knew not to mess around with. "Go back to the door. Keep quiet."

Clara slunk away, staring bullets at her brother as she went.

"Just a bunch of Drifters anyway," Wade said under his breath, trying to make himself feel better. "Nobody's gonna miss 'em."

"They're more important than you think; I've told you that a thousand times. Did you kill them all?"

Wade thought this was an odd question to ask until it crossed his mind that if there had been more than ten and one had ran away, this whole thing could come back to haunt him in a hurry. He decided it would be better to lie, then clean up the mess later if he had to.

"It happened really fast. They jumped me, and I lost control; that's it. Took maybe two minutes. But yeah, they were all dead when it was over."

The person on the video screen wasn't so sure, but he let it go. "And you disposed of the bodies?"

"God, this is so gross," Clara said. She opened the door and walked out, leaving Wade to deal with the situation on his own. Wade started to yell at Clara, but the person on the Tablet stopped him.

"Let her go. She'll be fine if you give her some space."

Wade returned his gaze to the Tablet, trying his best to stay focused.

"Yeah, I know where the bodies are buried. It was some work."

"You're lucky to be alive. Drifters are dangerous and unpredictable."

"A plague on the earth," the unseen female voice added. "I can't say I mind fewer of them taking up space."

There was a pause as the man looked at Wade for a long moment. "Did you know what you were doing, or did it feel like something else was in control?"

Wade didn't want to answer the question. The Wire Code had made him more violent and alert. He'd never felt that powerful; and it really had happened very quickly, like a bolt of lightning, and it was over: dead bodies everywhere, Faith sitting in the cart shaking uncontrollably. He'd given her a second Wire Code so she'd block out everything. It was risky, especially for a first-timer, and he'd felt badly doing it. But he couldn't let her remember what he'd done. Not an option.

"They attacked; I went for it," Wade said. "To be honest, it's all kind of a blur. I don't remember exactly."

The whole thing had been crazy, and while he thought Drifters were subhuman losers who were too stupid to live in the States, he couldn't wrap his mind around the idea that he'd actually put ten of them out of their misery.

"Stay away from the girl," the man in the video feed said. "It's a distraction you don't need right now. Get stronger, do the training, and be ready. I'm going to need you at your best."

The feed went dead, and Wade was pleased that the Wire Code hadn't come up. He breathed deeply, like he'd been holding his breath during the conversation and finally he was allowed to get it all out and feel what he was really feeling.

"Holy shit, Wade," he said to himself. "You killed ten Drifters."

His emotions were all over the map. Part of him was amped at how incredibly powerful he was. Drifters were bad people: killers, thieves, con men. He'd had that drilled into his brain for years. He was thinking about taking on fifty, a hundred Drifters. Bring on the ninjas, send in the mixed martial arts champ; he'd take them all at once without breaking a sweat. Another part of him was struggling to make sense of what he'd let himself become. He didn't feel like a guy who'd take out ten people in a matter of minutes without thinking twice, but that's exactly what he'd done. He thought of Faith, and what she'd think of him if she knew. He liked her, and that was becoming a problem. It wasn't in the plan, and Wade Quinn was all about the plan.

All those thoughts were swirling around a more central one occupying a huge piece of real estate in his brain.

Something was up with that Wire Code.

Wade snapped his Tablet to small, put it in his back pocket, and went in search of an answer he could only get from one person.

Hawk, you better shoot straight with me, he thought as he opened the door and started down the empty hallway. *Otherwise you might be number eleven.*

"You realize what he's done," Andre said. Gretchen stood at his side, unmoving but clearly pleased. Talking to the twins always got her blood boiling.

"He's started a war," she said. "I would have expected nothing less."

"It's not the timing I would have chosen."

"The games are only a month away. We stick to the plan. This changes nothing. And you should encourage him more. He needs to get used to this. Ten Drifters was just the beginning for Wade."

"I don't know. Meredith can be unpredictable. This may set her off."

"You worry too much. She's only one person, and she's surrounded by castoffs and fools. I think it's good Wade did this; it shows how stupid she is. If she thinks Drifters will be of any help to her, Wade has made it clear they're going to be useless in any kind of real confrontation. She's running scared. Trust me."

Andre couldn't look at his wife. She was striking in the meanest way he could imagine, a characteristic that had been enticing and powerfully attractive when they'd met. In situations such as this one though, he felt nervous about her energy. She wanted power, lots of it, and as fast as it could be gotten. And there was something else, a thing that Andre understood all too well that Gretchen did not.

Meredith was a lot more powerful than he was. If things got complicated, their hope rested with the twins. It was a risky bet he wished he didn't have to rely on.

"Where have you been?" Hawk hadn't seen Faith for a week. She'd gone off grid, locked the door to her house, vanished.

"I was sick. It happens." Faith hadn't felt right for days and decided to take her classes from home, give herself some time to regroup. It was allowed, and in some ways even encouraged, this idea of schooling on one's own. Mr. Reichert and Miss Newhouse only asked that she check in every day with her Tablet, let them know she was getting her work done, staying out of trouble. It had taken six days to shake the headaches and the bouts of fever. She'd felt adrift, lost to the world, unable to reconnect.

"You were already skinny enough," Hawk said. He

looked up at her face, which was bordering on gaunt. "You wanna hit the cafeteria? We have time, like fifteen minutes before the first bell."

They sat together eating pancakes and cold cereal, the only two things besides milk that were always available for breakfast at Old Park Hill. Ten or so other kids were there, too, scattered in little groups around the cafeteria, eyeing Faith like she'd come back from the dead.

"Can I ask you something, Hawk?" Faith asked, slurping on a spoonful of wet cornflakes.

"As long as you keep eating, you can ask anything you want."

Hawk was careful to look up every few seconds in case Wade or Clara appeared. He'd been dodging them like a secret agent for days, steering clear of any trouble.

"What do you know about Wire Codes? I mean, are they dangerous or just fun?"

Hawk's throat went dry.

"It's okay; you don't have to answer me. I thought maybe, you know, since you're all techie and stuff, you'd know more than I do."

"Why are you asking?"

"Because I think I might have been given one without knowing about it."

Hawk started pouring syrup onto his totally uneaten pancake.

"You've got a little lake forming there," Faith said, pointing her spoon in the direction of Hawk's plate. Hawk set down the syrup bottle and cut a corner of pancake free, stabbing it with his fork. He swirled it around in circles in the slop on his plate, which made him look like he was high or stupid or both.

"Forget I asked," Faith said, shaking her head and standing to leave.

"No, it's cool. Really, I just—well, I just hope you're not in any trouble is all."

A kid Hawk's size always had a certain level of paranoia, sort of like a Chihuahua trying to make a go of it in a family of four or five people without getting stepped on. But the pressure was definitely getting to him. Word in the halls was that Wade Quinn was looking for him; and whatever he wanted, it might involve rearranging Hawk's face. And now Faith was asking questions he wasn't sure how to answer.

"How would I know if I'd been given a Wire Code?" Faith asked quietly, sitting back down and leaning over the table toward Hawk.

"You'd know."

"How?" Faith asked. "Are there side effects? Like, is it possible I'd forget stuff?"

"Maybe. The first time can be unpredictable. How much does it feel like you can't remember?"

Faith shifted in her seat uncomfortably. She hated talking about her symptoms even more than having to grovel for information.

"Honestly? I can't remember anything from the night with Wade. It's a total loss."

Hawk understood more than he was saying. He knew the only way blank-slate memory loss occurred was if a person took a second Wire Code before the first one wore off. He also knew a dosage of that level, especially for a newbie, could cause irreparable brain damage. And there were other side effects, too.

No wonder she hadn't come to school for a week.

"Have you had headaches, right here?" Hawk asked, touching the center of his forehead.

"Yeah, feels like someone hit me with a hammer."

"Thirsty?"

"Totally," Faith said, and to prove it, she drank all the extra milk in her bowl and licked off the milk mustache.

Hawk didn't ask anything else, but Faith could tell she had her answer by the way all the color drained out of his face and he wouldn't look at her.

"So Wade gave me a Wire Code; you're sure?"

"I don't know *who* gave it to you. But yeah, you had a Wire Code. No doubt."

Faith was angrier than she could remember ever

being in her life. She wanted to find Wade Quinn and slap him across the face.

"That's what I thought," Faith said. Her voice shook with frustration at what she'd let happen to her. "Why would Wade do that to me?"

Hawk had a pretty good idea, but he didn't think it would help the situation to tell Faith what it was.

"I don't know," he chose to answer, because it was the only marginally safe thing to say. His stomach churned as he looked at the puddle of syrup on his plate. When he glanced up again, Faith had already left. Hawk couldn't stop thinking about the fact that it was the second Wire Code in quick succession, not the first, that made a person lose their memory. He'd told the Quinns never to do that because it was risky. The things a person did after experiencing two Wire Codes could be unpredictable and at times violent.

What was Wade Quinn trying to hide?

Chapter 10

The Smallest Guy in the Room

Hawk found Wade before Faith did.

"Why'd you do it?" Hawk asked. Wade was alone on the practice field, holding a metal handle attached to a four-foot-long chain. An iron ball, which was sitting in the grass, was attached to the end of the chain.

"Busy here," Wade said, not looking up as he swayed back and forth. "I'll have to rearrange your face in a second." The hammer throw was Clara's best event, but Wade was having some trouble mastering it. Working with the hammer always put him in a bad mood.

"My finger is hovering over a SEND button," Hawk said, undeterred as he stood his ground a few feet away.

"It's not the kind of message you want going out."

Wade shifted his gaze from the iron ball in the grass to straight up the length of the long, rarely used football field. "You know how far it is to the other end?"

Hawk felt a cool breeze blow against his shaggy hair, sending a chill through his body. "I can ruin you, Wade Quinn. Just tell me why you gave Faith two Wire Codes."

"It's a hundred and twenty yards, long ways," Wade said, staring back at the iron ball and tightening up the slack in the chain. He began to spin around in a circle, and the ball rose up in the air as he turned faster and faster. When he let the handle go he yelled, and the ball and chain ripped through the air like a rocket. Hawk couldn't help backing up a step or two as he watched it sail wildly through the air and land somewhere near the other end of the football field.

"Next time I'm going to throw that thing at *you*," Wade said. He had moved silently within two feet of Hawk and yanked the Tablet out of his hand. Hawk knew he should run, but the idea of leaving his Tablet behind was more than he could deal with.

"You were serious?" Wade asked dubiously. He stared at the Tablet screen and realized that Hawk was about to send a message to the authorities about Wade's Wire Code usage. "You were really going to rat me out.

Would have gotten yourself busted right along with me. Dude, you must be sick in love."

"Shut up, Wade." Hawk surprised himself—his voice sounded so angry. "She was just a conquest for you; is that it?"

Wade's emotions were already fragile. He'd been unable to find Faith Daniels, and he needed to know how she was doing, because deep down he did like her more than he was willing to admit. This stupid kid had some bad dirt on him. And on top of all that, he couldn't quite shake the feeling that maybe there had been eleven, not ten, Drifters that night.

"Our conversation is going to be a lot more useful if this thing isn't distracting you," Wade said. He whistled sharply, then held the Tablet over his head like a marker.

"What are you doing, man? Seriously, give me back my Tablet. I won't send it. Just leave her alone; that's all I'm asking."

"You act like you've got some control here, sport," Wade said, "That's like a joke, right?"

Hawk jumped up and down, practically climbing up the side of Wade's leg trying to reach his Tablet. It wasn't until Wade pushed him hard to the ground that Hawk heard the scream from the far end of the football field. He hadn't seen Clara there before—she must have been standing off to the side—but she was there now. She was staring at the hammer that was flying through the air in Hawk's general direction. If he could have made out her face, he would have seen that she was concentrating feverishly on the iron ball as it flew.

"Sort of pisses me off," Wade said casually. "She can really throw the hell out of that thing."

He held the Tablet out to Hawk, and Hawk thought for a brief instant that he might be able to get out of the situation unscathed. He reached out, already thinking about how stupid this had been and how fast he would run once he held the Tablet again. Just as his fingers touched the slippery glass, Wade pulled the Tablet away and flung it hard up in the air.

"NO!" Hawk shouted. He was up on his feet in a flash, running under the Tablet as it kept rising skyward.

If he'd been watching the hammer fly, he would have seen that it was about thirty feet from landing. He would have seen that as his Tablet was flying up in the air like a Frisbee, the hammer was changing course. It was turning to the right and rising, not falling. Hawk's Tablet reached its apex, and all Hawk could think about was staying under it, catching it before it landed with a thud on the football field. Unfortunately for Hawk, when the Tablet was five feet from landing in his hands, the hammer smashed into it, trailed by the chain and the handle. The Tablet burst into glass and electric light, smashed into a thousand pieces as it showered Hawk with shrapnel.

Wade shook his head and looked thoughtfully at the hammer where it lay lifeless in the grass.

"She is good with that hammer. No denying it."

When a Tablet split apart into so many pieces, it couldn't fix itself. Hawk's Tablet was gone for good.

"You're the biggest a-hole in the universe," Hawk said. He started to leave, but as he passed by, Wade grabbed him by the collar and held him firmly.

"Next time it won't be the Tablet. It'll be your face. I'm done with your Wire Codes. Some kind of bad mojo you're brewing up. Let's call it even and leave it at that. Tell me we have a deal."

Hawk was so mad he was shaking. He wished he were a bigger guy so he could wrestle Wade Quinn to the ground and punch him a million times. He vowed to have his revenge but nodded his ascent. If Wade Quinn would have been smart, he would have taken Hawk more seriously, because people piss off geeks at their own peril. They know a thousand ways to ruin a life, and they have plenty of pent-up nerd frustration just waiting for a reason to get out.

Hawk pulled himself free and yelled, "When are

you going to grow up, man?"

"Yeah, when are you?" Hawk heard Faith's voice as she approached the field. All he could think about was how much he wished she would leave it alone. He knew her well enough to know that wasn't going to happen, but he tried to shut her up anyway.

"It's fine, Faith. Just let it go."

Faith looked at Hawk as if to say *This isn't about you. It's between me and him.*

Wade's sister was walking up the middle of the football field. The scene was complicated enough, and he wished she'd just stay where she was. But then Dylan Gilmore appeared from the gym doors looking protective, and Wade started to feel outnumbered.

"Answer him, Wade," Faith said. She shoved him in the chest with both hands, but Wade barely moved. "When are you going to grow up?"

"I don't know what you're talking about," Wade said.

"Sure you do. You gave me a Wire Code. What else did you do to me that I can't remember?"

"It's not what you think," Wade said. "It's complicated." He wanted to explain what had really happened, but how could he tell her he'd wiped her memory because he'd killed ten Drifters—not because he'd taken advantage of her? So instead he turned the focus away from himself and onto Hawk. "He's the one you want to talk to. He *makes* the stuff. And he told me it was a really low-level set of codes—nothing big, just a fun time."

"You're lying," Faith said, but then she looked at Hawk and she just knew. "You didn't," Faith said, stunned and confused and angry.

"I'm sorry, Faith," Wade said. "But nothing happened. We only kissed, that's it. Seriously. When I figured out it was strong stuff, I took you home. I swear."

Hawk was speechless. He had no words to convey his immense frustration and shame. It was true; he had made the stuff, but only because Wade had forced him to. His Tablet was destroyed, and it would be days before the Western State would send a replacement. And Faith, the only friend he had left in the entire world, was looking at him like he'd ruined her life. As Dylan Gilmore arrived from one side and Clara from the other, Hawk started running. He had to, because he knew it was only a matter of seconds before he started crying, and that was an embarrassment he wasn't willing to risk.

Dylan arrived next to Faith at about the same time Clara arrived next to her brother. The four of them stood motionless—two on one side, two on the other—and stared at one another.

"Everything okay?" Dylan finally asked no one in particular.

"Everything's fine, right, Faith?" Wade asked, reaching a hand out toward her. She backed off but stopped short of leaving altogether. Dylan saw the smashed Tablet and raised a dark eyebrow.

"I'm guessing that's Hawk's Tablet. Looks like it got hit with a hammer. Literally."

Clara started laughing, but when she saw that Dylan responded with curious indifference, she swallowed hard and backed off. "Don't look at me. I don't even know that kid. It's him you want." Clara hooked a thumb at her brother and walked over to pick up the ball and chain.

"I'm doing this school a favor," Wade said, playing a risky hand but feeling like he was all in whether he liked it or not. "He's making Wire Codes, bad ones. I just put him out of business."

Dylan shrugged like it didn't mean much, then lowered the boom.

"I guess you'll have to find another dealer then, won't you? Too bad. I understand he was giving you what you wanted for next to nothing."

Faith shot a glance at both guys and put up her hands. "I've had it with this place. You people are crazy."

She started to leave, then turned and came back, standing in front of Wade. She looked up at him, and for a brief but fabulous moment, Wade thought she was going to forgive him. Then she slapped him, and the ringing in his ears sounded like a siren call.

"Don't you ever trick me like that again. And leave Hawk alone. He's just a kid."

She turned to leave but found herself face-to-face with Dylan, which forced her to look into his eyes for a split second. They were dark, deep, and worrisome, like he thought she might have gone too far. Faith was sick of everyone at Old Park Hill, and as she stomped away, she made sure everyone knew it. "And tell your sister she's a bitch!"

"I'm standing right here," Clara said. She was holding the ball and chain like she might swing it over her head a few times and aim for the back of Faith's head.

Dylan followed Faith off the football field as Clara stood next to her brother and handed him the hammer.

"Your turn to throw," she said, looking at Dylan like she wanted to reach out, take his hand, and pull him away from Faith. All she could think about was how it would feel to have Dylan look at her that way, like he wanted her. There was something about his dark eyes and that solid frame that made her think the unimaginable: Would he ever be into someone like Clara as much as he obviously cared for Faith? But it didn't change the way she felt: there was something about Dylan Gilmore that felt *powerful*—and she wanted it.

Faith wasn't just distracting Wade from the important work he needed to do. She was also standing between Clara and Dylan. And that, Clara began to realize, was unacceptable.

At one time, years before he'd met Faith and Liz, Hawk had been a sneaky little kid. By the third grade he'd fashioned himself a persona that allowed him to drift through school without being noticed. He'd gotten into the habit of finding discarded Tablets—all too common with eight-year-olds hell-bent on playing tag on the playground. Grade school kids don't keep a lot of interesting, private information on their Tablets, but it had been a thrill all the same to find some nugget of information he could use when he needed it.

Hawk was always the smallest guy in the room, and for the most part it hadn't bothered him at all. It seemed to him that the other small boys in grade school were trying too hard in order to make up for their size. They were all clowns or live wires, full of aggressive energy, their voices stuck at an annoyingly high volume. It wasn't in Hawk's nature to be obnoxious or hold center stage. He didn't talk much; but when he did, his comments were wry and cutting, the stuff of legend. No one wanted to be on the receiving end of a well-crafted Hawk comeback, so very few kids scuffled with him verbally back then. It was how he'd gotten his nickname. Hawks were quiet watchers; but when they were ready, they moved with purpose and struck with deadly force. It helped that Hawk seemed to know secret things about almost everyone, in part because he had big ears and listened to every conversation, but also because he'd been inside most of their Tablets at one time or another.

Unfortunately for Hawk, he'd lost every ounce of his early confidence in the sixth grade, and it had never returned. Grade school was so simple: stay quiet, provide a biting remark when required, sneak around as much as possible. But middle school had been like a wrecking ball on his quiet personality. He'd tried a cutting remark only once and chosen badly, finding himself with a bloody nose at the hands of a large, mean, popular kid. The incident had put a black mark of humiliation on Hawk that dogged him all the way to Old Park Hill. His quiet charm turned reclusive and weird. Other kids kept their distance and mocked him when he tried to fit in. One might say he was driven underground, deeper into himself, where he spent endless hours hacking into his Tablet. By the time he met Faith Daniels at Old Park Hill, Hawk was one of the few people in the outside world who had cracked the Tablet code. It was a dangerous thing to have done, he knew, because it gave him access to things he wasn't supposed to see. He hadn't told anyone, for who would he tell? His parents were as isolated as he was, content with their books and their writing. For them, the outside was a quiet place to be left alone for as long as the world would allow them the peace and quiet.

Hawk always liked the reason for his nickname: that he could strike at any moment, and the victim wouldn't see it coming. Though, to be fair, he hadn't struck anyone with deadly force in his entire life. He thought about it a lot, because he had long ago acquired the skills to inflict a lot of misery on his enemies, and he often reveled in these thoughts for longer than was useful. A little fantasizing about watching your tormentor suffer was fine, but that sort of thinking can get to be a problem if it becomes a habit. Hawk had thought of a thousand ways to ruin Wade Quinn's life since arriving at Old Park Hill. They'd both been there longer than Faith or Liz, and somehow they'd fallen into each other's orbit. Wade had gotten a taste for Wire Codes at his old school, and he knew from experience that it would be the really smart, socially awkward kid who would have the skill to get it done.

"Never made one," Hawk had said the first time Wade asked him to make a Wire Code, which wasn't exactly true. As a Tablet hacker of some renown, he'd played around with Wire Codes purely to see if he could make them. They were a witch's brew of crazy codes and hidden sites; and while no two of them were exactly alike, they all shared the same foundational coding designed to set the mind on fire.

"I tell you what," Wade had said as he stared down at Hawk during their first encounter. "Give it a shot. I'll pay twenty Coin just to see what you come up with."

Wade Quinn was the biggest badass Hawk had ever encountered in his life, and he could tell from experience that he was an alpha male of the highest order. This was the kind of guy who could literally destroy a kid like Hawk, but Wade was also that rare beast who could carry a kid like Hawk up the social ladder. Associating with the likes of Wade Quinn, especially in the form of something that instantly created dirt on the guy, had a certain appeal.

"No promises, but I can try," Hawk had said. "Give me a couple of weeks."

"Let's say tomorrow instead," Wade replied.

By this time Hawk's awkward nervousness had taken full bloom, and he yammered on for another few seconds before Wade walked away without so much as a good-bye. By 4 a.m. that same night, Hawk had created his first functioning Wire Code, a real junker; but he was able to deliver it the next day.

"Be careful with that thing," Hawk had said, only half joking. "It's radioactive. I really have no idea what it will do to your brain."

Wade had tapped out the transaction for twenty Coin on his Tablet, transferring the funds to one of Hawk's many untraceable accounts, and Hawk slipped the Wire Code necklace into Wade's hand. The deed was done. Hawk, the geeky quiet kid, was officially a drug dealer.

Standing outside of Faith's window at midnight wasn't something Hawk had planned to do; but there was something he had to show her, and it couldn't wait any longer. A week had passed since the incident on the football field, and he'd reverted back to his quietness, not talking to anyone at school and avoiding eye contact with the people he knew. It was an unusually cool night as he looked into Faith's window, trying to decide how to wake her. He wasn't fully aware that Faith's parents weren't in the picture, so as far as he was concerned, ringing the doorbell wasn't an option. He was thinking of tapping on the glass when she began to stir.

He watched her roll over and pull the thin covers up to her chin, curling into a tight ball in her sleep. Then the door to her closet began to open slowly, and he ducked low against the windowpane. At first he thought there might be a dog or a cat in the house, or worse, a coyote, which had been known to roam the valley. But how would a coyote get into Faith's closet? She'd never said anything about having a pet, either.

Hawk peered over the sill of the window, cupping his hands to his eyes for a better view through the shiny glass. What he saw made no sense, and he began to wonder if he was tired enough to be seeing things that weren't there. It was true he hadn't slept very much in the past few days, but he'd never hallucinated before.

A folded blanket was hovering a few feet over Faith's bed, and as Hawk watched, it began to unfold. A few seconds later the blanket was all the way flat, hanging in the air like a big magic carpet.

Hawk couldn't help himself from banging on the glass, because he cared for Faith and he somehow imagined the blanket was about to smother her. He watched as Faith stirred awake and rolled over onto her back. As she did, the blanket fell, landing softly over her entire body before she opened her eyes and looked around like someone might be in the room with her.

Hawk tapped on the glass once more and waved moronically, hoping Faith wouldn't chase him off by yelling for her parents.

"It's just me. It's Hawk. Nothing to worry about."

Faith breathed a sigh of relief and then seemed to

wonder how the blanket had gotten onto her bed. She went to the window and unlocked it, pushing it upward only a few inches and crouching down to talk.

"What are you doing here? It's after midnight. In case it wasn't obvious, I was asleep."

"No, I get it, I do," Hawk said, nervously shivering in the cold. "This can't wait. It's a timing thing, honestly. I wouldn't ask if I didn't have to."

"You're acting weird."

"I know, totally normal, back to my old self. Can you let me in? It'll only take a second."

Faith looked back at her bed like she were still dreaming, rubbed her eyes, then peered back out the window.

"Did you put that blanket on my bed?" she asked.

"I'm out here, remember?"

Faith looked dubious, but she raised her eyebrows and shrugged it off, pushing the window up high enough for Hawk to crawl through.

"You know, I do have a front door. For future reference."

"Didn't want to wake up your parents," Hawk said as he climbed through the opening and caught his tennis shoe on the edge, falling onto the carpeted floor. "Always liked carpet, much more forgiving than hardwood. Love the stuff."

"Uh-huh," Faith mumbled, shutting the window and crawling back under the covers before Hawk could say anything else. He stood in the dim light of her room rubbing the cold from his bare arms.

"No, you can't get in," Faith said.

Hawk looked like he was about to cry.

"If it's that big a deal, fine," Faith said. "Just stay on your own side."

Hawk shook his head back and forth like she'd misunderstood.

"I'm sorry, Faith. I blew it. I didn't think you were going to take those Wire Codes. They were for Wade."

"Uh-huh," Faith said, not sure how she was supposed to respond. She was tired, and she felt betrayed by one of the only friends she had in the world. What she really wanted at that moment was to fall asleep and forget about Wade, Hawk, Dylan—all of them.

"I need to tell you how it happens," Hawk said. "He doesn't ask me to make them. He *tells* me to. Try being my size with a guy like that telling you what to do. It's not easy saying no."

Faith's heart softened as she looked at Hawk. He looked so young and vulnerable. She was starting to feel like maybe she was being a little too hard on him. She still didn't know if she could trust him, but she was willing to listen. The truth was, she felt lonely, and

Hawk was very chatty. He'd do most of the talking anyway.

"Come on, get in," she said, pushing down the covers on one side of the bed and patting the sheet like she were trying to coax in a puppy.

Hawk leaped onto the mattress so fast it startled Faith fully awake. He didn't even remove his shoes, which she thought was gross and dumb; but he had the covers over his legs before she could say anything.

"Cold out there. Way better in here. Thanks for the invite."

Faith was pretty sure she'd just made a mistake. How long was this going to take?

"So you're not a notorious drug dealer then?" Faith said.

"No way, not that. Not even close. I'm very limited release, superexclusive. Only rich a-holes need apply."

"Right."

Faith ran her hands along the soft surface of the blanket.

"How *did* this thing get here? You sure you didn't do it?"

Hawk was nervous about how to answer, because obviously Faith didn't know her room was haunted. What else could have caused a blanket to drift over a bed like that and unfold? Was there any chance he had imagined it himself? His stress level had been off the charts lately, and it was dark in the room. Maybe he was losing his marbles.

"Probably the Wire Codes," Hawk lied. "Sometimes you forget little things for weeks after. You probably put it on and just don't remember."

"I guess. You know what the strange part is though? I was thinking about how cold I was, not really dreaming it, just wishing I had another blanket. And then I woke up, and there it was. Weird, right?"

Hawk shrugged like he had no idea what she was talking about.

"You know, if you want, I could probably sleep here for the rest of the night. My parents don't even know I'm out."

"You wish," she said sarcastically.

"Yes, I do."

"At least get your shoes out of my bed. That's gross."

Hawk's shoes hit the floor before Faith could take back what she had just given in to. For Hawk, it was the single most awesome thing that had happened to him in months. He took out his three-day-old Tablet and pulled it by its gleaming corners, stretching it until it snapped into its larger size.

"I brought you something. It's time sensitive."

"Sounds mysterious," Faith said. "Kind of like this

blanket on my bed. I'm telling you, I didn't put it here."

"Setting aside the fact that your room is haunted by items of home decor, I think you've got a nice place here."

Faith couldn't help but smile as Hawk looked around the room appreciatively. He was a huge nerd, but he was sweet. "What did you bring me? If it's a hug, you can put your shoes back on and hit the road."

Hawk pressed the screen on his new Tablet, bringing it to life. The light bathed the room in an eerie glow. Shadows danced on the walls as Hawk used both hands to program in some commands, bypassing several layers of security in order to reach the service he wanted access to.

"We can only do this for about two minutes before it fades out," Hawk said. "You'll need to make it quick. And listen, I don't know if I can ever do this again. The new Tablet had a back door installed, something I've never seen before."

Faith didn't have a clue what Hawk was talking about; but then he handed her his Tablet, and his meaning became clear in an instant.

Liz Brinn's face was on the screen, staring back at her.

"Liz? Is it really you?" Faith stammered.

A cute guy with sandy-brown hair squeezed into the

camera view. "Hey, Faith! Thanks for taking care of Liz while we were apart. I owe you one!"

"No problem," Faith said, laughing softly as her eyes began to fill with tears.

"Uh-oh. Your buddy's not doing too well," Noah said.

"Stop that," Liz said, playfully shoving Noah out of the way. Her cheeks were flushed with good health, and she looked happy.

"Hey, it's okay. Don't cry. Everything is fine, really."

Faith wasn't so sure. She'd really blown it on the night she'd been swept away by Wade Quinn. "I'm so sorry, Liz. I don't know what I was thinking. And I miss you. It's not the same out here all alone."

"You have Hawk; he's your wingman. He'll take care of you."

Hawk was basking in the glow of being called a wingman to a pretty girl.

"Wait, are you in bed with him?" Liz asked. "Whoa."

"It's a sleepover," Hawk said, leaning into the screen. "And she let me take my shoes off."

"Cool," Noah said from offscreen.

Faith shoved Hawk back toward his side of the bed with her shoulder as Liz started talking.

"We only have about a minute left. I just want you to know I'm okay. I found Noah, obviously."

"What's it like?" Faith asked. "The State, I mean. Is it as great as they say?"

Liz pondered the question for a few seconds. She didn't seem to know exactly how to answer.

"It's good, yeah. I mean, everything is clean and nice. And I have a billion channels on my Tablet; it's insane. We watch it all the time now. Plus there are cute guys by the millions."

"They all have rough hands," Noah said.

"He's lying," Liz said, rolling her eyes. "Anyway, I hope you get here soon. I know it's just a matter of time, but you can trust me on this—you're not going to hate it. It's a little bit, I don't know, boring, I guess. But it's good."

Faith knew exactly what Liz was talking about, because they'd imagined the States many times. They'd seen plenty of beautiful and exciting pictures and videos of the Western State, but they'd always concluded that it lacked the grit of real life. Something real was missing. Faith didn't know what else to say. She was so happy to see Liz; but she was sad, too, because she knew she'd never go to one of the States unless she was forced. The screen began to flutter with static.

"I'm really, really sorry, Liz. And I'm happy for you."

Like a dream that folds into the mist and is quickly

forgotten, Liz's image started to fade on the Tablet screen.

"I love you," she said. It was full of static, but Faith heard her say it, and then Liz was gone.

"I love you, too."

Hawk thought about reaching for Faith's hand, to try and make her feel less lonely, but he was pretty sure any sudden movements in her direction would get him kicked out of bed. It was a risk he wasn't willing to take, so he stayed perfectly still until Faith handed back the Tablet.

"How'd you do that?" she asked. "I didn't think it was possible to communicate with people on the inside."

"Technically it's illegal. Also impossible. I know because I've been trying since she left. The new Tablet was set wrong or something, who knows. All I can say is, it was a gift from the gods and it probably won't happen again."

Faith was overcome with appreciation for what Hawk had done for her. Hawk had given her an enormous gift she wasn't sure she'd ever be able to repay.

"What would happen if they caught you?" Faith wondered out loud.

"You know what's funny about that? No one really knows. I've done a lot of hacking over the past few years, but I'm always very careful to cover my tracks.

Best I can tell, people who mess around with this sort of thing and get caught just disappear. I don't know if they go up in smoke, but their Tablet identity vanishes."

Faith yawned. It was after midnight, and she was starting to fade as she slid down onto the bed and stared at Hawk.

"No funny business," she said. "Let's get some sleep and talk in the morning."

Hawk wanted to ask where her parents were and what they would think, but he let it pass. Either she was a very independent girl, which was probably true, or her parents were on a trip somewhere. Either way, he was much more interested in whether or not he had really seen the blanket move across the room or not. As he let his head rest on the pillow, he vowed not to fall asleep for at least an hour, just in case something else moved in the room. For safe measure, he set his Tablet on the nightstand, turned on the video recorder, and pointed it at the closet.

Four minutes later he was asleep.

Dylan Gilmore's brain was tired. His body was fine; there was plenty of energy there. But his mind, which he'd been putting through hell for months, was at loose ends. He was standing outside Faith's window, trying to understand why Hawk was lying in bed next to her.

Didn't see that coming, Dylan thought, Even though he was nearly sure the two of them couldn't possibly have a thing for each other, he felt the same stab in his heart that he'd felt when Faith and Wade had hooked up.

Dylan looked at his Tablet for the time and saw that it was after two in the morning. Normally he'd have work to do, but it was risky with Hawk in the room. He noticed the blinking red light on Hawk's Tablet and understood immediately that he was recording.

"Nice try, little man. But it's too soon for that."

As Dylan looked at the Tablet, it began to move toward him in the air. The window latch unlocked, and Dylan quietly slid the window open a few inches. The Tablet drifted through the opening, and Dylan took it in his hands, stopping the recording. He was about to delete the video file, but instead he scrolled through on fast-forward, stopping and backing up when something moved in the room. He let it run at normal speed for a few seconds, watching silently as Faith Daniels rose up in the air, the covers coming along with her.

"Interesting," he said, deleting the video file and sliding the Tablet back through the opening in the window. "*Very* interesting."

Dylan stayed by the window for two more hours, watching Faith Daniels and thinking about the progress he'd made. Things were moving faster than he'd expected, possibly faster than was safe given the circumstances. As he walked away at ten past four in the morning, he made up his mind about something. It had been a very long time coming, and months of exhausting work, but the moment had finally arrived.

It was time to tell Faith Daniels the truth.

Chapter 11

How Did You Get Me All the Way Up Here?

Every year the Field Games were held in different States around the world. It had been five years since the United States had hosted, and the Western State had created a state-of-the-art facility like nothing anyone had ever seen. Every event would be broadcasted live onto millions of Tablets via thousands of cameras. Field Games were even fed to Tablets owned by those sorry souls still living outside the States, although there was a delay to allow for editing. In the days leading up to the start of the Field Games, news reports streamed onto the Tablets twenty-four hours a day, preempting all other programming for endless speculation about the competitions.

"God, I'm tired of hearing them talk about the games," Faith said as she shuffled into a classroom with everyone else. "Get it over with already."

In the months since Faith had arrived at Old Park Hill, more students had stopped showing up. The population of the entire school was down to the classroom she was in, which held nineteen students, and one other room with another twenty kids waiting it out. Amy, whom Faith had avoided religiously, had been moved to her room a week earlier. She had different feelings about the games than Faith did.

"Hot guys running around in tights? Best show on my Tablet."

"Uh-huh," Faith murmured, trying not to get pulled into a conversation.

"Have you seen Wade jump? Oh. My. God. He's insane."

Wade and Clara Quinn still hadn't made an appearance at the warm-ups, also known as preflights.

"They don't talk about Wade or Clara," Faith said. She sat down in her seat, hoping Amy would move off and sit somewhere else. She didn't, taking the seat next to Faith and clicking on her Tablet.

"That's because the Quinns are on the outside. They don't even keep outsiders on the radar; you know that. But Wade told me people inside are worried. Last thing they want is someone from out here showing up to take the spotlight."

"Wouldn't matter," Faith said, growing bored with the conversation. "Once they're in, they're in. The State will spin it as another victory either way."

Faith glanced up and saw that Amy understood something that had somehow eluded her to that point. She wasn't the brightest bulb in the room, but even Faith thought it was impossible that Amy wouldn't have thought about it.

"Once Wade and Clara go in for the Field Games," Faith explained, "they aren't coming back. No one comes back. You know that, right?"

Amy looked flustered and started swiping her finger across her Tablet nervously. She had a thing for Wade even if Wade couldn't care less. "Of course I know that. But this is different. He said he'd come back. And if he doesn't, it's fine anyway. My parents are moving us in pretty soon anyway."

Faith doubted that, but she didn't want to totally ruin Amy's day, even if she deserved it for being dumb enough to pursue Wade, a very Amy thing to do. Faith knew that once Wade left for the State and became some sort of superstar, he'd never settle for someone like Amy.

"I thought your parents were on cleanup. Doesn't that last for a while longer?" Faith asked.

"You don't know what you're talking about," Amy said. "They can go whenever they want."

Faith and everyone else knew that wasn't true. Parents who signed up for cleanup got paid a lot of Coin, but they were on annual contracts. Amy had at least another six months outside and probably more.

"Ladies, how about we get to work? Would that be okay with you?" Miss Newhouse asked. Faith was more than happy for the out. She went straight to work notating an English lecture while a teacher on her Tablet explained the finer points of *The Grapes of Wrath*, a story Faith related to for its outsider, nomadic themes. She settled in, then glanced around the room looking for Hawk. He hadn't shown up for class. Her eyes landed on an empty desk at the back of the room where Wade should have been sitting. His absence was less surprising, because with two weeks to go before the games, he was almost never in class anymore. The word in the halls was that he and Clara were leaving in six or seven days, which suited Faith just fine.

Dylan was sitting in the back row in the far corner

of the room under the soft light from a window over-
looking the courtyard. He looked up, caught her eye,
and smiled. Faith smiled back awkwardly. Inside she
was nervous about how uncomfortable he made her
feel. . . .

When she looked back at her Tablet, a message
came in across the top of the screen.

Didn't make it in today, parents are
having a tough day.

Hawk almost never talked about his parents and
neither did Faith. It was a topic they both wanted to
avoid, so neither of them brought it up. It crossed Faith's
mind not to answer the message. It was a door she didn't
want to open because she was sure the topic would turn
in her direction in due time. Still, it was Hawk. How
long could she really hold out without telling him her
parents were Drifters?

Sorry. Did you get caught in the middle
of it or what?

Faith tried to pay attention to the audio stream in
her earphones as she waited for an answer, tapping out
a few notes on the lightboard.

It's complicated.

Faith messaged back:

Better to talk in person later?

She wondered if it was about leaving for the Western State. Most arguments with parents were. In some strange, unsaid way, the Field Games felt like a marker for everyone who remained outside. It was a national moment to shine, to show the rest of the world they were a unified people with the will to do what had to be done in order to survive.

Hawk messaged back:

My mom heard a rumor the States were going to stop letting people in. I've searched, haven't seen any sign of that. That's kind of intense if it's true.

It had never been a threat Faith thought too much about, but it was an idea she'd heard people talk about for years. China and Africa had closed their States years ago, and almost everyone had complied. Of the billions of people in China alone, only a scant few thousand were unaccounted for within a month of the announcement.

China had already built eleven interconnected States, and they were always working on more; but the rest of the country was empty. Africa, with its fourteen state-of-the-art States, was a vast landscape of deserts, trees, and animals nearly devoid of human life.

Faith thought of all the places in the world that were empty of people. She knew she could walk for days and days through once-thriving cities and not see a single person. It was what made her current location different. There were people, hundreds of them, all in one place on the outside, like they'd been herded there by a shepherd on their way to somewhere else.

Faith pulled up a program on her screen with an interactive map of the United States. There was a lot of empty space, with two circles that could not be missed. One was in the place where Nevada had once been, only the circle was bigger than that. It leaked out over Oregon and Idaho and what was left of California after the floods. This was the Western State, almost two hundred square miles, so vast it was almost unthinkable. To the east, covering parts of Kentucky, Arkansas, Missouri, and Tennessee, was another enormous circle; the Eastern State. It was just as big and getting bigger by the day.

The old high school was the tiniest of red dots, and seeing it sitting in the shadow of the Western State, Faith knew the truth of the matter.

She sent a message to Hawk:

We'll be overrun by the State pretty soon
anyway. Unless we move again. And I'm pretty
tired of moving.

And that was the bitter truth. The States were fine with letting people stay outside, but they couldn't be too far off into the unknown. They had to be reachable within a few hours of driving so the white vans from the State could return by nightfall. And the States kept growing, gobbling up more space as the population grew.

Another message came in, and Faith read it without really thinking:

I have something I need to show you. Meet
tonight at the old mall parking lot, 9 p.m. Thanks.

She was about to tap out a message to Hawk telling him that would be fine when she realized the message hadn't been from Hawk. It was from Dylan Gilmore. Her heart fluttered in her chest, and she hoped he wasn't watching in case she looked nervous. She began chewing on her pinkie nail without even noticing she was doing it, unsure of how to respond.

A message came in from Hawk:

You're probably right. Matter of time. What do
you think your parents are going to do?

As she'd expected, the conversation had turned to
her own parents, which was something she didn't want
to talk about. So she decided to answer Dylan instead.

What do you want to show me? And how did you
message me during a lecture? Have you been
talking to Hawk?

It was risky, but she was curious. The last time she'd
gone with a boy to see something he really wanted to
show her, she'd ended up consuming two Wire Codes
and blacking out the entire thing. There were times, in
her darker moments, when she imagined a lot of bad
things happening to her that night. Part of her felt it was
better this way, not knowing; but it was also hard not
being able to remember. She might spend the rest of her
life wondering.

By the time class let out forty minutes later, Faith
still hadn't gotten an answer from Dylan; and when
Miss Newhouse let everyone go, Dylan was gone before
Faith could get up the nerve to talk with him.

———

"I lied, but only a little."

They were not the comforting words Faith had been hoping for when she showed up in the empty parking lot of the old mall. She thought about turning around, leaving before this got complicated or dangerous. She stared at him from ten feet away, where she'd come up short and stood motionless on the cracked concrete sidewalk.

"That's a terrible opening line," Faith said.

Dylan smiled and took two cautious steps forward.

"Relationships are about trust, so I thought I'd better come clean right up front."

Faith was not impressed with Dylan's circular logic, but she did like the way he looked in his jeans and that leather jacket as he took two more steps toward her.

"Let me guess," Faith said. "You're really a vampire. You're a thousand years old, and you think it will gross me out. You're right."

Dylan let the comment slide as he arrived next to her and reached out for her hand. Faith pulled back.

"Oh no, you don't. Not until I get some truth-telling out of you. What did you lie about?"

"I have two things I want to show you, not one."

"Are either of them unpleasant?"

"I don't think so, but I'm wrong a lot."

"Not comforting."

Dylan smiled, and their eyes met for an instant, then he walked past her and kept going without turning back.

"Hey, whoa—you can't just leave me here."

"Come on then, I'll show you the first thing. Won't take long."

Faith wanted to follow, but she was afraid of where it might lead. What if she ended up in trouble again? Dylan had the appearance of someone even more mysterious and unpredictable than Wade Quinn.

You sure know how to pick 'em, Faith thought.

The electricity wasn't on at the old mall, so none of the streetlamps were shining down as she followed Dylan warily. All the old buildings were dark and shadowy, and for a split second she thought she might have seen a figure move on the other side of one of the broken windows. She started taking two steps to each of Dylan's one until she caught up.

"Do you ever worry about Drifters?"

Dylan didn't respond the way she thought he would.

"I've met a few Drifters. They're misunderstood."

Yeah, two of them are my parents. I know all about misunderstanding, Faith wanted to say but didn't. It was her secret, and she sure wasn't going to share it with a mysterious guy she barely knew.

"How are you at climbing?" Dylan asked. He was staring up at the back of the old Nordstrom, a notoriously tall building. Faith could barely see the outlines of a fire escape in the darkness.

"I don't climb on a first date. It's a rule I have."

Dylan looked a little disappointed, then he started up a metal ladder, leaving Faith to decide if she should follow for the second time in as many minutes.

"Both of the things I want to show you are on the roof," Dylan said, quickly up on the first landing. He was staring down at her, and their eyes locked. "You sure you won't check it out with me? It's safe, I promise."

Faith wasn't technically afraid of heights; she just hadn't been in many high places. There hadn't ever been much of a reason to get her feet off the ground.

"Do you ever wonder what it would have been like to travel in an airplane?" Faith asked, staring up at Dylan as his dark hair fell forward over his face.

"Yeah, would have been cool," Dylan agreed. "I tell you what—you come up here with me, and I promise I'll figure out a way to get you flying sometime in the near future."

"How are you going to keep a promise like that, Romeo?" Faith asked, putting her foot on the first rung of the ladder leading to the landing where Dylan stood.

Dylan didn't answer, choosing instead to continue

his journey up to the second landing before Faith could change her mind. It was a series of switchback stairs made of metal grating the rest of the way up; and before Faith made it to the first landing, he was already three more landings up in the air. Dylan leaned over the railing and called down.

"You're slow."

"Sorry to disappoint you."

Faith was naturally competitive and genuinely curious. All her reticence went out the window as she took two steps at a time on her way to the top of the old Nordstrom building. She only made the mistake of looking down once, when she arrived at the fourth landing, and it took her breath away. After that she kept her focus upward, yelling for Dylan to wait more than once. She was having fun though, so much fun in fact that it didn't occur to her that the situation wasn't that dissimilar from her night with Wade Quinn. She was only fifteen minutes into her date with Dylan and already she was climbing up the side of a building.

"Okay, now you're impressing me," Dylan said as Faith arrived on the tenth platform with him.

"I bet you say that to all the girls," Faith said, catching her breath as she looked up the side of the building. "That part looks scary."

Getting to the roof required a final ascent on a

ladder with at least thirty rungs, and this time, Dylan wasn't going to leave her behind.

"You go first. I'll catch you if you fall."

"Why am I not comforted?"

Dylan flashed a smile at Faith, his eyes sparkling like little diamonds in the soft light. Maybe it was the altitude or the cool air, but Faith definitely felt light-headed for a moment as she looked at this mystifying boy.

"How did you get me all the way up here?" she asked, not expecting an answer.

"Keep going; it will be worth it."

Faith smiled back at Dylan, turned to the remaining ladder, and decided to take the rungs as fast as she could. If she was going to go first, she was going to get there in time to really check things out before he got there. She climbed fast, finding herself halfway up the wall in no time. If she had looked down at that point, Faith might have lost her nerve. The stars and the moon left everything behind her on the ground in shades of gloomy gray and black. There were very few lights as far as the eye could see, but one thing was for sure: it was a long way down.

"You keeping up down there or am I too fast for you?" Faith said, hoping to find that he was still standing on the platform below her. Dylan didn't answer, so she kept going, faster still, until she had her hand on the roof of the building, the cold, concrete rail slick on her palm. Faith pulled herself up and looked at the roof. There was a table set for two, a gas barbecue, and candles. But those weren't the most surprising things about the roof of the old Nordstrom.

The most surprising thing was that Dylan Gilmore was lighting the candles.

Chapter 12

It's Not Just a Burger

"How'd you do that?" Faith asked. She was starting to feel afraid, like she'd been given another Wire Code or something worse and the whole experience was a trick of her imagination. Dylan, the ladders, the landing, the table—was any of it even real?

Having lit the candles, Dylan opened the grill and struck another match. When he turned to Faith, the orange light of the flames was dancing on his face.

"There's another way up is all," he began. "I'm making hamburgers; I hope that's okay. I'm afraid the patties were frozen hockey pucks an hour ago. Best I could do was raid the Old Park Hill cafeteria freezer."

"What do you mean, another way up?" Faith asked. She was still standing on the ladder.

"I promise I'll tell you after dinner. It's just another way, not a big deal."

The hamburger patties had thawed out before Dylan put them on the grill, and they sizzled when he placed them over the flames. White smoke billowed softly into the night air, and Faith was suddenly aware of the lights off in the distance. She wasn't sure if it was the lights or the smell of the food or the fact that her legs were getting tired that finally led her to climb off the ladder and onto the roof, but it didn't really matter. She was on the roof with Dylan now whether she liked it or not.

"The lights are the first thing I wanted to show you," Dylan said. He flipped the burgers and closed the grill, then looked toward the far edge of the rooftop. There, a glowing orange filtered through the distant trees. Whatever its source was, it looked massive, like the sun were about to rise over the horizon and light the world on fire.

"Is that what I think it is?" Faith asked, awestruck at the size and shape of the soft light.

"The Western State. It's only a hundred miles away now, give or take."

"It's closer than I thought," Faith said. The fear rose in her voice.

"They don't mess around," Dylan said. He went back to cooking the patties in silence, adding thick slabs of cheddar cheese to each one and watching them melt. Faith kept staring at the light. There were no mountains or high places near Old Park Hill, which was why the school had been given its name to begin with. By hill, they'd meant bump. It wasn't much of a climb up to the campus, and the campus was surrounded by tall trees on every side. The roof of the Nordstrom building was much higher, and there was nothing but a flat parking lot down below. The trees were far enough in the distance to let the light through from a hundred miles away.

"I think these masterpieces are ready," Dylan said, placing each thin burger on a white plate.

Faith let Dylan pull out her chair for her and sat down. There was an orange disk in the center of her plate but no bun.

"It's not really a burger without bread, ya know?" Faith joked. She knew bread was hard to come by.

"I thought about using pancakes, but that just seemed wrong. And it's not just a burger. It's a *cheese*-burger. Big difference."

"I do like me some cheese," Faith agreed, nodding at the bunless wonder on her plate. She picked at the gooey corner and pulled up a string of cheese, wrapping it around her fork like spaghetti.

"It's getting really close," she said after chewing on some burger.

"I heard it's growing by ten miles a month in some areas," Dylan said. That made it sound even scarier.

"So you think Old Park Hill will be gone in less than a year?" Faith asked.

"They're prepping land as close as thirty miles that way," Dylan pointed off the end of the roof with his fork. "I don't think it will be even a year before they allocate this land for the States. Takes a lot of space to hold a hundred million people, right?"

"Yeah, I guess so."

They ate in silence, Faith taking small bites just to be polite while Dylan put away his entire cheeseburger.

"This is really nice," Faith said. "Thank you."

"Don't let the State scare you. It's for a good reason. Saving the world and all that."

"Is it the wall that makes it glow like that?" Faith asked. There was no reason why Dylan should know, but he seemed to be aware of things about the State that others weren't, so Faith asked.

"I think so, yeah. Weirdest thing ever, but pretty cool."

Faith nodded. All she knew was that the States were surrounded by movable walls that weren't really walls at all. They were more like energy fields rising into the sky that kept things in and kept things out. As the States grew, the walls moved out, taking up whatever space they wanted.

"There's something else I need to show you," Dylan said. "It's a little more important."

"Let me ask you something first," Faith said. "How did you hack into my Tablet and send me a message today during class?"

Dylan shifted nervously in his seat and shrugged, but he could tell that Faith wasn't going to let it pass.

"Hawk isn't the only one who knows how to mess with a Tablet. Let's just leave it at that, okay?"

Faith nodded slowly. She was starting to think Dylan was mysterious, romantic, *and* brainy. Not a terrible combination.

"Okay," Faith said apprehensively. "What else do you want to show me?"

She held her hands in her lap, wondering where this was going. The night had been dreamy and exciting, but it had also put her on edge. Seeing the Western State that close made her worry for herself, her parents, everyone she knew. There was something diabolical about the way it was coming toward her.

"First I need you to do something for me," Dylan said. He leaned forward but didn't touch the table and looked at Faith as if nothing else existed in the world, which happened to be true. At that moment, Dylan's entire universe was filled with Faith and Faith alone.

She held his gaze, and even in the dimness of the candlelight, her eyes sparkled in shades of blue and green. Her lips parted and she started to speak, then held back with a sigh, tilting her head ever so slightly as if to say *What is it you want me to do?* She pushed her long, blond hair behind one delicate ear and waited for the answer.

"Close your eyes."

The request was a little unnerving for Faith. She had a hazy memory of Wade Quinn asking her to do the same thing or something like it. "Why?"

"Just humor me, will you?"

Faith had the feeling that Dylan was going to surprise her with flowers or a present. She liked the way he was treating her. Faith was thinking all those things at once as she closed her eyes and smiled.

"Now what?" she asked, nervous but excited. She imagined feeling his lips on hers as he leaned over the table and kissed her, but instead she heard his voice.

"Now seriously, you have to keep your eyes closed for me no matter what I say. Can you do that?"

"I guess so," Faith said.

"Think about the glass on the table, the one you

were drinking out of. Remember it?"

"Yeah, I remember. It had water in it."

"Okay, good—now imagine it, in your mind, doing something other than what it's doing right now."

"You mean, instead of just sitting there on the table? This is weird."

"I know, I know—just do it for me, please. Keep your eyes shut, think of the glass. Think of it doing something besides sitting there."

If Faith had opened her eyes, she would have watched the glass tip over on its own, spilling water across the white tablecloth. She heard the clank of the glass as it happened and, opening her eyes, started to get more worried. She had imagined the glass tipping over, and the fact that it was lying on its side, all the water poured out, could mean many things. Maybe Dylan had somehow read her mind and pushed the glass over in order to surprise her. Or possibly he did this trick with girls all the time and knew that most of the time people who closed their eyes and thought about what would happen to a glass of water thought of it tipping over. And there was another option, the one that scared Faith the most. Dylan could have given her a Wire Code that she couldn't remember, and the entire evening was being filled with hallucinations she would eventually forget she'd ever experienced.

Faith thought of these many alternatives as she watched Dylan peel off his leather jacket and hang it on the back of his chair. His arms were powerful looking, with wisps of soft hair along their surfaces.

"Okay," Dylan said. "Now put it back the way it was."

"Pardon me?" Faith said. "You don't have to close your eyes this time. Just think of the glass. Think about setting it back up again. Don't worry about putting the water back in."

Don't put the water back in? Faith thought. *Is he crazy or am I?*

Faith pushed her chair away from the table but didn't stand up.

"Did you know Wade gave me a Wire Code—no wait, *two* Wire Codes—without telling me?"

Dylan didn't speak, only nodded. A silence ensued, then he spoke, just above a whisper. "Put the glass back where it was, Faith. I need to see you do it."

"Either I'm crazy or you drugged me. Which is it?"

"Neither. No one's crazy, and I don't give people Wire Codes. And Wade Quinn is a huge jerk for about a million other reasons." Dylan took a deep breath and tried one last time. "Please, just put the glass back where it was. You can do it."

"Maybe it's you that's crazy," Faith said. She stood

up and turned in the direction of the ladder leading down to the fire escape.

"Faith, listen to me—"

"NO," Faith yelled, thinking of the few sips of water she'd taken when it was still in the glass. "You put something in my drink, didn't you? Were you going to take advantage of me? Is that it?"

"You don't understand."

"You're just like Wade Quinn, only worse. And your burgers suck."

Faith was angry and confused as she looked at the glass where it lay on the table. Thinking of the glass, she swished her arm fast in front of her. The table was five feet away; but as she moved her arm, the glass flew with lightning speed, as if a blistering wind had picked it up. It flew ten feet through the air, then smashed violently onto the roof, shattering into a thousand pieces.

"We're going to need to get that under control," Dylan said. It wasn't clear whether or not he was pleased or merely logging the event in his mind.

Faith was shaking her head, on the verge of tears as she backed up.

"Why are you doing this to me? Do you get some kind of sick pleasure out of it?"

"Faith, listen to me—it's not what you think."

"I bet it's not."

Faith turned on her heels, hoping she could escape whatever was happening to her before it was too late.

"You're going to remember this tomorrow," Faith heard Dylan say. She was almost to the retaining wall that wound its way around the roof of the building when Dylan appeared out of nowhere in front of her. He was standing on the ledge looking down at her. Had he appeared all at once, out of thin air, or had he some-how moved there before Faith could see him do it? It was dark enough that she couldn't be sure.

"What's it going to take to get you to stay with me?" Dylan asked.

Faith was so angry and scared that she wanted to scream. Dylan had slipped something into her water glass or who knew what he'd done. All she knew was that none of it could be real, and it would only get worse. She was so mad, all she could think about was shoving Dylan off the roof. And as she had this thought, Dylan reeled back, lost his balance, and fell out of view.

"Dylan!" Faith yelled. The nightmare was going deeper inside her, and for a flash of a second she saw bodies flying into lockers in the abandoned high school building—a flashback of a lost memory with Wade—and then it was gone. She was going crazy; that's what it was. She felt this with more certainty when Dylan's voice rose up from behind her.

"I don't think you're going to believe me, are you?" he said.

She wheeled around, putting her hands against the low wall around the roof.

"Please, Dylan. Just take me home. You're *really* scaring me."

Dylan looked visibly wounded, like he'd made a horrible mistake he wished he could take back.

"You're special, Faith," he said. "And important. More important than you know."

"Stop lying to me!"

Faith climbed up onto the ledge and carefully stood up. There was a breeze that made her wobble, and Dylan reached his hand out toward her.

"If you jump, I'll make sure you don't land badly. You can count on it."

She wasn't thinking about leaping off a building; she'd only wanted to get as far away from Dylan as she could. She wanted to run away, but couldn't. Looking back and forth as her hair tangled in the breeze, she began to cry. Glancing down, Faith realized she wasn't standing over the ladder, which would have put her fall only ten feet away to the first landing on the fire escape. What she saw instead was a long drop into darkness. The wind kicked up without warning, and she leaned in toward it, losing her balance as she tried to correct.

"I wish you hadn't done that," Dylan said as he watched her arms flail, and she disappeared over the edge, screaming her head off. He closed his eyes and lowered his head, then he returned to the table and sat down. He could hear her screaming as she rose up in the air, far over his head. Faith flew across the expanse of the building some twenty feet up into the darkness, then she stopped directly over her chair and hung in the air.

"Let me know when you're ready to come down," Dylan said.

Faith kicked and screamed in the air, which made her flip and pitch in different directions. When she finally stopped, she was breathing heavily, a soft wind blowing through her blond hair. She looked like a ghost.

"I'm going to lower you slowly now. If you start kicking you might hurt yourself, so please, stay calm until you're sitting again. You can still run away if you want to."

Faith didn't move a muscle or say a word. She was still afraid, but she was starting to feel Dylan's calm confidence in the air all around her. She felt, in a strange way, as if he was holding her in the air, like he had his arms wrapped around her. "Dylan," she said as she slowly lowered toward the chair she'd sat in.

"Yeah?"

Faith didn't speak again until her feet were on the ground and she was sitting in the chair. She breathed a sigh of relief at not being dead, then looked directly into Dylan's eyes.

"I believe you. Now tell me what the hell is going on."

Dylan couldn't help but smile at her. Faith's hair was all over the place, and her shirt had twisted around just enough to look like she'd been sleeping in it all night. Faith reached across the table and took his hand. She wanted to be sure this wasn't a dream or a nightmare she was trapped in; and feeling the soft skin of his palm, she felt a little bit more certain that it was all going to be okay.

"Promise not to freak out anymore?" Dylan asked.

"I do. Or I mean I'll try. Let's not have me flying around anymore. That'll help."

"Done," Dylan said.

And then he told her some, but not nearly all, of what she needed to know.

Chapter 13

Hotspur Chance

Once Dylan had established the minimum-required trust, he told Faith the first of many secrets.

"You can move things with your mind. Not with any kind of precision or skill, but you can do it."

Dylan let this information sink in while he tried to fashion a way in which to explain everything to her. He'd thought about this moment through long, endless nights standing outside her room in the cold, but somehow the words were harder to find than he'd expected. Behind the bedroom window she'd always looked so soft and warm, all limbs and wild hair, a sleeping beauty waiting to be woken up. But now she was awake and turning out to be more complicated then he'd imagined.

Faith stared at her fork, her brow narrowing and her full lips tightening as she concentrated.

"Make sure you know where you're sending that thing before you think too much about it," Dylan said, intuitively sensing what she was up to. "You don't want to find that thing sticking out of your forehead. Or mine."

Faith didn't heed his warning, and the fork was gone from the table in a flash, over the side of the roof and off to places unknown.

"Headed for Wade's ass," she said.

Dylan laughed softly. "You'd have to run that errand the old-fashioned way. If you don't know where he is, it's not going to know where to go."

"So where did the fork go?"

Dylan shrugged. "It'll stop when it hits something, which could be another human being. Better call it back."

Dylan made a slight motion with his hand, and a moment later the fork was on the table. The tongs were bent backward.

"Guess it hit something hard," Dylan said. "Bummer."

"I didn't know you were so fond of forks."

"You're funny when you're not screaming."

Faith was starting to settle down. She ran her fingers through her tangled hair, trying to tame it as best she could, then gave up and put it in a loose ponytail that wouldn't reveal her two small tattoos. She looked at the broken glass on the roof of the Nordstrom building.

"You do realize this is completely ridiculous," Faith said.

Dylan nodded, gathered his thoughts, and tried to explain.

"Do you remember the lessons about the early stages of the States? You learn that stuff pretty young, like second grade."

"And they keep teaching it," Faith added. "Not that you'd know. It doesn't seem like you're really into taking classes on your Tablet."

"I'm flattered you noticed. Humor me and tell me what you learned in school all these years."

"What does any of that have to do with the fact that I just made a fork fly off the edge of a building *with my mind*?"

"So you don't remember anything about history? I guess the rumors are false. I heard you were pretty smart."

"Better watch it. I can put a fork in your eye without

even moving my hand."

"No, you can't. But that's not important at the moment. Tell me what they've been teaching you. Best to start with what you think you know."

Faith was annoyed with Dylan's confidence, but he knew a lot more than she did. She was smart enough to play along, at least for the moment.

"In 2025 the California coast slid into the ocean, killing three million people. That about where you want me to start?"

"It's the right marker, yeah. Let's take it from there."

Faith leaned back in her chair and put her arms across her chest, looking at Dylan like he were a substitute teacher.

"You already know all this stuff. Why do I have to repeat it?"

Dylan was silent. He picked up his glass of water and took a drink, waiting patiently.

"Hotspur Chance," Faith said, nodding to Dylan as if to say *Why would I go into detail about this guy? You know this already.*

"What about him?" Dylan asked.

That was it for Faith. She decided to get it all out in one long explanation instead of waiting any longer for Dylan to let her off the hook.

"California slides into the ocean, setting off alarm

bells all over the world about global warming. So they get the smartest people they can find from all over the place and stick them all in the same building for three years. No one talks to them; no one hears from them. They're just working in isolation like they're on the moon or something. When they come out, they've appointed a leader, Hotspur Chance, a scientist from Oklahoma, of all places. Guy isn't autistic, but he's got some personality issues, so he doesn't talk much. What he does do is prove beyond any shadow of a doubt that the world is totally screwed, and it's going to happen way faster than anyone would have imagined. There are a lot of charts and computer simulations that ninety-five percent of the scientists worldwide agree with. The five percent who don't are idiots, which apparently means that five times out of a hundred even dumb people can attain a degree in the sciences. Not long after Hotspur Chance shares the findings, New Orleans is gone and so are another million people. That pretty much shut the last five percent up."

"Then what?" Dylan asked. He'd turned attentive instead of condescending. He was looking at her with those big, dark eyes, hanging on every word.

"Uh . . . ," she stammered, looking down at the table and spinning her plate in little turns with her fingers. "Hotspur Chance and the rest of the group went back underground or whatever. They'd proved that global warming was going to destroy vast areas of the world in under a hundred years. That was the big news. A couple of coastlines were one thing; but according to Hotspur Chance's report, it was going to get a lot worse, and fast. There would be no way to stop it entirely—the world was going to get tougher to live in no matter what—but there was a way, if we were fast enough, to stop the damage."

"How?" Dylan asked. "How did he propose we do this?"

"States. That was the short answer."

"But why States, what was his reasoning?"

"They all agreed on building States—every country, every scientist—for a lot of reasons. Getting everyone into small spaces would open up vast portions of land. They estimated that the North American landmass would need to be eighty-three percent empty, seventeen percent full in order to survive. That's not including agriculture, just humans. Everyone had to populate in the same places, *huge* places. And those places had to be created from scratch as clean, modern, perfect atmospheres for living. No more gasoline-fueled cars; those would fall under a worldwide fossil fuel ban. Using gasoline or oil would have to land you in jail or worse; that was critical."

"And people really bought into this?"

"Not at first, no. But then there was the global drought, followed by sections of Japan and China going under sea level. And the 2029 quake—that was what really did it. The earthquake really woke a lot of people up."

"So far you're doing great. What happened next?"

"Well, that's when Hotspur Chance and all the other scientists went back to work. Only this time they invited the smartest engineers, planners, and architects to join them. There were thousands of people working in relative secrecy for a while. I mean, people knew what they were doing, but they lived on a closed campus and didn't release reports or news very often. The world kept falling apart while they worked."

"How many of the thousands of people who went in came out at the end?"

Faith thought this was a weird question.

"I guess I don't know what you mean. A lot of them never did come out; they just kept working. Hotspur Chance was the only person the public saw very much of."

Dylan nodded like he understood and motioned for Faith to go on.

"The first States were started in 2032, and people began moving in a few years later. The States were designed to grow outward as more people arrived, but I don't know too much about what they're like on the inside. You know, since I've never been in one."

"And what percentage of the world population now lives in a State?"

"More than ninety percent. It's shocking, really. Just twenty years, and the world is nearly empty. Crazy, right?"

"It shows what we can do when we put our mind to it, but, yeah, it's a lot of people."

Faith shrugged. "I don't know; I guess it's perfect and clean and fabulous inside. My parents are so head-strong about it. They'll never go inside the State. I think that part of them may have rubbed off on me."

"It's not a crime, living inside a State."

"Might as well be. Can't drive, can't burn wood, no pets, can't go wandering off into the middle of nowhere in search of some peace and quiet."

Faith was always bothered by the conformist aspect of the States. It wasn't in her nature to walk in the same direction everyone else was walking.

"Freedom is pricey, no doubt," Dylan said, then he turned his head sideways slightly and looked at Faith like he were trying to read her mind. "Did you ever hear anything about the intelligence movement?"

"The what?"

Dylan nodded perceptively, like Faith's ignorance was the only answer he needed.

"Another time," Dylan said. "I understand what you know."

"How'd I do? A-plus, right?" Faith said.

"You're about half right. And the half you got wrong has a lot to do with why you can pick up a glass with your mind and shatter it on the ground."

"Sorry about that, by the way. Was it expensive?"

Dylan smiled and shook his head. "No, not expensive. I found them in the back room of the Target just down the street."

Dylan put his hand out across the table, reaching toward her.

"Can I touch your wrist? It will help me explain."

"We're all done with the history lesson, and now you want to hold hands with the teacher?"

"My turn to teach you, if you'll trust me."

Faith's heart danced nervously inside her chest. There was something mystifying and dark about Dylan that made him very attractive. But the mysterious, good-looking type had been recently banned from Faith's life. Wade had set her on edge, and she wasn't going to let another jerk get under her skin.

Faith looked at her spoon, which hadn't been used, and thought about having it do something other than sit there. The spoon moved slowly up in the air, then settled in Dylan's hand.

"So no hand, just a spoon?" Dylan asked. He didn't get an answer, just another shrug of Faith's shoulders.

"I have trust issues."

Dylan looked off toward the Western State glowing in the distance.

"A lot more happened in those years behind closed doors than Hotspur Chance let on. I'm not going to tell you everything right now; it's not my place to do that. But I can tell you a little. Hopefully it will be enough, for now."

"Sounds fair," Faith said. Faith felt herself gently moving. It started in her feet, which lifted off the roof as light as a feather. She felt weightless and soft, but an energy was building deep inside her. It was a feeling she'd never had before, and something about it made her grab hold of the chair she sat in.

"What's happening? What are you doing to me?"

"Better if you don't hold on to anything," Dylan said. He backed away from the table and stood up. "You'll have to drop it eventually."

The feeling inside Faith's body magnified like a ripple on the water, growing larger and larger, until Dylan gave her a funny look and her whole world changed in an instant. Like a rocket, she shot straight up in the air, taking on speed as she went. She forced her eyes open and saw that Dylan was right in front of her, rising up in the air as she was. It was dark and cold; and looking down, Faith realized she was sitting in the chair, her white knuckles a grip of steel around the bottom edge.

"You really should let that thing go," Dylan said as they came to a stop.

Faith was so terrified she couldn't speak. Her breath kept catching in her throat as she alternately glanced down and shut her eyes in terror. If she could have seen herself, she might have laughed at the silliness of a girl who was floating a few hundred feet off the roof of a building holding on to a chair.

"This will all get easier, I promise," Dylan said. He reached down and touched the back of her hand, and she flinched, letting one side of the chair slip from her fingers. She tried to hold on with her other hand but couldn't, and a second later the chair fell out of the sky. There had been something about sitting in a chair that had felt safe, like she wasn't really this far off the ground with nothing to hold her up. As she heard the chair smash into pieces below, Faith finally lost it. She grabbed for Dylan, turning him around like they were floating in water, then she pulled him close and wrapped her arms and legs around his broad back. He didn't say a word, just let her calm down and hold him that way as he stared off into the distance. He put his hands on hers where they were gripping his T-shirt in two fists.

"You're not doing this; I am," he said. "And I'm really good at it. There's nothing to worry about."

"Easy for you to say," Faith whispered. She was still shaking—maybe he'd gone too fast.

"I'm just going to start talking," Dylan said. "You don't have to do anything. Don't think about where we are or what we're doing. I've got you, and I'm not going to let you fall. It took me a long time to find you, much longer than I thought it would. Like I said before, you're a special person. I'm guessing that's obvious by now."

Dylan felt Faith let out a small laugh.

"I don't know if I can deal with this."

"You're strong. You'll be fine."

Faith loosened her grip slightly, felt the same weightlessness she'd felt on the ground.

"I'm still scared," she said.

"Do me a favor and keep your eyes open," Dylan said. "I want you to see something."

Faith lifted her head off Dylan's back and peeked over his shoulder as he turned in the air. They had been facing away from the Western State, but now they could see it full-on. It was more beautiful than she'd expected: a vast city at night, like a whole universe sitting alone in the blackness of space. The wall, which wasn't really a wall at all, glowed soft and yellow. It looked like a wall of fog caught in a perfect beam of moonlight.

"Wow," Faith whispered in Dylan's ear.

"Yeah. Wow."

Faith wondered where in all those white buildings her friend Liz might be. The State was so huge, miles and miles across and full of the tallest skyscrapers she'd ever seen. Even from a hundred miles away, from the height she was at, Faith could see that the Western State was an entire world unto itself.

"I'm going to take you home now if that's okay," Dylan said.

Faith didn't speak. She wouldn't have known what to say. The night had already been so far beyond where her imagination could take her that flying home and listening to Dylan's voice began to feel okay. It felt good to lie on his back as he went, and she began to relax. He told her that she should never try this on her own, not yet. And that she had to be careful not to move things with her mind unless the two of them were together. It was dangerous and especially unpredictable for someone who was as untrained as she was.

As they arrived in the darkness outside of Faith's house, she wished it wouldn't end. Standing on level ground turned out to be more of a letdown than a comfort.

"You like the flying," Dylan said, turning to face her. "I thought you might."

"It's all right, I guess." Faith laughed.

"I promise I'll tell you more really soon. It's going to take a little bit of time, so you'll need to be patient. And I'm not the one to tell you everything, but someone else will. Promise me you won't try to move anything unless we're together. Please?"

Faith nodded, though she was dying to get into her house and start throwing pillows around her room with her mind.

"How long have you been watching me?" Faith asked.

Dylan wouldn't answer her question.

"I can train you, but only on the roof, where we were. Meet me there tomorrow, just after dark?"

"You're not going to pick me up?"

"Afraid not. We really need to keep this to the roof as much as possible. Deal?"

Faith nodded, Dylan smiled, and then he was gone.

As Dylan hovered above her in the darkness, he worried about what he'd done. It was sooner than they'd discussed, and he hadn't asked for permission. He wasn't sure how he was going to explain to Faith that he'd been watching her every night for months. And there were much more serious things he worried about, too. He knew a catastrophe could invade the States at any time. And he knew he was about to put Faith Daniels in serious danger.

Dylan would have liked to go home and rest, but he knew that wasn't an option. He would let Faith have an hour or so on her own before returning to her window, and there he would spend the rest of the night.

He'd trained her to move things with her mind. She was clumsy, but it was a start. What Faith didn't know was that she'd only discovered half of the abilities she would need. There was something even rarer and more important still hidden inside her.

If he could help her find it, there was a chance she'd live through the coming fury.

Chapter 14

Let's Not Tie Our Shoes

"But we just got here," Faith said. "They can't be serious."

She was sitting in a classroom, exhausted and confused from her night on the roof of the Nordstrom building with Dylan, when she heard the announcement on the PA system.

"Once again," Mr. Reichert repeated as Faith looked around the room at all the stunned students. Her gaze fell on Wade Quinn, and she turned away quickly. "Old Park Hill will remain open for two more weeks, at which time you will be reassigned. Officials from the Western State will be contacting parents and guardians to make arrangements. Thank you, I hope you all make the most of your last days at Old Park Hill."

Faith knew what this really meant. Every time a school closed, the numbers got smaller. She was convinced the State used the closings in order to encourage parents to leave the outside behind. Half of the students in the room, more than likely, wouldn't make it to the next school. She missed Liz more than ever and wondered, for the first time, whether she should simply give up. If it wasn't for the bizarre events of the night before with Dylan Gilmore, she would have decided then and there to put a stop to her endless waiting.

"I've enjoyed our time together," Mr. Reichert continued, though he sounded tired and unsure, as if he, too, had run out of reasons to stay. "Let's do our best to have a nice final run, business as usual."

So that's it then, Faith thought. *Old Park Hill will be closed by a week from Friday. Perfect.*

Faith glanced around the room once more, searching for Hawk but finding Dylan Gilmore staring at her from the back row. He shrugged, gave her a little smile, and went back to whatever lesson he wasn't really listening to.

"I say we have a party," Wade Quinn said. Faith rolled her eyes, but everyone else in the class including the teacher seemed to think it was a good idea. "Come on, you guys!" Wade continued, lathering up the crowd.

"A real end-of-the-world bash. What do you say, teach?"

Miss Newhouse looked around the room like it wasn't really her call. "I'm only here to observe. As long as your work is getting done, I don't have a problem with a going-away party. It'll be mine, too. You were my last assignment."

"Wait, you're not even *from* this school?" Faith asked. It hadn't occurred to her that the school might be run by teachers from somewhere else.

Miss Newhouse laughed softly and shook her head. "No one is from here, Faith. Everyone at this school has been moved just as many times as you have."

Like on cue, a commercial break appeared on everyone's Tablet, interrupting whatever individual lecture they were all ignoring. This one focused on the newly released entertainment options for everyone living inside the States. Five new movies were premiering on all State Tablets throughout the week, featuring the biggest-name actors, and a new Tablet series was starting on Friday. This was one of the toughest things about living outside. All the newest, best content was excluded from Faith's Tablet because she wasn't on the closed State network. More and more of the really good stuff wasn't making it out at all; and even if it did, there was a long wait.

"Outside the States?" the commercial asked. "Catch a sneak peek at what you're missing, tonight at 8:00

p.m. Pacific Standard Time. This you're not going to want to miss!"

Harsh, Faith thought. It was how the State eventually wore people down. They never forced anyone to leave; they just lured the holdouts in with an endless stream of cool stuff you couldn't get if you didn't join. At the end of every commercial message, they flashed a message for about ten seconds: *Ready to call the State home? Just let us know; we'll be right over to pick you up.* A button on the screen said home. Faith had been in classrooms where people had pushed that button on their Tablet, only to find that their parents were the ones who had to make that decision, not them.

"It's been a pleasure serving you," Miss Newhouse said when the commercial was over, but it was obviously she'd had enough. She hadn't really taught a class in years, and the commercials had done their work on her, too.

"Why'd you stay out here so long?" Faith was surprised to hear Dylan's voice from the back of the class. She'd never heard him speak in class before. Faith couldn't help remembering what it had felt like to wrap her arms around his back as they flew through the night sky.

Miss Newhouse straightened her blouse and tried to put on a good face.

"Because I'm a teacher. I wanted to teach."

There was a long silence as everyone stared into their Tablets, and then Dylan said something no one expected, least of all Miss Newhouse.

"So teach us something."

Miss Newhouse looked like she didn't quite know how to process the request. *Teach? You mean, like a subject?* her face seemed to ask.

"Tell us something we don't know," Dylan prodded, leaning forward on his elbows, waiting for an answer.

"I thought we were planning a party," Wade said.

A few of the students chimed in support of the party-planning route, but Miss Newhouse didn't say anything. She started nodding her head up and down slowly, like she'd come to some important conclusion, then she looked out at the class, and the confusion in her expression was gone.

"You don't need me," she said.

"Already knew that," Wade joked, getting a few scattered laughs. But it was more sad than funny. Miss Newhouse pressed the screen on her Tablet, and everyone understood that she was about to abandon them. Wade sat up straighter in his chair, looking at Miss Newhouse like she was about to make a decision that would change not only her life, but also his.

"Should have done this a long time ago," she said,

moving toward the door. "Because you're right, Mr. Quinn. You don't need me. You don't need *anybody*. All you need is your Tablet."

A few seconds later Miss Newhouse was gone, and everyone expected Wade to take control of the group. He sat there in silence. Everyone did. And then he looked up, smiling, as if a great adventure was about to begin.

"Looks like our party just got started," he began as he walked to the front of the room. He nudged Faith on the shoulder with his hip as he passed by, trying to be flirty, but the only thing Faith felt was disgust. It was at that moment that her own resolve began to crumble. Even if her parents were still out here, she was getting to the point where she couldn't go on with business as usual any longer. She decided then and there, as Wade called out instructions about music and drinks, that when Old Park Hill closed and the students who remained were reassigned to a new school, she wouldn't be attending. Inside or outside the State, school just didn't make sense anymore.

Faith couldn't stand listening to Wade take over the class, so she stared at the floor instead, hoping it would just be over soon. Her shoe was untied, and though she'd been told not to, she couldn't help thinking about the laces. The edge of one side lifted off the floor slightly, and when it did, she heard a cough from the back of the room. When she turned, she saw Dylan staring at her, shaking his head slowly, as if she'd done a very dangerous thing.

Clara Quinn was a perceptive girl. Nothing at Old Park Hill got past her. She felt things other people didn't feel and knew things other people didn't know. And as the school got smaller, she was spending more time in the proximity of Faith Daniels. She was, in fact, in the same room when her brother boldly took over the class. She was there when Miss Newhouse left the room. She understood the gravity of that decision as much as Wade did, even if no one else had a clue.

She'd long been crushing on Dylan Gilmore. He had a certain kind of energy she liked. She could imagine the two of them doing all sorts of crazy things. It was a preoccupation. But he was so quiet and brooding, getting him to talk was like pulling teeth. She was extremely beautiful and highly athletic, a goddess among mortals. And she knew this, which didn't contribute to a winning personality. And so she couldn't bring herself to court Dylan Gilmore. She only watched him from afar and thought of him in her quieter moments alone. It was for this reason that she'd experienced a series of two unexpected events that felt connected, though she knew they couldn't be. She'd watched as Dylan coughed, looked up, and shook his head slowly, like he was warning someone to stop doing whatever it was he or she was up to. Simultaneously—and this was the strange part—she'd felt something.

A *pulse*.

Soft but real.

Someone had moved something. She knew this because she had been told to be ever aware, ever searching for a pulse that was not her brother's or her own. It was a feeling she could sense better than her brother, although he, too, could feel it if he had half a mind to pay attention, which he had not been doing very much of late.

Clara looked around the room, wondering, *Did Wade do that? Was it someone else? Or am I so bored I imagined it?*

She couldn't definitively know the truth, but looking back at Dylan once more, she was troubled by the fact that he had seemed to respond to it as well. Either that or the timing had simply been coincidental. It wasn't until after class while she was walking with her brother that she got her answer.

"Did you move something in there?"

Luckily for Faith Daniels, Wade had been crazy enough to pull up songs on his Tablet with his mind instead of his finger. He'd only done it that way for a few seconds, but, yeah, he'd probably sent out the pulse Clara felt.

"Do you remember when you did it?"

She sometimes let Wade's pulse fall away into the background because she felt it so much. The one she'd felt was stronger, like something fresh and wild.

"Nope, don't recall. And you should stop being so paranoid. We're leaving soon—I mean *really* leaving; know what I mean? Stay focused on the games; it's important."

"Important to whom?" Clara asked. "And what do I need to focus on? I can't lose."

"Yeah, but you could win too big. Remember, we gotta control ourselves. That's the hard part."

Clara nodded. She understood completely. Hanging around with a bunch of untalented normals was sucking her will to live. It was demeaning to constantly lower her standard of ability.

She kept thinking of how Dylan had coughed and nodded, how he seemed to be paying more attention to Faith Daniels all the time. The thought of Dylan choosing Faith over her was unthinkable. It was beyond sickening.

It was a lucky thing Wade had been reckless in class. And even luckier that he couldn't really remember when or exactly how he'd moved something with his mind.

Faith had Wade to thank for being alive. Because if Clara Quinn had known what Faith could do, Faith would not have lived to see the party Wade was planning to throw.

Chapter 15

Like a Pebble Hitting a Pond

Hawk waited until the sun was almost down before heading to the abandoned building on the campus to do some recon. He'd been curious for over two weeks about the night Wade and Faith were together, but he'd been putting off any sort of investigation until things cooled off a little bit with Wade. Then he'd heard that the school was about to close for good, and he knew time was running out. If he didn't get in there soon, he never would. And it was important that he discover everything he could about that night.

"What were you up to in here, Wade Quinn?" Hawk asked out loud. He'd made quick work of the security system and found himself walking down a darkened corridor with streaks of pale light on either side. Another fifteen minutes and it would be completely dark in the empty wing of the school.

Hawk wasn't just smart, he was intuitive. He would have made a fine detective, because he had an objective eye that could log everything he was seeing, parsing it out for hidden meaning. There was less light as he turned the corner and found the hallway where Wade had been riding his go-cart for fun. He examined the cart itself, which had some significant damage. One of the wheels was off, and the welded metal frame was on its side propped up against a wall. The stretchy cord that had been used to launch the cart snaked around the floor like a long-abandoned whip.

Hawk's Tablet was equipped with a variety of lighting options, and he chose one that illuminated the space, but not too brightly. The hallway glowed like it were being lit by seven or eight candles all bunched together in his hand.

Hawk spun one of the remaining attached wheels, which was at eye level because the cart was partly overturned, and started walking. Some of the lockers had violent marks on them; and examining them more closely, he determined that this had not been caused by the cart. There were dents that looked like they'd been made by shoulders and heads. The damage looked more like it had been caused by human bodies crashing into the lockers at high velocity. As he scanned the floor, Hawk found more items: two shotgun shells; metal buckshot pellets scattered around the floor; and, most curiously, dried blood. The blood was just a smear in the dark; and since the lockers were red, it was easy to see how it could be missed in a haphazard cleanup effort.

"Whatever happened in here, it was some kind of fight," Hawk said.

"You better believe it, little man."

Hawk whirled around and saw, to his great misery, that Wade Quinn was leaning heavily against a locker at the far end of the hall. His voice echoed menacingly down the long, empty space. Hawk turned and started running back toward the upturned cart, hoping to find an escape route. At the end of the hallway he turned left, and as he did, he thought he felt a soft wind over his head in the near darkness. He came up short when he saw Wade standing in front of him a few feet away.

"How'd you do that?" Hawk asked.

"I'm fast; what can I say," Wade joked. "Either that or you're really slow."

Hawk ran back in the direction he'd come from; and when he came to the cart, he grabbed it by the top edge and flipped it back down behind him, hoping it might slow Wade as he took chase. There was a door to a classroom to Hawk's right; and as he passed by, the door opened, and he was sucked inside against his will. It felt like he'd been made as light as a feather, swept up on an unseen wind.

I'm starting to think someone slipped me a Wire Code, Hawk thought.

The door he came through slowly closed behind him without a sound, and he crawled across the floor until he came to the teacher's desk. Before he knew how he'd gotten there, Hawk huddled under the middle of the desk where the teacher's feet were supposed to go. He leaned back and peeked over the edge of the desk, watching as Wade's shadow moved past the glass in the center of the door.

"Maybe you're quicker than I gave you credit for." Wade laughed, the sound of his voice leaking in under the door. "But I'll find you. And when I do, we're going to have another talk, you and me."

There was a long line of windows on the far wall that revealed the darkened courtyard of the school. Hawk thought about opening one of them and crawling out. But it was a long way from the desk to the windows, and he was afraid to get up. He heard a noise behind him, close enough to take his breath away, and he was sure he'd come out from under the desk to find Wade Quinn standing there. How he would have gotten there, Hawk didn't know. But he was starting to think anything was possible in the unpredictable world of Old Park Hill. He took in a big, silent breath, then turned to look for what had made the noise. He spied a door to what must have been a storage room behind the teacher's desk. The door was partway open, and through the crack, only darkness lay beyond. He wondered if Wade had somehow entered the room without being seen, then opened the door and hidden inside. He could imagine himself in there, the darkness, the much bigger guy, the door closing behind him.

"Hiding is just going to make this take longer, Hawk," Wade said. He sounded less menacing, friendlier, but Hawk knew all too well that this was only one of Wade's many weapons of persuasion. "Come on, man—I'll put the wheel back on my cart and take you for a ride. You're gonna love it."

Knowing Wade had not somehow arrived in the darkness behind the door, Hawk made his move, crawling as fast as he could along the cold tile floor. He opened the door a little wider and crept through, then he pulled the door closed and heard it click shut. He held his breath in the dark, hoping he hadn't been heard.

"Running out of patience here, Hawk," Wade said. He was standing out in the hall, Hawk could tell, and he cursed himself for letting the door click shut as he closed it. He was too afraid to shed any light on the storage room with his Tablet for fear that Wade would see the light under the door in the classroom. He could hear Wade coming closer, probably about to look under the desk, and then he'd be at the storage room and it would be over.

Hawk slid his Tablet into his back pocket and started feeling around with his hands out in front of him. He was careful not to move too quickly, shuffling around in a circle, feeling the shelves. At the back of the room he found another door, and, turning the handle, he opened it slowly. The smell of the room took his breath away, and he began to gag, but then he heard a tapping on the door leading out to the classroom.

"No way you're in there, right, Hawk?"

Hawk sucked in a giant gulp of breath and passed through the second doorway into more darkness. When he closed the door behind him, he risked taking out his Tablet and shining a light on the situation. Wade still hadn't come through the first of the two doorways, so at least for a second it was safe. He immediately wished he hadn't seen what the room contained the moment a soft light bathed all the dead bodies. He'd stumbled onto Wade Quinn's idea of a burial ground. He hadn't used a shovel to bury the Drifters he'd killed. He'd just piled them up in this room and left them to rot. Hawk turned off the light on his Tablet and placed it back where it was safe, not because he couldn't stand to see what he was seeing, but because Wade had opened the first door. By the time he got to the second door, Hawk had done the unthinkable: he had gotten in with the bodies, hiding among the trench coats and the shotguns and the rotting limbs. When Wade opened that second door, he shined his own light on the grizzly contents of the room.

"I knew I should have buried these damn things," he complained, turning up his nose at the smell of death. "God, what a mess."

And with that he slammed the door shut and went looking for Hawk elsewhere in the building. Hawk didn't move for another five minutes, just to be sure, and in those minutes he came to understand that his life was not going to be as easy as he might have hoped. It had always been difficult, but it was getting harder still; and he was becoming part of something bigger than himself—something he was pretty sure might get him killed. When he felt sure Wade Quinn had abandoned his search, Hawk crept out of the closed area of the school. How Wade had done what he had done was unclear, but there was no doubt Wade had been responsible.

If he could have seen outside the long line of windows of the classroom, Hawk would have noticed that Dylan Gilmore had been watching everything that had happened inside the room. The moment Dylan knew that Hawk was safe he was gone. He had another place to be, and he was already running late.

"You're nowhere near ready to be doing that, and there are other risks, too," Dylan said as he landed on the roof behind Faith. She was standing at the railed ledge, staring off into the distant light of the Western State, and hearing his unhappy voice startled her.

"A little warning would have been nice. You scared me half to death."

Dylan walked away toward the table they'd sat at the night before. He'd arranged some things there that he needed her to work on, but, sitting down, he doubted they should be on the roof at all. "I shouldn't have told you. It was too soon."

Faith was irritated. Getting back up to the roof in the dark had been a harrowing experience, and when she'd finally made it to the top, she'd found herself alone. For all she knew he was going to stand her up. Or worse, the whole event really had been a bad dream or a bad trip. *Maybe*, she had thought as she stood there staring out at the light, *I really am crazy*. Dylan's insensitivity bordered on cruelty.

"You're being kind of a jerk."

"I've been called worse."

"I bet you have. Lots of times."

Faith walked to the table and sat down hard in the chair, looking off toward the ledge where the ladder was, thinking about whether or not she should just leave. Dylan wouldn't look at her, wouldn't speak. It took about ten seconds for Faith to break the silence.

"Okay, so I blew it; but seriously, what's the big deal? I moved my shoelace. So what!"

Dylan looked straight at her, all business.

"They can feel you."

"What? Who?"

"It doesn't matter who," Dylan said. "I told you not to move things unless we're up here. Please, trust me on this. You *can't* do that again, ever."

"It matters to me," Faith said. She understood she'd made a mistake, but she was also starting to feel like she was being played. "I need to know what's going on, Dylan. Put yourself in my place. I'm moving things with my brain! It's not exactly normal."

Dylan peeled off his jacket and hung it on his chair. He had on a flannel shirt and began rolling up the sleeves.

"Time to go to work," he said, ignoring Faith's plea. She leaned back and folded her arms across her chest.

"Screw that."

Dylan had finished rolling up the sleeve on his left arm and began doing the same to the right. The table was arrayed with all sorts of colored balls, blocks, and cups of different colors.

"Move the yellow ball into the blue cup," he said.

"Move it yourself. I'm tying my shoe."

Dylan leaned under the table and saw that the untied shoelace on her left foot was, in fact, busily tying itself back into a perfect double loop. He was more than a little surprised at how well she was able to do this, given how little training she'd had. When he sat back up, all the balls, blocks, and cups were gone. Faith smiled sarcastically, then everything that had been sitting on the table fell out of the sky and landed, one by one, on Dylan's head. Luckily for Dylan, the balls and blocks were made of foam, and the cups were plastic.

"Very funny," he said, instantly putting every item back on the table in the places where they had been. One ball was missing, a green one, which bounced off Dylan's head and rolled away on the roof.

"You missed one," Faith said.

"I can see you're going to be a model student."

Faith didn't answer. She was not going to let Dylan

run the show, at least not without getting some answers first. Dylan could see he wasn't getting anywhere, so he resorted to bargaining.

"If you move the yellow ball into the blue cup, I'll tell you why you can only use your newly discovered skills up here on the roof of an empty building."

Faith stared at Dylan but didn't move. She raised an eyebrow and smirked, and the yellow ball lifted off the table. It lifted in front of Dylan's face, then floated around his head three times before peeling off and landing in the blue cup.

"Slam dunk," she said. "Your defense stinks."

The ball came out of the cup and returned to where it had been, which was all Dylan's work, and then he leaned back in his chair like he were going to take a nap.

"Try again," he said, taunting her enough that she momentarily forgot she was owed a reward. She went to work again, thinking of the yellow ball, but nothing happened. She kept trying to make it move, but it had turned to granite on the table. Not only that, but each of the three cups on the table popped up in the air and landed on top of the ball, one after the other. She kept trying to move the ball, and it kept sitting there. Dylan was vastly more powerful than she was. It was nothing to force the items not to move even when Faith was giving it her all.

"The reason we have to do this up here," Dylan said as he made the cups dance in the air like they were being thrown by an invisible juggler, "is because up here, no one can feel what we're doing."

"Why not," Faith asked.

"As long as we're higher than other carriers, they can't detect a pulse."

"So whoever you don't want finding out about me is down there while we're up here?"

Dylan nodded, setting down the cups on the table. "Signal won't carry up or down very far. But side to side at the same level, a pulse will ripple out about thirty feet. Think of it like a pebble hitting a pond. The ripple only goes out, not up and down. That's what a pulse does."

"You keep talking about a pulse. You mean like the one in my neck?"

Faith felt the soft space under her cheek, searching for the tiny tremor under her skin she knew was there. Again, Dylan wouldn't answer unless Faith participated in some work. He made her stack the blocks, move the balls into different cups, get all the foam items floating at once. Dylan was surprised at how quickly she learned and how precise she was with her movements.

"My head is starting to hurt," Faith said after about fifteen minutes of work. She held her hand on her temple and looked down at the table.

"That's normal. It will get easier, and you'll get stronger. Right now you're moving things that weigh almost nothing, but it's a start."

Faith smiled softly and placed her hands flat on the table. Dylan was blown away when he felt himself moving, rising slowly in the air until he was lying flat on his back ten feet over the table.

"Impressive," Dylan said. But then Faith felt a sharp pain in the side of her neck, and suddenly Dylan was free-falling. He should have landed on the table, sending the balls and the blocks and the cups flying everywhere. But instead he only fell until he was an inch away from landing, then hovered in the air, turned over, and sat himself back down.

"You might not be ready for something as heavy as me," he said. "I've got a huge head."

Faith laughed nervously. She touched her neck again, thought of the pain, which bore a strong resemblance to being stuck with a tattoo needle.

"It's nothing to worry about," Dylan said. "Think of it as a growing pain. Over time it will happen less and less."

Faith nodded and smiled weakly. When he said things like that, it made her think about how her life wasn't ever going back to the way it was.

"How many people can move things the way you and I can?"

Dylan took his time answering, and even when he did, it was vague.

"More than just you and me."

"That's not much of an answer. What, like a thousand?"

Dylan laughed. "If there were a thousand carriers, it wouldn't be much of a secret. It's rare. Until we know more about your skill set I think I've told you everything I can."

"Don't make me pick you up again. I might drop you a lot farther next time. I'm unpredictable."

Dylan was starting to get a good feeling about his student. She was whip-smart and fast on her feet, and she didn't mind working hard once he had her focused. But he was running low on time; and time was one of those things that, once it was gone, there was no getting it back. He would need to make the most of every second he had before the school closed.

In the nights that followed, Faith was diligently trained by Dylan. She asked a lot of questions, all of which Dylan answered the same way: you'll find out in time. Faith wanted to know why she and Dylan were carriers, who else had the power, how it had been discovered, and on and on.

On the next night Dylan worked with the cups, balls, and blocks, teaching Faith how to pick them up and move them at different speeds and in different ways. By the third night the items had been replaced with pool balls, blocks of wood, and metal cups. She found these items more difficult to work with. They caused the sharp pain in her neck to reappear several times, all the items crashing down onto the table at once. At the end of a particularly grueling night of exercises, Dylan removed all the items from the table but one black pool ball. It was a number eight. Faith would always remember this, long after Dylan used it to teach her a hard lesson.

"You've been asking me about the pulse," Dylan said, rolling the pool ball back and forth on the table in front of her. "You have a special one, very rare. It's what allows you to do these things. And I have the same kind of pulse, so I can do the same things."

Faith could tell by the way he was looking at her that there was something more he was trying to say. Their relationship was becoming more intimate that way— they could tell what the other was thinking, sometimes just by looking into each other's eyes.

"There's something else about the pulse, isn't there? Something you're not telling me?"

Dylan nodded, then lifted the eight ball with his

mind. It hovered a few feet up in the air as he set his hand flat, facedown, on the solid table beneath it. He blinked, and the ball fell like it were held up by a string and the string had been cut. When it reached his hand, the ball moved sideways, rolling across the table and landing on the floor with a loud pop. Before it bounced a second time, Dylan moved it back onto the table with his mind and picked it up.

"There's more than one pulse," he said. "There's a second pulse, much deeper than the first."

"A *second* pulse?" Faith asked. "But that's impossible. No one has two pulses."

"You don't have to believe me, but I'll tell you what it does and why it's so important just the same. If you're a carrier, you have a second pulse, but it takes a lot of work and special understanding to bring it to the surface. It's hidden deep inside you, and it's the most important part of being a carrier. Want to know why?"

Faith's head was reeling, but she was very curious and desperately wanted answers. She nodded, said nothing, hoped for some new insight.

"Put your hand on the table, like I did," Dylan instructed.

"Are we back in school again? I thought you were going to tell me a secret."

Dylan didn't respond, which was his way of saying

he was done talking until Faith did what he'd instructed her to do. Faith rolled her eyes, feeling tired of being told what to do. But she laid her hand flat on the table, palm down, hoping for *something*.

"Now promise me you won't move," Dylan said. "No matter what."

"I won't move."

Dylan tossed the black ball in the air, and it stopped about ten feet over the table. It spun around in circles but otherwise stayed in the same location. He knew she wouldn't be able to keep her promise, so without her knowledge, he held her hand in place with his mind. No matter how much she might want to move it, nothing on Earth could make that happen as long as Dylan didn't want it to. He let the ball free-fall, and as it approached Faith's hand, she couldn't help but try to move her hand out of the way. Her arm wrenched back, tightening at the elbow, but her hand didn't budge. When the pool ball hit her squarely on the knuckles, she yelled in pain. Without thinking, she used her power to pick up the ball again and throw it in the direction of Dylan's chest. He in turn moved the ball back toward her, catching her in the sternum.

"Stop throwing that thing at me!" she yelled.

"I will if you will."

Faith hated being manipulated more than anything.

She wanted to get up and leave, but she couldn't. Her hand was still stuck to the table.

"How long are you going to hold my hand down?" she asked.

Dylan leaned forward.

"Throw it as hard as you can, right at my forehead."

"You're crazy."

Dylan moved the ball so it clocked Faith on the side of the head. Not too hard, but hard enough that she definitely felt it.

"Do it. Hit me with the ball. Use everything you've got."

Faith's face turned angry: her eyes narrowed and her lips pursed. The eight ball flew behind her, then back toward Dylan like it had been shot out of a cannon. When it arrived at his forehead he didn't flinch, didn't move, didn't care. It seemed to hit him, but he didn't react. The ball appeared to bounce off his forehead. As it ricocheted forward it found Faith's shoulder. The impact hurt worse than the shots to the chest and hand put together.

"Ouch! Okay, that one really hurt. That's gonna leave a bruise."

"Probably so. Sorry. I didn't mean for that to happen. But it makes my point. Accidents happen when you do this stuff. *Bad* accidents."

He stood up and came around to Faith's side of the table, leaning back and sitting down on its edge, tossing the eight ball between his two hands.

"How's your head?" Faith asked. It felt like they'd had a small war in which they'd inflicted minor wounds on each other for no reason.

"I have a second pulse, Faith," Dylan said. "You don't."

Faith seemed to finally understand that there was something fundamentally different about the power in Dylan's hands than in her own.

"Wait, you mean you didn't feel that at all?"

"It didn't actually hit me. Came pretty close though."

Faith ran out of words and looked up into his eyes, confused.

"The first pulse for a carrier is what gives us our ability to move things, but the second pulse is just as important. It senses everything around it. It knows when something is going to hurt and deflects it."

"Use the force, Luke," Faith said in a monotone voice, only half joking.

"You're not too far from the truth. Watch."

Dylan was gone in a flash, flying straight up in the air.

"Dylan?" she called, staring into the starry sky above, but it returned only cold silence. Another ten seconds went by, and Faith stood up, wondering if this was a test she was supposed to understand but didn't. At least Dylan had freed her hand from the table.

"Dylan?" she called again, then more to herself than to him added, "You are one mysterious dude, Dylan Gilmore."

And then she saw him. He was diving headfirst at shotgun speed, like he wanted to drive his head into the roof of the Nordstrom building and split his entire body wide-open. She tried to scream, but nothing would come out. Her head tilted down, watching the tucked arms and the rigid body. When his head hit the roof, it was like something out of a movie, an asteroid hitting pavement, dust and debris clouding up around the impact. Faith fell to her knees, then flopped over onto her left hip and put her bare hands on the roof. A state of shock pulled at her insides and drawing each breath was a struggle. Her mind told her he was gone, that he'd made a calculated error. Dylan was dead, and she was alone with endless questions she could never answer for herself.

The dust settled quickly, leaving the soft light of the stars and a few candles that had been set around the foot of the table. Dylan wasn't there. His body had gone through the roof, leaving a tattered opening about the size of a manhole cover. She crept a little closer, until she was surprised by the black eight ball, which popped out of the hole and rolled toward her, stopping just shy of her knee. She picked it up, examined its smooth surface, feeling the slick marble against her fingers.

"I might have gone a little overboard there," Dylan said. He was shaking the plaster and dust out of his mop of dark hair and brushing off his shoulders as he drifted up and out of the hole he'd just made in a building.

"Ya think?" Faith asked, but then she was up on her feet, running to him, hugging him tightly. When she pulled away, Dylan looked a little stunned, which she didn't quite know how to respond to. Being Faith, she resorted to cleverness in the face of confusion.

"You smell like building. New cologne?"

Dylan smiled as she brushed the dust off his V-neck T-shirt, black this time, which she had liked from the moment he showed up.

Dylan looked deeply into her eyes, like he was searching for something he couldn't find but wanted to very badly. "That's the second pulse. You could drop a car on my head, but it knows. I'd be fine. What you have is only half of what you need."

"You mean I'm no good to you, no help, unless I can have a car dropped on my head?"

It was a funny way of putting things, but Dylan

PULSE ◄◄◄

basically agreed, nodding with a half smile on his face.

"But why would anyone want to hurt me?"

Faith asked the question, but she also suddenly understood something that had only been a whisper of a thought—until Dylan had used his head to drive a hole into the roof of a Nordstrom building.

"You're recruiting me," she said. "For something more than just fun and games."

Dylan didn't answer. He didn't betray any feeling about what she was suggesting as he returned to the table and sat down. "Let's get back to work, see if we can't get you lifting heavier stuff."

Faith was starting to realize that the only way to the answers she needed was to keep going. If Dylan wanted to be difficult, fine; he could be difficult. But soon enough she'd be too powerful for him to control. Then she'd get her answers whether he liked it or not.

"Let's do it," she said.

They spent the rest of that night and many nights after working on Faith's first-pulse abilities. Within a few more days she was lifting bowling balls and fifty-pound weights. And she was flying and carefully landing on her own. She was so immersed in the building up of her own powers that the answers to her questions started to matter less and less. She felt stronger than she'd ever felt in her life, and yet there was a growing

243 ◄◄◄

fear taking up more and more of the space in her heart. Seeing a bowling ball fly through the air started to have the unnerving effect of making her duck even when it was nowhere near her. The mere thought of having it clobber her before she could move would take over, and she'd lose concentration. It was one thing to move objects that couldn't do any harm if they went astray, such as foam blocks and plastic cups. It was something else entirely when things got heavy enough to kill her.

But more than that, Faith was starting to feel things for Dylan she couldn't deny. She kept telling herself, over and over, not to let her feelings get involved. And the longer she spent time with Dylan, the more she was intrigued by the idea that he had something she didn't. Between the two of them, he alone had a second pulse.

"I don't see why I can't come, too," Hawk said. It was the last day of school, and he was angling for an invitation to wherever Faith had been disappearing to every night. "Especially tonight. It's the end!"

"I told you already; it's not my call. Dylan says no. I even asked him."

That wasn't exactly true. Faith had asked if Hawk could know about carriers, and Dylan had said absolutely not. She'd never asked if Hawk could come up to the roof.

"Dylan, Dylan, Dylan," Hawk repeated. "When you fall, you fall hard."

"Oh, come on, I'm not that bad. And we're just talking, taking it very slowly."

"Mmmm-hmmmm," Hawk said.

The hall had seemed empty as they entered the school, heading for their last day of class at Old Park Hill. But they'd walked past Clara Quinn, who was standing off to one side, staring into her Tablet. She snapped the screen small, placed it in her hip pocket, and advanced on the pair.

"Taking what slowly?" she asked Faith. Faith tried to move around Clara, but Clara was a tall, strong girl, and she kept stepping in front of Faith as she tried to get by.

"Aren't you supposed to be leaving for the games or something?" Faith asked. What she really wanted to do was throw Clara through a door. Just knowing she was capable of doing it gave Faith more confidence than normal.

"We're leaving in a couple of hours," Clara answered. "Have to stay for Wade's blowout, right? Can't miss that."

"I'm in charge of music," Hawk said. "DJing is my new thing. I think you'll find I'm pretty good at it."

Clara completely ignored Hawk and bore down on

Faith with her piercing eyes. Faith took a step forward, glaring at Clara's face, and asked her to please step aside.

"You and Dylan seem to be getting along fine," Clara said.

"Why do you care about anything around here anyway? You're in the Field Games. After today we'll never see you again. Just *leave*."

"Whoa, Faith, take 'er down a notch." Hawk pulled gently on her shirtsleeve, but she jerked free.

"I think I'll stand over here," Hawk responded, backing away. "By these lockers. In case I'm needed."

As usual, Amy showed up just in time—she could see a fight about to start and, loving the idea of Faith getting clobbered, hung back to watch.

"Amy," Clara said. "Get the hell out of here. Now. You, too, squirt."

Hawk was about to toss off a retort, but he thought finding Dylan might be a better idea. He and Amy double-timed it down the hall as Clara took half a step toward Faith.

"I'm only going to say this once," Clara fumed. Her voice was quiet but oh-so-confident, like a girl who could knock out a gorilla with one punch. "I've had my eye on Dylan Gilmore since we showed up at this godforsaken shit hole. Stay away from him. 'Cause I'm coming back, and when I do, I'll be wearing some new gold around my neck. I think that's going to impress him a little more than your clever banter."

"I have a better idea," Faith said, and then she lost it. She knew it was wrong. She knew it would make Dylan mad and might get her kicked out of the Nordstrom Rooftop Club for good, but she'd had enough of Amazon Woman. Faith imagined throwing Clara Quinn into a wall of lockers, then throwing her to the other side of the hall, where she'd hit more lockers. A flash of a memory appeared in her mind, of seeing Drifters doing the same thing, and then it was gone. When she shook her head clear of the memory, Clara Quinn was slumped on the floor to her right. Faith's first thought was to run, but she was seized by a sharp pain in her neck that nearly doubled her over. She looked to her right, expecting to see Clara, but the space she'd occupied was empty. Somehow Clara had gotten up and moved in the flash of an instant. She was standing behind Faith, whispering in her ear with a menacing voice.

"I see we have a player," she seethed. "Interesting. *Very* interesting."

Faith's throat started to tighten like someone was wrapping a pair of cold hands around her neck and slowly adding pressure.

"Can you take it as good as you dish it out?" Clara

asked. Her voice was soft in Faith's ear. All at once Faith felt herself being thrown against the wall of lockers. Her shoulder hit first, then her head jerked sideways and slammed into metal. Faith blinked her eyes hard, trying to clear the ringing in her ears. Clara's voice was back.

"Let's keep this our little secret, okay? You're a freak, just like me. Only I see you're just half the package."

Faith felt a quick jolt to her side and thought she'd been kicked, but when she looked up, doubled over in pain, Clara was halfway down the hall calling back, "Stay away from him. I mean it."

Faith flew across the floor, slammed into the lockers she'd just thrown Clara into, and slid to the floor. She stayed there for only a few seconds, regaining her strength and standing as she wiped the tears from her eyes. She thought of three things then; nothing else mattered.

First, Dylan couldn't know what had happened. He'd never forgive her.

Second, and this was huge: Clara Quinn had a pulse. She could move things with her mind.

And third, she had to find a second pulse so she could kill Clara Quinn if she ever came back.

Chapter 16

Hammer Throw

Everyone, including the few remaining souls on the outside, watched the games. They were a slimmed-down summer Olympics, streamlined to include only the individual events. The games were all about the one man or the one woman who was better than all the rest. There was no traveling from State to State, not domestically nor internationally; but world records were still set and broken at just about every game. All the States across the globe held the games during the same seven-day period, with twenty-four-hour live coverage on dozens of Tablet channels.

There were twenty core events in which men and

women competed separately:

- *100-, 200-, 400-, 800-, and 1,600-meter footraces*
- *javelin, discus, shot put, and hammer throws*
- *high jump, long jump, triple jump, and pole vault*
- *100 hurdles, 200 hurdles, 400 hurdles*
- *three fighting events: wrestling, boxing, and judo.*

The twentieth event was a modernized decathlon blending all sixteen core events into a three-day competition. It was the decathlon that Wade and Clara had been training for in the gym and on the field at Old Park High. It wouldn't have been practical, given their unusual skills, to practice within a State training center. There were cameras everywhere and thousands of athletes. And besides, competing in the Field Games was not about winning for the people who funded Clara's and Wade's training. It was about much more than that.

The twins arrived with no fanfare whatsoever, virtually unseen as they crossed under the wall in an unmarked white van. Automobiles were rare inside the States, where there were very few roads for driving. Mass transportation, with thousands of miles of high-speed light-rail, carried millions of people from place to place.

No one spoke as they drove. Wade and Clara made little attempt to take in the view of the world outside for, really, there wasn't much of anything to see. Roads were covered by circular, white tubes; oncoming vans were infrequent. The road was flat and straight, the white tube oppressively low over their heads.

After about twenty minutes, the van pulled off on a marked exit down a secondary tube and came to a stop. Clara and Wade gathered their things and entered a building through a set of sliding double doors. None of the usual checking in at the hotel desk took place. Instead, Wade and Clara boarded an elevator, which was glassed in on all sides.

"Here we are," Clara said as she pushed the button marked 300.

"Yeah," Wade said. "Here we are."

The building they had entered was 301 stories high, one of the taller buildings in the Western State. As they began their ascent, the glass elevator emerged onto the outside of the building after the first few floors, allowing them a spectacular view. At first they only saw buildings surrounding them on all sides. Modern, sleek structures of metal and glass that rose so high they couldn't make out the tops. But soon enough, as they passed the halfway point, gaps in the buildings started to appear. There were white skywalks everywhere, spanning from one building to another. The higher they went, the more connecting spokes there were. From the sky, it began to look like the buildings were all trapped in an enormous spiderweb that went on for hundreds of miles: thousands of sleek skyscrapers connected by layer after layer of white passageways.

"Pretty cool," Wade blurted out as he leaned his forehead against one of the windows of the glass elevator. "Last week they surpassed four million connecting passageways. Blows the mind."

Tops of lower buildings started to appear, bright green and teeming with life. The giant roofs were used to grow much of the food consumed in the Western State. All the rooftop farms were managed mechanically to plant, grow, and harvest without human intervention. Distribution was handled through automated delivery systems that put fresh fruit and vegetables in every residence on a regular schedule. Advances in soil and seed management produced constant, not seasonal, new harvests.

In the elevator, Clara pulled out her Tablet, snapped it large, and turned it on. She was hoping to send a message to someone as they rose up in the air, but she was surprised to find that her Tablet had reset while they traveled. The operating system had been updated, and she was tied into the G12 network.

"Hey, check your Tablet," Clara said. "We're on the grid. Lots of channels."

Wade snapped his Tablet open and started scrolling through the channel guide. By the time they reached floor 250, they'd both realized how much they'd been missing. Their old network had delivered what amounted to decades-old reruns, lectures, and propaganda about everything anyone on the outside was missing. Now that they were inside, the options were endless. What they both wanted to do was curl up on a couch and watch new shows for weeks on end, but a message on Wade's Tablet brought them back to reality before they could even begin to enjoy the idea of lazing around in their rooms.

"He says we need to be at the practice field in two hours," Wade said as they arrived at the three hundredth floor and the elevator stopped.

"What else does he say?" asked Clara. She stepped out of the elevator into a corridor lined with doors and turned left.

Wade laughed. "He says not to overdo it until he tells us to."

"Figures," Clara said, stopping at a door just off the elevator. She minimized her Tablet and held the screen next to a reader on the door. There was a soft, buzzing sound, and the door unlocked. "If he has it his way, we'll never show anyone what we can do."

"He wants us to contact him as soon as we settle in," Wade said, snapping his Tablet small and placing it in his pocket. Unlike Clara, who could turn moody and sullen when the pressure was on, Wade was dizzy with excitement as he went to the plateglass window and stared at the view below.

"Come on, Clara. You have to be excited when you look at this place."

Clara stood next to her brother, trying not to feel manipulated by forces outside of her control. What she really wanted to do was start throwing things around the room with her mind, but she knew that would solve nothing. Looking down, she saw the location for the Field Games, a stunning spectacle of modern architecture. Buildings towered all around the edge of a rooftop field. The striking green color of the grass overpowered the sea of white and silver. There was seating for 100,000 around the edge of the track, and on top of all the surrounding buildings another 50,000 seats. Hundreds of millions of people worldwide would watch the games on their Tablets or on larger screens in their apartments, but 150,000 would see them compete live. Clara thought of those people, especially the lucky few who would be seated near the field, and mulled over something she'd been contemplating for days.

"Let's contact him," Clara said. "I want to start warming up as soon as we can."

Wade was happy to see his sister come out of her funk, if only a little, and went straight to work setting up a connection. The G12 network wasn't available outside the Western State, but Wade had been instructed in how to get around that little problem. With a few keystrokes, he was tied into multiple networks at once, and a few seconds later he and Clara were sitting on a couch staring at two people. One was Mr. Reichert, the other Miss Newhouse. They were no longer using those names as covers though, and they were no longer running Old Park Hill, which had closed the previous day.

"No trouble getting settled in?" asked the man. His name was Andre Quinn, and though he really did have something of an egg-shaped head and a bad haircut, he was a formidable presence when he wasn't pretending to be a washed-up school principal.

"No trouble at all," Wade said. "And we can see the field from our window. Amazing!"

Wade's father smiled proudly. He loved his son's childlike exuberance. Unlike his sister, who could be difficult, Wade wanted nothing more than to please his father.

"Remember," Andre Quinn warned, "this has to be handled delicately. If you compete at too high a level, our plans will be harder to manage. Don't draw undue attention."

Clara hated this part of "the plan." She knew she could win every single event without even trying. Having to pretend that she was lame like every other athlete on the field was going to be very tough. And the plan had been bothering her for a long time, primarily because she didn't fully understand what it was.

"I don't know why we have to throw these events," Clara said. Arriving in the Western State and seeing the facility had turned up the volume on her competitive nature. "What's the point of even doing this if you're not going to let us compete?"

"There's a job to do. Drawing attention to yourselves is the last thing we need," Andre's wife said. Her name was not Miss Newhouse and never had been. This was Gretchen Quinn, and she was always the bad cop when it came to dealing with Clara. "This is not about winning, Clara. At least not yet."

Clara rolled her eyes. She couldn't stand her stepmother and thought she was a power-hungry idiot. "Whatever you say, Mommy dearest."

"That's enough, Clara." Andre was all too happy to let Gretchen deal with Clara's behavior, but there was a line he would not let Clara cross. "We're at the beginning of a long journey. It's a marathon, not a sprint, and it begins with small steps. These ridiculous Field Games are not going to mean anything by this time next year. And I promise you, by then you'll have more power than you know what to do with. Trust me on this, Clara. I know what I'm doing."

Clara did trust her father, even if his taste in women bordered on insane. But Clara had a plan of her own, one that had been swirling around in her head ever since Gretchen had come into the picture. *Just you wait,* Clara thought as she glared at her stepmother. *I'm going to come for you; and when I do, you'll wish you'd never been born.*

"When you warm up, keep it normal, nothing out of the ordinary. Stay near the back of the pack during the decathlon, and do as we've instructed when the time comes. Remember, you're not there to win games. You're there to do a job."

Wade felt a small pang in his chest as he thought about all the work he'd put in training for the games. It was nowhere near the amount a true Field Games athlete would invest, but still, there had been a lot of endless afternoons jumping over a bar or throwing a metal ball. There had been many moments of extreme boredom in which he'd asked himself why in the world anyone would dedicate himself to such useless endeavors. And yet, deep down inside, he wanted to win. It would take all his self-control not to position himself on the top podium when the opportunity arose.

"Always remember, this isn't about us," Gretchen said, her cold gaze alternating between each twin. "We have the power to change the world, to mold it into what it should be. We are not to waste such power. Am I understood?"

Clara and Wade nodded obediently, looking at their father for any additional guidance he might provide.

"You are now firmly entrenched in enemy territory. Don't forget that. And don't for a second let your emotions get away from you. Get the job done and come home."

Wade was just about to sign off, but Clara stopped him.

"There's a girl from Old Park Hill, a friend of mine. I'd like her to have a seat. A good one, close to the field."

Gretchen saw this as a way to appease her unpredictable stepchild and immediately latched on to it. "I have someone on the inside, won't be a problem. Tell me her name."

Gretchen turned her attention to a Tablet at her side, where she scrolled through a list of seats she had access to through an associate in the State.

"Liz Brinn," Clara said. Wade shot her a look of surprise, but Clara ignored him and went on. "She was a really close friend; this would mean a lot. And she'd want to bring another person, if that's not asking too much."

Gretchen didn't like the idea of Clara having a close friend at Old Park Hill, but she let it slide. If this small gesture could build some much-needed goodwill between the two of them, so be it.

"I'll have two tickets sent to her, both right on the field. A213 and A214, in case you want to say hello. Does that make you happy?"

"That's perfect, thank you, Gretchen. It really means a lot."

Clara could be charming when she needed to be, and all appeared to be in order when the call ended.

Andre and Gretchen had moved to a new location ten miles to the north of Old Park Hill, where they could watch the Games unfold in peace and quiet.

"They're nearly seventeen. We shouldn't have to treat them like children any longer," Gretchen said.

"Well, it was a nice gesture all the same," Andre responded. "You know how unpredictable she can be. Better safe than sorry."

Gretchen looked at Andre without a shred of emotion. *The apple doesn't fall very far from the tree,* she thought. And she was right. Andre had been calm for many months, but he could be as unpredictable as his daughter.

If things didn't go as planned in the Western State, there was no telling what he would do.

"Charity case, happens every year."

Wade heard one of the other athletes use those very words as he began warming up at the high jump pit in the training facility an hour later. There were four other jumpers, and they all seemed to agree: Wade was the one from the outside, a concession to help the needy feel better about themselves. It galled him to think about what total losers they all were, and to take his frustrations out, he made them look like amateurs on every single one of their warm-up jumps. Wade would watch them elevate, then when they were right over the bar, he would use his mind to move the jumper's legs down and knock the bar off the stands. He did this to all the other jumpers, messing with their heads as they looked at the fallen bar and thought, *What the hell?* When the guy who'd made the lame comment stepped up for his first jump, Wade took special pleasure in making him trip on his approach and fall flat on his face. The guy didn't even make it to the bar.

"You guys warming up at six-six? Really?" Wade asked. "Huh."

On his first jump, Wade couldn't help himself. He cleared it by a foot and a half, a dangerous sign of talent that hovered in the area of the world record. Then he walked past the group and over to the throwing area. "I guess once is enough."

He continued the routine at each of the warm-up stations, relishing every jaw-dropping stare he got as he showed them all who they were dealing with. The complicated part of all this posturing was the fact that it was really messing with Wade's head. Clara had already made her case as they walked to the practice field: they should do what they wanted to do, not what witchy Gretchen and their dad said.

"Who does she think she is?" Clara had said, adding, "There's no reason for us to do what she says."

Wade had tried to convince her that it was their duty to follow through with the plan.

"They've been training us for what, three years? It's not our problem, Wade. It's not our war; it's theirs. I don't see why we have to be pawns on someone's chess board."

But Wade always had to remember that Clara was incredibly persuasive. If she'd been arguing the other side of the case, that they should stick to the plan and do as they were told, she would have been every bit as convincing. And the problem with Clara, as he'd come to know over time, was that she was notorious for changing her mind.

Still, he had to admit, it felt good to trounce a bunch of talentless normals. What fun it would be to sweep the games, take every event in the decathlon, and break all the world records while he was at it.

By the time he and Clara were settled in for the night, awaiting the morning alarm that would send them onto the field, he still hadn't decided which course of action he was going to take.

Liz Brinn couldn't believe her luck. She'd only been in the Western State for a little while, and already she'd managed to secure two tickets to the Field Games. And not just any two tickets, *field* level tickets. She was the talk of her social circle. No one could believe she had them. A bidding war broke out to buy the second ticket that went as high as six thousand Coin, a huge amount of Tablet cash she could have used to buy a whole closet full of new clothes. But it never really crossed her mind to sell the extra ticket. She knew it was a fluke, a once-in-a-lifetime chance to see the Field Games live and up close.

"Where'd they come from?" Noah had asked her when Liz video-called him. Noah lived twenty-one buildings over, and it took almost an hour to traverse

PULSE ◀ ◀ ◀

the passageways in order to meet up, which they tried
to do at least once a day. But she'd been so excited, she
had called him straightaway.

"It says they're a gift from the Field Games com-
mittee. I guess they do this sometimes for newbies
like me."

"What if it's a hoax? Maybe they're not even real,
and we're going to get turned away at the gate."

"Come on, Noah. You know that's not true. Just
embrace it. We're going to the Field Games!"

The States were very hard on cybercriminal activity, even if it amounted to nothing more than a prank. If
they caught you doing things like that, Coin would just
disappear out of your account without warning. Your
job assignment might go from entertainer to window
cleaner. It happened. Liz and Noah were going, and they
would be sitting close to the field itself. Still, it wasn't
until they were in the fourteenth row off the field that
Noah finally gave in. They were holding hands, which
Liz loved, and he leaned in for a long, warm kiss.

"I can see you like these tickets," Liz said.

"I can't believe this is real. It's incredible. They're
going to run right past us."

It was a perfect summer morning, warm and soft,
with a blue sky overhead. They both pulled out their
Tablets and reviewed the list of events. First would be a

series of men's decathlon finals, then the women would be throwing in the field in the finals of their decathlon. Liz shook her head, amazed at the turn of events.

"I didn't expect to see Wade and Clara Quinn in the finals. I had no idea they were this talented."

"They're in all the news feeds right now. Everyone's talking about the twins from the outside." Noah was scanning through news on the Field Games as he talked. "How well did you know them? You think you could get an autograph?"

Liz didn't have a clue how to even find Clara or Wade, and she definitely didn't want anything to do with them. "Honestly, Noah, they're both class-A jerks. I hope they lose today."

"Really? Everyone is totally into them. They seem so cool."

"Trust me on this one. I went to school with them, and they treated everyone else like nobodies. They don't care about anyone but themselves."

As they were talking, one of the athletes started jogging up the track in their direction. A roar of cheering rose along their route, and the athlete waved, smiling.

"Speak of the devil," Noah said, standing up since everyone in front of them was doing the same thing as Clara Quinn approached. To Liz's surprise, Clara turned at the stands and walked fourteen rows up to where she and Noah were standing. Their seats put Noah right on the edge of the walkway; and when Clara stood next to him, he was awestruck.

"You're . . . wow, you're—"

"Tall?" Clara said, but it was more than that. In the morning light and the fresh air, Clara Quinn looked vibrant and powerful. Her newly cut hair was shorter than she'd ever worn it before. Her arms were ripped, and her broad shoulders cast a shadow across Noah's face. She was easily six inches taller than he was.

"You cut your hair off," Liz said, suddenly starstruck herself as fans leaned in from every direction.

Clara messed up the blond froth of hair on top of her head and shrugged as if it didn't matter. "It was getting in my way, so I figured, why not? New home, new look, right?"

"Sure, yeah," Liz said, nodding nervously. Clara was bigger than life, much more intimidating to look at than she ever had been in the tiny world of Old Park Hill. On the world stage, Clara Quinn was more than holding her own. She was owning it.

"Anyway, I just wanted to stop by and say I hope you enjoy the seats," Clara said. "I'll try not to embarrass you."

Liz couldn't believe what she was hearing. "*You* sent me the tickets? But why? We weren't even friends."

"Really?" Clara said, crunching up her nose, which made everyone who could see her laugh. "I thought we were. My mistake, I guess."

Before Liz could find a better response, Clara was walking down the steps, signing Tablets with her finger on screens being held out to her. Everyone kept asking Liz what she knew about the twins. *Were they supercool? Were they like normal people? How did they get so good at these events outside the State?*

Liz mostly ignored them until the first event was called and everyone sat down, focused on the men's running finals that were about to take place. Before the first race began, the president of the Western State stood up, along with a group of dignitaries. He waved to the crowd from his box seat, which sat directly across from the seats Liz and Noah were in. Everyone stood, saluted, and began to sing.

"The president is sitting right there," Noah whispered into Liz's ear. "Like a hundred yards away. This is crazy cool."

Liz was glad she'd made Noah so happy, and she was excited to be there; but her heart also ached for her best friend. If Faith had been inside the State, there was no doubt Liz would have asked her to attend, not Noah. Faith would have understood about Clara and

Wade. They would have had a good time cutting them up behind their backs, talking about old times. They would have laughed a lot. Noah put an arm around Liz as the music concluded and pulled her in close.

"Let's get this party started!" he said, all smiles and good cheer.

The first few races blew by in heats of seven runners. Liz and Noah were positioned straight across from the finish line, where the runners were at maximum speed. These were superathletes of the highest caliber, people who had dedicated every ounce of their existence to training for the Field Games. The rules allowed for a maximum of ten competitions, and the year a competitor began was the starting gun. It didn't matter if they took four or five years off for injuries or whatever; ten years after their first games, competitors were no longer eligible. It was rare to see an athlete over thirty, because most athletes started competing in their late teens.

When Wade entered the starting blocks for his heat of the 100, he waved once to the crowd. He was wearing a black skullcap that covered his entire head, with matching running shorts and a skintight top. The crowd went wild with enthusiasm, a reaction that surprised Liz. She'd been on the outside not that long ago, and she'd always felt like everyone inside the State thought outsiders were nobodies. There were so few people left outside, but the general idea was that being out there meant you weren't part of the club. She was starting to realize that living in the States was like being chosen— not them choosing you, but you choosing them. When Wade and Clara Quinn stepped into the Western State for the first time, they chose these people. Nothing else mattered. The fact that they'd come from such humble beginnings and found themselves competing in the finals made them superstars. It didn't hurt that Wade and Clara were both good-looking Amazons. Wade had started the games with a head of long, blond hair held back with a wide black bandanna. Liz thought it made him look like a girl, but she was definitely in the minority. Girls in the State ate it up, gossiping endlessly about the hot young star who had magically appeared from the outside.

Wade went through the motions of warming up, peeling off the skullcap and setting it behind his starting block. He'd shaved his hair into an athletic cut, which produced a gasp from girls around the stadium until the cameras zoomed in and images of Wade appeared on jumbo screens. He flashed a Hollywood smile, and everyone could see that he was even better looking without the long locks that had totally entranced them. Tablets lit up with the Wade hair debate, a ridiculous spectacle that threatened to overshadow the Field Games themselves.

Liz had to admit, the Quinns were a PR machine. They knew how to lather up a crowd. She shook her head with some dismay at the idea of the Quinns looming large over her existence in the State. She could imagine their faces plastered all over the passageways and the Tablets and inside the high-speed trains. They'd probably leave sports behind, become actors and musicians, and lodge into Liz's life like a cancer she'd never be able to hide from.

"Gross," she said under her breath as the runners settled into their starting blocks.

"You okay?" Noah asked. Liz nodded and smiled. What did it matter? Soon enough Faith would show up, and the two of them could make fun of the twins all they wanted for the rest of their lives.

The starting gun went off, and everyone in the stands bolted to their feet for a better view. The world record for the 100-yard dash was under seven seconds, so everyone knew it would be over almost before it began. All of Wade's competitors were like machines, uncanny in their speed and strength, as if some sort of magic had turned them into more than just humans. But this would be a race that no one would forget for another reason. It would be played and replayed, slowed down and put in reverse, forever after. Whole Tablet sites would be dedicated to what would quickly come to be known as "the Race."

Wade Quinn, the mysterious kid from the outside who had shown up so unexpectedly with his confident smile and good looks, pulled out in front when the gun went off. By the time the rest of the field had gone two steps out of the blocks, Wade was halfway to the finish line. It happened in a flash, like he hadn't run there at all but had somehow been transported there. But later viewings in slow motion would prove that his legs had indeed carried him to the halfway point in under two seconds. Had he kept up that pace, Wade Quinn would have smashed the 100-meter record, cutting it nearly in half. But later evidence of his facial expressions in slow motion would show that he had seemed to force himself to slow down. He'd slowed so much that all the other runners not only caught up, they passed him, which knocked Wade out of the competition for good without a medal. Still, everyone would say from that day on that no one had ever run a 50-meter dash in double the time Wade Quinn had done it. And there was endless speculation that one day he would return and crush the world record for good.

Wade controlled himself after that, letting himself

finish midfield in the rest of his events. The thought of losing when he could have so easily won pounded into his soul in a way that he'd never experienced before. Letting the win slip through his fingers when he could have annihilated every single one of his competitors with ease was almost too much to bear. And yet he knew his slipup in the 100-meter—the way he'd used his powers to force himself down the track without so much as barely thinking about it—had been a scary eye-opener. Had he imagined himself at the finish line instead of the halfway mark, he would have blown the existing record to smithereens in such grand fashion it would have almost certainly caused a wide and endless investigation. It was not the kind of situation that his father or Gretchen would have appreciated.

As he walked off the track, defeated soundly in every event he had competed in, Wade pondered the fact that he'd almost let his sister get to him once again. She'd tried to poison him with thoughts of seizing the Field Games by the throat and choking the life out of every sickeningly normal competitor. Why should they stand by and do nothing? This was their time to shine. They'd earned it, living outside with Drifters and scum and garbage. They deserved to win! Wade had let these kinds of thoughts sink in. He'd held them deep inside and turned them over and over in his mind. He could see himself crossing every finish line first and jumping higher than anyone had ever seen. He could feel the heat coming off the crowd, the power of their adulation. These thoughts made him warm and happy inside. These were things he badly wanted. It was a miracle that he'd been able to stop himself when he did; and really, he didn't completely understand how it had happened. Not until he saw Clara after, and she smirked at him on her way to the throwing area.

"That was taking it a little far, don't you think?" she asked him. He understood immediately that it had been she, not himself, who had dropped him to last in the race. Clara had used her own power against him, slowing him down when he'd gone so disastrously out of control.

"Look, brother," Clara said, wrapping her hand around the center of a javelin and pointing the tip at his chest. "You're stronger than I am, always will be. But you're reckless. You might have just shown the world something it's not supposed to see. Not yet."

"You were the one who said we should crush these losers. What happened to that idea? Did you lose your nerve?" Wade asked. He hated the idea that she had intervened in the race. It felt like a violation of the rules, an unsaid thing they should never do to each other.

"Your problem is that you have no control," Clara

said, touching the end of the javelin to his chest. A crowd of a hundred and fifty thousand was watching, wondering what the two of them were talking so intensely about and why Clara was pointing a javelin at her brother. "You don't know anything about subtlety. You're a loose cannon. And in the end, that's exactly what might get us killed."

Clara walked away, but she smiled first for the cameras. She made it look like they had a harmless sibling rivalry going. Wade was totally confused, which tended to be the way his sister always made him feel.

An hour later he would find himself more confused still. The memory of Wade's brief and unexplainable move to the front of the pack was about to be pounded into the dirt by Clara Quinn.

Clara didn't think she was smarter than just her brother. That wasn't saying much. She felt smarter than pretty much everyone on the planet. Her bravado, unlike Wade's, had as much to do with outwitting people as it did with beating them physically. There was only one person who would later claim to understand all the reasons behind her decision making on the final day of the Field Games, and that was Gretchen. She alone knew the mind of Clara Quinn in ways that no one else did.

Unlike her brother, Clara had no true illusions of

grandeur when it came to something as meaningless as throwing a javelin or a hammer. Nothing about athletics had the allure of true power. In the events that followed, Clara Quinn threw an average javelin, raced an average heat in her finals, and threw a below-average hammer into the middle of the field. They were not stunningly bad results for a newcomer from the outside; in fact, they were still quite remarkable. She'd gotten what she had come for—respect—and that was enough for the time being.

There was one woman, a particularly overinflated twenty-five-year-old, in whom Clara had taken a keen interest from the start of the games. She was the one woman in the field of competitors who was abnormally large. She was, as far as any normal human being would claim, something of a giant.

"You're *huge*," Clara had said the moment she met Fleet Sanders. "No, seriously. You're like a building."

Fleet was six feet six, and two hundred and twenty pounds of pure muscle. Rumors of synthetic steroids and blood doping swirled around Fleet like hornets at a picnic, but no one had ever been able to make anything stick. She held several world records, most notably in the hammer, which she threw like a Greek goddess. She was also alternately described, depending on the setting, as manly, homely, or "ogre-like."

"That supposed to be a compliment?" Fleet asked Clara.

"In this place, yeah," Clara conceded. "What are you, two forty?"

Fleet couldn't tell for sure if Clara was being nice or condescending, but it didn't really matter. Clara was extremely beautiful, and that alone made Fleet hate her. Fleet was prone to random outbursts of rage, and there was something particularly irritating about a pretty girl competing against her in something as masculine as the hammer throw. She shoved Clara with both hands with the speed of a featherweight boxer, knocking Clara clean off her feet and onto her back.

"You're really fast for such a chunky girl," Clara said, laughing and shaking her head. She knew she was being cruel, but she couldn't help herself. As much as Fleet hated pretty girls, Clara hated bullies even more. Of course, Clara herself was one of the biggest bullies ever—it was a curious blind spot no one in her life understood.

Fleet raised her huge leg in order to stomp on Clara's chest; but when she went for the gusto, there was none to be had. Instead, against her will, she fell backward as if she'd slipped on a sheet of ice, crashing down on her back. Clara was up in a flash, standing over her, smiling sarcastically.

"Enjoy yourself today, Bertha. It's going to be a day to remember."

"I'm gonna kill you," Fleet said, standing up with alarming speed and staring Clara in the face.

"I'd love to see you try, but it looks like they're calling your name. Why don't you put all that rage to work on the hammer instead of wasting it on little old me?"

Fleet was breathing out of her nose like a rodeo bull. She hadn't been so angry in a long time; and sensing an opportunity to put her anger to good use, she marched straight to the hammer-throwing ring.

"I'll deal with you later," Fleet said, pointing a massive finger in Clara's direction.

"Can I count on that?" Clara asked.

Fleet Sanders looked across the field at the adoring fans. They didn't care that she was a freak of nature, a girl of highly unusual size. They also didn't know all the lengths to which her coaches had gone to train her into a machine. They didn't know about the thousands of hours she'd spent alone in a gym, working every conceivable angle that might give her an edge. They would never know that she hadn't taken any strength-enhancing drugs, not ever. If they could see what middle school had been like, they'd understand why later, when she was done throwing, she planned to do her almighty best to murder Clara Quinn with her bare hands.

"Enjoy that throw," Clara yelled from the sideline nearby. "Hope it's not your last."

Fleet picked up the handle of the hammer, a thick metal rod that vanished inside her gorilla-sized fist. She took one more look at Clara Quinn, thought about throwing the hammer in her general direction, and began her initial turn. With the hammer throw, the athlete stands on a square of concrete that has a rounded lip on the inside edge. The idea is to spin around in circles, holding the chain and the weight at the end like a tetherball on a rope. Fleet Sanders was known for a perfect rotation, one that made the distance of her hammer throws on a par with most men's. When she came around for her last spin, the ball at the end of the chain was moving with tremendous speed and force. Letting it go with a scream, Fleet stumbled at the edge of falling out of bounds but held her ground. She knew by the way it had felt leaving her hands that it was going to be a massive throw, maybe even a new world record. She was thinking about how happy this would make her, how she would rub Clara's face in it while she was simultaneously choking her to death, when she saw the hammer veer off course.

"No, that's not possible," Fleet said, words that were barely audible to anyone else around her. The hammer was drifting dangerously out of bounds as if it had been picked up on a sharp wind. Later, people would testify to just that, though it had been a perfectly calm day.

"Oh no, there was a big wind," one attending fan would say. "You could feel it, up in the stands. A gust like you wouldn't believe. Damn near blew me out of my seat. It was there and then gone. Poof! Just like that."

It was true about the wind; Clara was smart enough to throw in at least the hint of a reason why a hammer might change course so dramatically. Physics aside, the hand of God is always a good direction to place blame. Who could say for sure? The hammer spun on a chain in the air, maybe a big gust could send it flying like a Frisbee fifty yards off course. Either way, it had been the longest throw by any man or woman in the history of the Field Games. Not that it would matter, since, of course, it was way out of bounds.

The people who sat close enough to the victim said that it sounded like a tree being broken in two when it hit. But then, the sound of an iron ball slamming into a skull was something that couldn't adequately be described. And what it had done to the head was something out of a horror movie. There was only the one victim; no one else was hurt. But the one person was demolished. It was impossible to fix what had gone terribly wrong.

The president of the Western State, who sat center

stage at the events, looked on in horrified amazement just like everyone else. He was directly across the field from the carnage and had a pretty good view of what would later be described as the worst disaster in the history of the Field Games. The president would never have guessed the truth of the matter, that the hammer had been meant for him. It had long been planned that he would be the first of many State officials to fall. And it would have been completely untraceable. No one could have connected the flying hammer to the person who was really controlling it. If not for Clara's growing hatred for Faith Daniels, she would have followed the plan. It was true she disliked being controlled by her stepmother, but it was Faith who had pushed her over the edge. She would have done what she was told; she would have killed the president with the power of a hammer. He was lucky to get off the field alive.

Clara didn't bother looking in the direction of the catastrophe. She just walked away in the opposite direction. She knew the news would never reach outside the State, nothing negative ever did. But she had a special plan for sharing the information out there. A plan she rolled over in her head as she came up short in front of her brother.

"Welcome to the club," Wade said. "Any reason why you decided to go rogue? That's usually my job."

"Figured I'd take the lead there for once in my life," Clara said. "Killing the president was Gretchen's insane idea. It would have put the whole world on high alert. It would have been a mistake."

Wade looked off in the direction of the incident, then across the field, where the president was being evacuated.

"She's going to be pissed. You ready for that?"

Clara's lips curled into a half smile as she started walking away. She was still on board with the plan, but she was also a born leader. She was tired of following Gretchen's orders.

"I've been ready for a while."

PART THREE

SECOND PULSE

Chapter 17

How Deep Does This Rabbit Hole Go?

Faith felt off, like everything she'd learned from Dylan had found a way to escape into the open air and fly away. She'd been feeling that way all day, a tragic sadness welling up in her chest that made her want to cry. She didn't know why this was so; but as she walked in the darkness toward the old mall, she tried to think of all the reasons for her depression.

Life at Old Park Hill was finished. She'd left schools before, lots of times. But this was different, because she knew in her heart of hearts that whatever school had been, it was over now. There would be no more classrooms, no hallways, no teachers in the flesh. All

the desperate feelings of wanting to belong and traveling through angst-filled passageways were behind her
now. So that was one reason for feeling blue: the bloody
death of what little childhood she'd had was officially
over.

She would never go back inside the abandoned, ivy-
covered grade school again, either. She didn't know why
there was such certainty in this, only that it was so. It
was pathetic, she knew, a weakness she couldn't overcome and didn't think she ever would, but she loved the
old picture books. They were one of the only things in
the world that made her feel happy. When she was with
them, all the bad feelings went away. She had been able
to escape for a few precious minutes at a time, but she
would escape no more.

As she approached the ladder leading up to the
roof of the Nordstrom building, Faith knew there was
something more that made her feel so sad. But what she
really missed was a person she could tell her secrets to.
The one person she could tell about her crazy Dylan
dream, in which they were skinny-dipping, and her
legs were wrapped around his lower back. She missed
the person she could tell anything to and who wouldn't
judge her and she wouldn't be nervous or afraid of. That
person was Liz. Faith would catch herself holding her
hand out to the side, searching for a hand to hold and

finding only empty space. To her surprise, Faith eventually realized that it was she, not Liz, who needed that hand to hold on to. The fact that it was gone pierced her heart every time she reached out for it. Deep inside, in the part of her heart she tried to ignore, Faith knew she would only survive if she could continue telling herself that someday, even if it was way off in the future, they would find each other again.

It was a warm night, so she set her backpack on the cracked pavement and sat down on a curb. Faith was on the back side of the building, staring into the empty space where trucks used to deliver crates of suits and ties, dresses and fancy shoes. Out of the darkness came a shadowy figure, moving slowly toward her. It was unexpected; but all the same, she understood what his arrival signaled.

"Your timing is terrible," Faith said, not ready to get up and start moving.

"My apologies to the queen," Clooger joked, bowing his head of dreadlocks. He could be sarcastic when he wanted to be, which wasn't often. Faith had forgotten how huge he was and how pale his skin, which shone down on her like a small moon against a black sky.

"I was supposed to meet someone else here," Faith said. She had a hunch Clooger's appearance was all part of a plan.

"My instructions are to retrieve you. That's what I know."

Typical Clooger, Faith thought.

This was a moment she knew would arrive, but she still couldn't be sure her connection with Dylan and the arrival of the Drifter in front of her were connected, so she kept probing.

"Did my parents send you? They said they'd contact me when the school closed down."

Clooger looked in the direction of the school, which landed his gaze on the back of the Nordstrom building about four feet away. "School's closed down. You're being contacted."

"Do you have to be so cryptic? Can't you just tell me what's going on? Please, Clooger—throw a stray girl a bone."

Faith had known Clooger awhile, and she knew when she'd gotten to him. His massive shoulders would lower slightly, and he wouldn't look her in the eyes. He did this with no one but Faith, a rare letting down of his guard.

"Come on, big guy," Faith said, tapping the curb next to her. "Have a seat. Let's talk it out."

Clooger smiled, which was even rarer than seeing his shoulders droop, but he had no intention of sitting down on the job.

"All that stuff you've been doing up there," Clooger said, raising his chin to the roof of the building. "I'm here to get you because of that, not because the school closed down."

"You know about that?" Faith was shocked, but she also realized there might not be a conflict of interest after all. Maybe Dylan and the Drifters were connected; but if they were, he'd never said anything about it.

Clooger wouldn't answer, but he was staring her straight in the eyes again, shoulders back like the soldier he was. She'd gotten all she was going to get out of him.

"You left the Tablet behind?" Clooger asked as Faith got up and threw on her backpack. "It's important. Can't have that thing showing up where we're going."

"I put it where Dylan told me to."

"Who's Dylan?" Clooger asked, but Faith was having none of that.

"Nice try, Sasquatch."

"Ouch."

Faith looked up at Clooger as they began to walk. As tall as she was, Clooger still towered over her by close to a foot. The trench coat draped over him in a way that squared off his whole body like a refrigerator.

"My parents okay?" Faith asked as they walked along the sidewalk. She had no idea where they were going, but she assumed it would be a long way on a dark night. Clooger set his face like it were made of stone and kept on, unwilling to engage in any further conversation, at least for the moment. This left Faith to think of her parents more than she usually did. It wasn't that she didn't care for them; she wasn't as coldhearted as that. But Faith had always been so independent, so hell-bent on taking on the world by herself. It had been years since she'd felt anything approaching the need for someone to take care of her. When they'd come to her and told her their plan, she'd taken it in stride, knowing that as always, they'd be out there if she needed them.

"I actually sort of miss them a little bit," Faith said, her voice betraying a happiness she hadn't intended to show. "Even if they are wackos. It'll be good to see them again."

Clooger took offense in a way Faith hadn't expected. "You shouldn't talk about them that way."

He turned around the side of a building, heading down a narrow alleyway that cut into the mall.

"You can't be serious," Faith said. "No way the encampment is in the mall."

"Unexpected. That's the way we like it."

Faith had assumed all along that her parents and all the other Drifters were hiding somewhere in the woods outside of town; but the more she thought about it, the more it made sense that they'd be using a fortified structure such as an empty mall as a place to hole up and not be seen. The fact that it was so close to where she'd been living all this time made her feel like her parents really had been watching over her, even if she'd assumed they weren't.

Clooger halted at a door and took a set of keys out of one of his many pockets.

"There will be some surprises in here. Better take a deep breath and prepare for a long night."

Faith did as she was told, sucking in a giant breath of fresh air and closing her eyes for a moment. She hadn't seen her parents in almost four months. It would be good to see them. She was determined not to get into a fight about their views versus her own. She would let them hug her; it would be fine.

"Take me to your leader," she half joked when her eyes were open again, and Clooger unlocked the door. He invited Faith to go first, and she stepped into darkness.

Clooger had a flashlight that performed like the batteries were about to die, so Faith's initial introduction to the inside of the mall was dim and half seen. They passed through what must have been the immense space of a department store, where clothing racks sat empty or tipped over on their sides. It was like walking through a forest of metal limbs reaching out to touch her, piles of abandoned clothes tripping her up as they went.

"Watch your step through here," Clooger said when she balanced herself on his arm. "Best if we leave no trace."

He shined his light on a cash register, which struck Faith as an ancient and useless item. She had read about them but had never seen one up close and tried to imagine inserting paper money into a drawer in exchange for a pair of underwear. Weird was the word that came to mind, but it also made her think specifically of her mother. Faith had fought with her endlessly in their last days together.

"We didn't always have Coin, you know. That's part of how they control us," she had been fond of saying.

"You just don't get it," Faith would respond. "Who wants to carry money around? It makes no sense. It's dumb."

"The Tablets are dangerous. I'm only trying to protect you."

But Faith knew better than that. Her mother and her father hadn't been trying to protect her. They had been holding her back. They wouldn't even touch their Tablets, and they'd often hide Faith's in the house to keep her away from it. It made her so angry that she would scream at them, telling them they were out of touch and didn't know anything.

"I'm fine by myself. I don't need you to tell me what to do," she would say. Then she'd find her Tablet and escape into her room, locking the door behind her until morning, when she could leave for school and be rid of them.

There had come a point when their ideas about life diverged so dramatically, it was like the very old poem Faith had read about two paths heading off in different directions, never joining up again. She touched the hidden tattoo on the back of her neck and wondered how she'd ever gotten so far down a path her parents wouldn't take. And a glimmer of hope, that somehow, against the odds, the paths were about to come together again.

Faith had let her thoughts drift so far that it came as something of a shock when Dylan appeared in front of her, standing at the top of an escalator going down. He looked happy to see her, and she surprised herself when she ran up and hugged him. He put one arm around her—a half hug she took as a sign of confusion on his part—and she leaned back, smiling.

"Finally decided to invite me to your place, huh?" She glanced around. "It's big. Could use some decorating."

Dylan smiled back, then looked up at Clooger. "I'll take it from here. Next assignment?"

Clooger nodded, and, without speaking a word, he turned and walked away.

"Bye, Clooger," Faith called out. "Thanks for picking me up."

Clooger waved without looking back, and a few seconds later he was enveloped in a quiet darkness. "He stops in and sees me once in a while," Faith said as she held the slick rail and slowly descended one step at a time. "Just to make sure I haven't burned down the house or fallen down the stairs."

"He's a good man," Dylan said. He used the light of his Tablet to guide the way, which gave off a much brighter beam than Clooger's crummy flashlight had.

"How come you get to have your Tablet and I had to leave mine behind?"

"This one's been altered; yours hasn't. Can't bring tracking devices in here."

Faith knew that most Tablets were equipped with powerful GPS technology that told the State exactly where you were. It made sense not to bring something like that into a secret hideout, but she longed for her Tablet just the same. It really was like having a limb cut off without its constant stream of messages, shows, music, and so much more.

"I didn't realize how hard it would be going without it."

"That's how they control us. You know that, right?"

Faith thought Dylan sounded an awful lot like her parents, and for a moment she recoiled at the idea that Dylan was more like them than he was like her. Anger welled up inside her chest at the idea that Dylan had probably been spending time with her mom and dad, being indoctrinated into their crazy worldview. As they came to the bottom of the escalator, she wished they could be on top of the building, not underneath it, moving things with their minds, together in their own little world.

Dylan turned to her when they'd cleared the last step and took one of her hands in his. It sent an electric jolt into Faith's heart, and she realized her feelings for this boy were even stronger than she'd supposed.

"Listen, Faith, this isn't going to be easy," Dylan said. "I just want you to know I'm here for you. We're going to get through this together."

Faith cocked her head sideways, something she did when she found herself experiencing a very specific kind of emotion. She called it an upside-down mixed-up feeling, and that's what it was. Confused, afraid, apprehensive, directionless—it was all those things rolled into one.

"I don't know what my parents told you, but if this is some sort of twisted intervention, it's not for me. Let's go back to the roof. That was more fun."

"You should make peace with your mom and your dad," Dylan said, which had the reverse effect of making her pull her hand away in frustration.

"You're the second person who's said that tonight. Whatever they're telling you, it's not me—it's them. We don't see eye to eye, and we're not going to. It's not a big deal."

"Okay," Dylan said. He didn't pursue anything more about her parents. "Everything is about to change, and none of what's coming is easy. Are you sure you want to know everything?"

"Put yourself in my shoes," Faith said without hesitation. "I recently discovered I have the power to move whatever I want just by thinking about it. Hell yes, I want to know everything! What kind of question is that?"

Faith was having a familiar feeling of rebellion in the pit of her stomach. She didn't realize how hard this was for Dylan, how much harder it was going to get before the night was over, or how her reaction was pushing him away.

"Come on, there's someone you need to meet," Dylan said. He put his firm hand on the small of Faith's back and guided her forward. Faith calmed down as they walked, but with each step she was struggling with the idea of seeing her parents. It would not go well, she knew this now, and it was putting her in a defensive mood she'd have trouble letting go of.

"Did you know your training started the day after your parents left?" Dylan asked. It was a subject he'd wanted to bring up but hadn't had the courage to. With time running out, he wanted her to hear it from him, not from Meredith.

"I don't understand," Faith said. "You mean the stuff we've been doing on top of the Nordstrom building? That training?"

Dylan nodded. He was hoping that a couple of small revelations would make the blows to come slightly less overwhelming. "It started the night after your parents left. In fact, if you want to know the truth, it's *why* they left."

"Why do I not like where this is going?" Faith asked. She stopped in her tracks, fearing the worst. Something had been going on for a long time, and her parents were involved. It was the last thing she wanted to hear.

"It took a long time to find you, Faith. *Years*. And we're out of time. I knew what you could do because I can feel it when there's a pulse hiding out there. I felt you long before we ever met."

"This is starting to sound creepy."

Dylan looked up, breathed a sigh. Then his eyes were back on Faith like he wished he didn't have to explain. "The first time you moved something by thinking about it was in your sleep. That's the way it starts. I was patiently waiting to feel it happen; and when it did, I found you. That was four months ago."

"Four months? Wait, so you've been . . . what? Watching me or something? And my parents are in on it?"

"Faith, please—I'm trying my best here. The only way to draw this power out of your subconscious is to help you. That's something I can do by watching, thinking certain thoughts, focusing very specifically on you. So yeah, I've been watching you sleep. For about four months."

"Okaaay," Faith said. It was voyeuristic, and Faith wasn't exactly sure how she felt about it. "What do my parents have to do with this?"

"Catch this," Dylan said, and then he threw his Tablet out into the darkness like a Frisbee. Faith reacted intuitively, a flash appearing in her brain as the Tablet came back and landed in her hand.

"If I hadn't spent those months showing you what to do while you slept, you wouldn't be able to do that. And it wasn't going to work if your parents were in the picture. Don't ask me why, because I don't know the answer. It just goes faster if you're isolated. I mean *really* isolated, not just alone. Like I said, we were very short on time. They understood what was at stake."

"Why didn't you tell me any of this sooner?" Faith asked. She felt manipulated, used.

Dylan couldn't tell her the truth. She was possibly the most important person on the planet, but he didn't know how she might react to news like that. He decided to stop while he was ahead.

"Just don't blame anything on your parents. You're going to wish you hadn't done that."

"Stop taking their side. You don't even know them."

That wasn't exactly true, and Faith knew it. Dylan had been with her parents for the past four months, listening to them go on and on about how terrible Tablets were and how the States were evil and who knew what else. It made her furious, but she decided to hold it in. It would be more satisfying to use it on her parents when she saw them. "Lead on, Prince Charming," Faith said sarcastically, handing Dylan's Tablet back to him.

They started walking again, this time without talking to each other. Dylan was afraid he'd make another mistake, and Faith was laser focused on all the things she was going to say to her parents when she got the chance. They came to a door, which opened with a swipe card Dylan produced, and there was yet another set of stairs.

"The person you're going to meet . . . she'll tell you everything," Dylan said as they walked down a steep staircase together. "I'm warning you up front, she can be a little on the cold side. It's just her way; don't take it personally. The good news is, she's on our side."

"I didn't realize there were sides," Faith said. She wanted to ask about this mysterious new person, but she decided to stay quiet. She was thinking about how long Dylan had been watching her sleep at night and how brooding and distant he'd been at school. And what had her parents told him? She didn't even want to think about it. At the bottom of the stairs, a final door stood open.

"She knew we were coming; otherwise this one's usually locked. She's got the only key."

"How deep does this rabbit hole go?" Faith asked, wondering all over again if all the circumstances of the past month were nothing more than an elaborate, Wire Code–induced dream.

She could see that there was light inside. The ceiling was lower than she liked, but as they rounded a corner to the right, things opened up. The ceiling was higher, and the room was forty or fifty feet deep. They were in a basement with concrete walls and old-fashioned lightbulbs hanging from exposed beams. At the far end of the room, sitting in a red chair with a high back, was a woman. Three folding metal chairs sat around her in a semicircle. They were all empty.

"Time for me to go," Dylan said. "I'll come back for you."

"Wait, you're leaving me here? With *her*?"

Faith wanted to grab him by his leather jacket and make him stay, but it was not in her nature to be weak. She would see this through; and if push came to shove, she would put whoever sat in the red chair through the wall. Faith looked across the long, empty expanse of the dimly lit room, trying to size up the situation. When she turned back, Dylan was gone.

"Come, sit down," a voice called to her. It was a woman; that much was obvious. Faith was determined to find the answers to her questions; and if talking to this person was the way to get it done, she would sit in one of the chairs and listen.

And so she did.

Chapter 18

I Brought This for You

A green apple sat on one of the metal folding chairs and, on another, an unmarked envelope with a splattered wax seal. This left only one unoccupied chair, which Faith stared at for a long time before dragging it noisily toward her across the concrete floor and sitting down.

"Your chair looks more comfortable than mine."

Faith spoke first because the woman, for whatever reason, seemed happy to let an awkward silence fill the basement. Whoever she was, she wasn't like anyone Faith had met before. Her face was at once delicate and threatening: skin so paper-thin that Faith could see the veins in her forehead, blue eyes that never wavered

from their chosen target, dark hair held back by a slen-
der, black band. Her lips were pale but full; and when
she spoke, very little else moved. Not her gaze, not her
hands, not her flawlessly straight nose. Only her wil-
lowy eyebrows betrayed her feeling, and hearing Faith
comment about the chair, they rose with what appeared
to be either surprise or concern.

"Would you like to trade places?" The woman
asked.

"Who are you, and why do you live in a basement?"
Faith asked. She was not going to let herself be tricked
or bullied.

"So we'll stay where we are then, good. I'm Meredith; didn't Dylan tell you *anything*?"

Meredith leaned back slightly in her chair, crossing
her long legs.

"He told me some, but not enough. He said you
would tell me more."

Meredith kept staring at Faith. She seemed to be
trying to decide something, but it was difficult to say.

"I live underground because it's safe. Also I'm a
troll."

Faith was taken aback. It sounded like Meredith
was making a joke, but that couldn't be right.

"You should see me out of these shoes. *Hooves*.
Ghastly."

Faith didn't want to smile, but she did. "You're not what I expected."

Meredith leaned forward slightly. She had a way with slow, small movements that made Faith wonder if she was made of plaster.

"Dylan tells me you're a quick study. I'd like to see that for myself, if it's all right with you."

Faith didn't like the idea of being tested, but deep down inside she was dying to show Meredith how powerful she was. She was thinking about what was in the room that she could move—the chairs, the apple, the envelope, Meredith—when Meredith moved with a kind of speed Faith had rarely seen before. She was sitting in the red chair, and in the blink of an eye she was missing. Before Faith could turn around searching for her, the chair flew up in the air, hovered over her head for a moment like it was deciding if it should fall on top of her or not, and then it, too, was gone. Faith found herself staring at an empty concrete wall and two folding chairs, one with the envelope sitting on top and one with the green apple.

"Could you put the chair back where it was? Let's start there."

Faith spun around and saw Meredith at the farthest end of the room. She was standing next to the red chair. "Don't overthink it. Just put it back for me. I'd appreciate it."

Faith thought about the red chair flying across the room and ending up where it once was. The chair didn't move. It sat there like it was bolted to the floor.

"Wait, something's not right. This usually works."

Faith focused her mind as hard as she could, scrunching her eyes to mere slits as she willed the red chair to move. When nothing happened, Faith became frustrated and turned away from Meredith just in time to see the green apple fly away. Faith heard the *pop* sound when Meredith caught it at the far end of the room.

Meredith held out the green apple, letting it balance on the palm of her hand.

"Let's try this instead."

Faith didn't bother turning around. She knew the apple had arrived in Meredith's hand and hoped she could do something about it. She thought of the apple, her emotions tied up in knots, and then she felt the apple brush by her head and slam into the concrete wall, bursting into pieces.

"Were you trying to do that, or was it an accident?" Meredith asked calmly.

Faith felt like she was failing whatever test she was being given and used her mind to try the red chair again. This time she felt the sharp pain in her neck, which buckled her over. When she recovered, both

Meredith and the red chair had returned.

"It's okay. Red is a common problem at the beginning. Nothing to worry about. Not yet anyway."

"So you're like me," Faith said, intrigued but also afraid. The woman before her was clearly a lot more advanced in her ability than Faith would probably ever be.

Meredith ignored the question. "Science is a tricky business, especially when people are in a rush. Normally there are rules, regulations, a lot of red tape. A paper trail is an awfully nice thing to have when you can get one."

"I'm going to assume you're telling me this for a reason."

"There was a moment in history," Meredith went on, "when there was no time for regulations, documentation, *anything* that might slow progress. You know what I'm talking about, don't you?"

"Dylan and I discussed it. He said I had some of my facts wrong. I asked which ones, but he wouldn't say. Apparently it's above his pay grade."

"I'm encouraged to see you still have your sense of humor," Meredith said, though Faith was quite sure it wouldn't make it through the rest of their conversation.

"Hotspur Chance was given authority to do things no man should be allowed to do. So begin there—no rules—and imagine what might happen. Then you must always remember that Chance was not an ordinary man. He was one in a trillion, by all accounts the smartest person who had ever lived. The reason this is important is because it makes him—and his motives—unknowable. Even if you doubled the IQ of the smartest people on Earth, they would be halfwits compared to Hotspur Chance. And when you get into that kind of thinking, one has to imagine a certain godlike quality."

"You mean he had a god complex?" Faith knew what this was from one of her many classes, though she couldn't say for sure exactly how she'd come by the information.

"No," Meredith said. "I mean he is, in a sense, like a god to us whether we like it or not. He understood the universe, our world, our bodies, our minds—all in ways that go far beyond what we know of ourselves. It might have a way of compromising one's morals."

Faith felt like Meredith was dancing around all sorts of things she didn't really want to say or wanted Faith to figure out on her own. It was maddening how she wouldn't just say what she meant. Either way, Faith wasn't getting the information she wanted and decided to play along.

"Everyone worships the ground Hotspur Chance walked on, but he had ultimate authority to do whatever he wanted," Faith said. "He put the smartest people in the world into a facility and removed every rule that had ever been made about tampering with DNA, cells, reproduction, weaponry, human testing—all of it, anything he could think of, absolutely no rules. No documentation, no one to answer to, and unlimited access to resources. Whatever he wanted, he got. No questions asked."

Meredith was pleased with the response. She was getting somewhere.

"And out of that came the States," Faith concluded. She mulled over the rest of her answer before saying it. "Did Hotspur Chance make me like this?"

"How we got to you is a little more complicated than that, but yes. He and his associates saved the world—a worthy goal—but they unlocked some other things in the process."

"What did they unlock?"

"They found the pulse first and, realizing its devastating power, quarantined those who had it. There were twelve. You can probably guess who one of them was."

"Hotspur Chance."

Meredith nodded slowly. "They weren't just able to move things with their minds; they were also violent. There's no record of why this was so; but a week later, only one of them was alive."

"Hotspur Chance," Faith said. It was starting to feel like a mantra, this man's name on her lips.

"He was the first to find the second pulse, the one that could move things and also be unmoved. Dylan explained this, am I right?"

Faith nodded. "He has it, too. Nothing touches him. He was disappointed that I didn't get it."

Meredith's expression indicated that she, too, was disappointed.

"Shortly after that, we know only two more things that occurred: the plans for the States were developed in great detail over a stunningly short amount of time, and the first Intel was created."

"I've never heard that term. Intel?" Faith said. She did remember Dylan saying something about an intelligence movement. The two things sounded connected, but she didn't mention it.

"Remember, no rules, no regulations," Meredith said. "It was an anything-goes environment."

Meredith paused, her gaze locked on Faith. "Hotspur Chance found a way to bond his own DNA to existing people. They were his hosts. He needed more brain power, and he needed it fast. These people were called Intels."

"That's terrible," Faith said. "He was like a parasite. How many people did he infect?"

"Interesting choice of words," Meredith said. "I pre-fer to think of them as still who they were, only much smarter. And remember, without the Intels there would be no States. Sometimes a terrible thing is required in order to fix a great many problems."

Meredith looked at the envelope sitting on the chair, then back at Faith. She had known this would be a dif-ficult transaction, because the contents of the envelope had the power to change Faith's life forever.

"In a moment, two people are going to sit in these empty chairs. After that it's going to get tougher. Are you ready?"

Faith knew her parents were about to enter the room and lord over her their weird ideas. She tried to tell herself that it was fine. She hadn't seen them in four months, and deep down she did miss them. She only wished the circumstances could be different. Somehow, it felt like her parents had set everything in motion without telling her. Now they'd ambushed Faith in a basement with the help of crazy Meredith.

"Take the envelope. Keep it for a later time," Mer-edith said.

"Before you bring them in, I have a question," Faith said, leaning over and taking the envelope and holding it in her hand.

Meredith didn't signal her willingness to answer or

not, so Faith went ahead.

"How many people are there like us?"

Meredith lowered her chin slightly, smiling softly.

"I don't know how many they have."

"They? What do you mean, 'they'?"

Meredith ignored the question.

"It's complicated."

"Did you know it's impossible to get a straight answer out of you?"

"So I've been told."

Faith heard the door open at the far end of the room. It was a heavy door with a squeak that echoed annoyingly across the emptiness. She couldn't bring herself to turn around and watch her parents approach. Instead, she closed her eyes and reminded herself to make the most of this. She was determined not to pick a fight even if she felt manipulated or belittled. She would not give them a guilt trip for leaving her. She would take comfort in the knowledge that they loved her in their own way. She wouldn't make the same mistake she'd made with Liz, because who really knew when someone could be swept up into the Western State and never be seen outside again?

Faith opened her eyes and stood. She could feel her parents getting nearer; and putting on a brave face, she turned in their direction with her arms held out.

"Mom? Dad?" she said, but even in the dimmest of light, she knew it wasn't so. This was not her mother and father coming toward her; it was Dylan and Hawk. The two of them didn't speak as they each sat down, one on either side of Faith's chair. Hawk had been carrying a cloth bag at his side, which he set on the floor next to him.

"Where are my parents?" Faith asked. She sat down in her own chair and flashed a brief smile at Hawk. She was happy, but confused, to see him.

"Go ahead," Meredith said. "But shut the door first. And lock it."

Dylan didn't look at the door they'd entered as Faith heard it shut, the deadbolt turning coldly into place. It struck her then that the door was red, a detail that hadn't seemed to matter until this very moment.

"The night you were with Wade Quinn," Dylan said, never taking his eyes off Faith, "he gave you two Wire Codes because he didn't want you to remember what happened. A team of Drifters were in that building, keeping an eye on everything, making sure you were safe. Some of those Drifters had a first pulse, and one of them accidentally moved something."

"Okay," Faith said. "What's that got to do with my parents?"

"They were in that group of Drifters. They were

there the night you and Wade entered the building."

The first thing that crossed her mind was *Oh no, they saw him take advantage of me. That can't be good.*

"I'm not the only one with a second pulse," Dylan said. "Wade has it, too. He knew the Drifters were there."

Faith's mind flashed with an image of Drifters flying against walls, their brains being bashed into lockers. She shook her head, and the image was gone.

"Don't say it," Faith said. She touched the secret spot on her neck where the tattoo of the battered hawk lay hidden.

"Wade Quinn killed ten Drifters that night," Meredith said, unwilling or unable to let Dylan carry the heaviest part of the load. "Two of those Drifters were your parents."

Faith's hands began to shake as she stared at the concrete floor. The envelope fell out of her hand, and she looked up at Hawk, who would not look her in the eye. He was so small and young, like a little brother she wanted to protect. And yet all she could think of was how much she wanted to throw him into a wall.

"I know it's hard," Meredith said. "But try to control your rage. Don't let it get the better of you. You'll only regret it."

Faith clenched her fists and tried to clear her head.

Her parents were dead. Wade Quinn had killed them. It was him she needed to punish, not Hawk. Hawk was her friend. She looked at him again and saw that he had his hand buried in the bag he'd brought with him, an alarmed look on his face. He had hold of something she could not see.

"They understood the risks," Meredith said. "And they didn't die for nothing. The envelope is from them."

"I'm sorry," Dylan said. "It wasn't meant to happen this way."

Faith was so angry she didn't know what to say. She wanted to lash out at everyone in the room for dragging her family into things they didn't understand. She wanted to take back the way she'd felt about her parents. She was owed a chance to talk with them and make things right, to say the things she was supposed to say. But she'd never have that chance now.

"She's still calm enough," Meredith said. "Better finish."

"Stop confusing me!" Faith screamed. "I hate you!"

"You're about to hate me more," Meredith said; and for the first time, Faith heard a glimmer of compassion in her voice. "Hawk received a message from inside the State today. Your friend Liz is also gone. I'm not going to sugarcoat this, because you're going to find out and it's better if you do so in a secure location. She was hit with a hammer during the games. It was thrown by a woman with no known connections to our . . . *situation.*"

It couldn't be true. It was too much agony in the space of too little time. And yet Faith's mind was reeling with so much violent emotion, she couldn't get to a place where remorse waited. She watched as Hawk removed a large swath of red fabric from the bag he'd brought with him.

"Was Clara Quinn on the field when it happened?" Faith asked.

Meredith and Dylan didn't answer as they watched Hawk drape the red fabric over his shoulders like a warm blanket.

"Tell me!" Faith screamed. She stood, and the chair beneath her flew up in the air behind her, careening across the room and smashing into the wall. "Was she on the field?"

Dylan stood and moved between Faith and Hawk. "She was."

That was all Faith needed to hear. Suddenly she knew the truth. Liz had no strategic value in whatever game was being played. It was Faith whom Clara was trying to hurt, no one else.

"So Wade Quinn killed my parents. And Clara Quinn killed my best friend. Is that where we stand?"

"Dylan?" Meredith said. Her voice betrayed fear, which Faith wanted more than anything to seize on.

"Everyone in this room is on your side," Dylan said. "We all want the same thing you do."

"And what's that?" Faith asked. The chair Dylan had sat in lurched forward, then blasted up in the air, its legs twisting and turning toward Meredith. Meredith raised a hand, and the chair flew in the other direction, crashing into the wall.

"Better get this under control, Dylan," Meredith said. "Or you might be the only one that gets out of here alive."

Faith didn't want to move. She tried to hold her ground, willing herself to stay; but she was drifting closer to Dylan, and she couldn't get it to stop.

"Leave me alone! Don't touch me!" she screamed. But before she could stop it from happening, Dylan had his arms wrapped around her. All the rage inside her tried to get out as she fought to break free, but there was nothing in the world that could have made Dylan Gilmore let her go. He held on as she kicked and screamed and tried to hurt him any way she could. When she finally went limp in his arms, all the anger turned to regret and sadness, she whispered something in his ear that only he could hear.

PULSE ◀ ◀ ◀

"It's my fault. They're all dead because of me."

Dylan knew it wasn't true and so he held her tighter still, whispering over and over again, "Not true. Not true. Not true."

Minutes passed.

"Let her go," Meredith said. "It's over."

Meredith understood more than anyone else what the end of a pulsing rage looked like. She'd lived through plenty of them. Dylan slowly let Faith go. When Faith looked at Hawk, he was still covered in the red fabric. He removed it, stuffing it into the bag as he took something else out.

"I brought this for you," he said softly.

He handed over his most precious possession, *The Sneetches*, which he had taken from the old grade school on the night he'd been there with Faith and Liz.

Faith reached out her hand and thought of Liz, how she loved to sit and read in the abandoned library for hours on end. She held it to her chest and tried to imagine a world in which Liz and her parents didn't exist.

Meredith took a breath and decided the room was safe once more.

"We come now to another one of those unfortunate moments," she began. "Where there is no time."

Faith felt a kind of sad relief at the idea of putting

315 ◀ ◀ ◀

off the pain of having to process all her feelings. This war she'd stepped into unwillingly had given her at least the smallest mercy.

"There are those who want to destroy everything the States seek to create," Meredith said. "Everything good that came from Hotspur Chance *is* the States. Hold other things against him, but not that. Nothing is perfect; but without the States, humankind would be in far worse condition and only getting worse. They're a brilliant invention, and they need to be protected at all cost."

"It's our job to keep them safe," Hawk said.

"No offense," Faith said, "but what have you got to do with any of this?"

Dylan looked a little sheepish, like he'd kept a secret from Faith. "He's a third-generation Intel. Very rare."

"Why am I not surprised?" Faith asked. Her mind was reeling with questions about how this was possible, but she was pretty sure in time they'd tell her how Hawk had come to be the smartest boy on Earth.

"Faith," Meredith said, and then she reached out and took her hand. Faith was surprised to find that it was very soft, and suddenly she was crying, unable to stop the tears from coming. "If we can find your second pulse, we can turn the tide. It's in you—Dylan can feel it. The question is, How deep? You, Dylan, and

Hawk—you three might prevail against a great evil."

Faith understood. She only had a single pulse. If a hammer hit her in the side of the head, it wouldn't matter how many she'd thrown the other way. She'd be a goner. It was only the second pulse that mattered in a real confrontation, and somewhere hidden inside, she had one.

"Take the envelope; read it later," Meredith said, lifting it off the floor with her mind and letting it hover in front of Faith. "It's from your parents."

"Can I please sit outside, on the roof?" Faith asked. "I can't stand it down here. I need to think. Alone."

Meredith looked at Dylan for some reassurance. *Could she be trusted not to do anything stupid? Had she calmed down enough?*

"Promise me you won't go anywhere else," Dylan said. "Just to the roof, and don't fly. I'll come find you in an hour, and we'll get going."

"Going?" Faith asked.

Meredith was convinced it would be okay to give Faith an hour, but that was the limit. Clooger was already gathering the rest of the Drifters for their long trek south.

"We can't stay here any longer, and besides, there's no reason. We need time to train where no one can find us."

The deadbolt on the red door turned, and Faith started to leave. She was suffocating with information, and all she really wanted was time alone.

"You might as well take this, too," Hawk said, pulling Faith's Tablet out of the bag he had carried in. "The tracking's off now, so you can't be traced. And I've made a few other adjustments. Like you can get more shows now. Unfortunately, there won't be any more free pants."

"I was really going to miss this thing," Faith said. "Thanks."

A few seconds later Faith was out the doorway, up the old escalator, and into the fresh air of a cool night.

When they were alone in the basement room, Meredith turned to Hawk. She trusted him the most, for he was an Intel. He was ten times smarter than Dylan and Meredith put together. "If we can't unlock her second pulse, the war is over before it begins."

Hawk seemed to be calculating something in his head as his eyes darted back and forth. "I thought the book would do it. My timing must have been off by a nanosecond."

"Feelings are hard to pinpoint," Meredith said. "Better follow her; make sure she doesn't go looking for trouble. This one is more unpredictable than most."

"And powerful," Dylan added. "She's something else."

Meredith stared at the open red door for a long moment before saying what they all knew.

"Without her we haven't got a chance."

Chapter 19

Second Pulse

Faith set *The Sneetches* on the wooden table where she and Dylan had done so much of their work. Carrying the book around was a burden, unlike her Tablet, which fit in her back pocket and never failed to deliver entertainment when she needed it. She'd followed the instructions, using the fire escape to climb up to the roof, but she still felt too close to other people. She needed real seclusion, the kind she could only get if she went higher still.

The orange glow of the State was strong and clear as Faith flew straight up, higher and higher, on the rocket power of her own thoughts. She knew it wouldn't take much of a mistake to end up with a broken leg or worse whenever she decided to come down, but she didn't care. She needed somewhere to be alone—really alone— and the higher she flew the more isolated her world became. What she wouldn't give for a second pulse— with that, Faith could fly right over the State, find Clara and Wade Quinn, and throw punches all night. She allowed herself to imagine picking up a bus and drop- ping it on Wade Quinn's head. She thought glorious, useless thoughts of putting Clara through a brick wall.

"I'm sorry I wasn't there to protect you," Faith said, the words falling like petals into an empty sky. She was saying it to her mom, her dad, her best friend. She hung in the air, thinking about the price she'd had to pay, and for what? She hadn't asked to be like this. She hadn't asked Dylan to stand outside her window invading her private dreams. No one had bothered to explain any- thing to Faith until it was too late. They would have her in their little army whether she liked it or not.

Faith screamed louder than she'd ever screamed before. The sky devoured every bit of sound before it reached the ground. She could have pitied herself for at least another hour had she been given the chance, but screaming had turned her mind into a sheet of white noise. She started falling; and not having a lot of experience with the weight of her own body falling through open space, she panicked. Arms and legs were dangling in every direction, turning her sideways and upside down, tumbling through space. The top of the building she would soon hit was dark enough that she couldn't say for sure how close she was to impact. And for one last, dreadful moment, she thought about letting it happen. It would be less painful. One moment, a split second, and it would be over. No more regrets about how she'd failed, no more guilt about broken relationships she'd willingly chosen not to fix. No more anger about how unfair it all was.

Three thoughts kept her from dying that night.

Faith.

The meaning of her name haunted her like a ghost from another world, flying in the air all around her. There was something, not nothing, on the other side of death. An eternity in which everyone felt sorry about her tragic ending was not the kind of afterlife she looked forward to.

Hope.

As she plunged toward her death, she saw Dylan's face the way he sometimes looked at her, and she couldn't imagine leaving him behind. Something below the surface of her mind told her Dylan could heal all the terrible scars she carried. And she saw Hawk's face, too. He could never replace Liz, but he had the intangible quality of being comfortable. She could sit in a room for ten hours and simply be with Hawk. He was easy that way, and she needed that. It could sustain her through the minefield of feelings she navigated on a daily basis.

And in the end, there was the fire that threatened to overwhelm her.

Revenge.

For better or worse, the fuel that would keep her from death was vengeance. She would destroy the Quinns or die trying. It was the thing that cleared her mind and slowed her descent. Revenge got her to stop flailing around, center her mind, and come to an abrupt halt three inches short of plowing her face into the roof of a clothing store.

She went straight to the table and picked up *The Sneetches*, then sat on the ledge of the building, letting her legs dangle as she gazed at the orange light of the State. Turning her attention to the book, she read each page slowly, savoring every word like each one might be her last. With the turning of pages she tore them out one by one, tossing them into the open air and watching as they fluttered back and forth like broken wings plunging into the abyss. When all the pages were gone and only the spine remained, she felt the empty weight of what she'd done and kissed her childhood good-bye.

Faith, hope, and revenge.

These words would be her mantra. These would carry her into a war she hadn't chosen and didn't understand. Her sadness would be replaced with an all-consuming mission. She didn't have the strength to read the letter tucked safely into her back pocket. It would have to wait for its turn at firing shotgun rounds at her heart. She'd had enough for one night.

As Faith's emotions realigned, she felt a buzzing in her back pocket. Someone was trying to find her, and while she wasn't ready to be found, she didn't think it was a good idea to vanish. If Dylan or Meredith or Hawk was trying to locate her, it would be less trouble to simply answer. It might buy her a little more time alone.

She took out her Tablet, not bothering to snap it into a larger size, and read the message.

I've come back for you. Let's finish what we started. Old Park Hill.

The message wasn't signed, but it didn't need to be. Faith knew exactly who it was. Clara Quinn was back. How she'd gotten out of the State after going in she didn't know, but what did it matter? Clara was at the school, and the two of them had unfinished business.

Faith's mind was so full of rage and confusion that she didn't even think about the danger of what she was about to do.

She left her Tablet there on the ledge with the spine of the book and dived off the roof of the building.

"What do you mean she's not there?" Dylan couldn't believe his ears as he stood inside the mall among a group of Drifters packing up their belongings. Hawk was there, too, busily tapping out code on his Tablet. He switched tasks immediately, searching for other Tablets in the area.

"I've searched the perimeter and the roof. She's not here," Clooger said. He spied something along the ledge on the far side of the roof and moved toward it with lightning speed, something he rarely did. Clooger was like all the Drifters—he had a single pulse, not a second pulse—but he preferred traditional weapons of war. He'd take a grenade over throwing a car across a parking lot any day of the week. Explosions were his thing.

"Hawk, anything?" Dylan asked, hoping Faith had taken her Tablet with her. He'd hated letting Hawk do it, but he hadn't told her everything about its tracking. It was true that the State couldn't track Faith's Tablet any longer, but that didn't mean Hawk couldn't keep tabs on where it was.

"Her Tablet's on the roof," Hawk said, looking up. "Could she have left it there?"

The idea of going anywhere without a Tablet was so alien to Hawk that he couldn't wrap his brain around it.

"Found the Tablet," Clooger said. "But no Faith. She left it here."

Dylan had a bad feeling. He never should have let her out alone in the state she'd been in. More than anyone else—even more than Faith herself—Dylan understood the wild power of her emotions. With only one pulse to rely on, she could get herself killed in a million different ways.

"Check the messages," Hawk said. "She had activity about eleven minutes ago."

Clooger tapped the screen, but Faith had set the security to her thumbprint. There was no getting inside without Faith. "It's locked, set to thumbprint. You want me to bring it back or keep looking for her?"

"Keep looking, I'll be there in less than thirty seconds," Dylan said. He turned to Hawk. "How long?"

Hawk was typing furiously, working his way through a string of commands that would bypass Faith's security. "Three minutes, maybe less."

"Call me when you have something."

Dylan was gone in a flash, out the door and flying across the parking lot. He tried to imagine who would have sent her a message. Who was he not thinking of? Did she have some other friends on the outside?

When he arrived on the roof next to Clooger, his heart sank.

"Left this, too," Clooger said, holding out the spine of the book with all its pages missing. Both of them looked out over the empty sky and tried not to imagine the worst.

"She's probably just walking around," Clooger said. "Clearing her head. It was a lot to deal with all at once."

"Where would she go?" Dylan asked, though he knew Clooger would have no idea. Then he had an intuition that seemed to make some sense. "Stay here in case she comes back."

Dylan ran for the other side of the building, his final step hitting the ledge, and leaped up in the air on his way to the old grade school. She'd destroyed one book; maybe she'd find some comfort in being surrounded by more of them. A minute passed before Dylan found himself standing in front of the ivy-covered building. There were large boulders next to the playground where kids used to climb, and picking up one of them with his mind, he hurled it into the front door, blowing it clean off its hinges. Dylan was already through the open door and into the abandoned library before the boulder came to stop in the principal's office.

"Faith?" he called out. It was dark in the library, so he set his Tablet to act as a light and held it out. Faith wasn't there, and this so frustrated Dylan that he yelled her name again, sending every book flying off every shelf with the power of his emotions. "Faith! Where are you?"

The room was alive with the sound of pages ripping and spines crashing into one another. Dylan stood in the middle of the storm of books, arms out wide, taking out his frustrations on the useless artifacts of the past.

"Dylan, where are you?"

Hawk was back, a small voice coming from the Tablet in the din of violence. Every book dropped to the floor at once, a carpet of pages surrounding Dylan as he answered. "The old grade school. Anything?"

"She's back, Dylan. It's my fault. I didn't even think—"

"Hold on, who's back? What are you talking about?"

There was a short pause, then a breath of frustration on the other end. "Clara Quinn. She's back. And I think she might know about Faith."

Dylan's blood turned to ice. If Clara knew, Faith didn't have a chance.

"Where is she?"

"Old Park Hill, at least that's what the message said."

Dylan was moving fast, but even at his fastest, it

would take a few minutes to reach the school. "Don't go anywhere; hold on."

Dylan switched frequencies to Clooger. "Old Park Hill, bring everyone."

Clooger didn't hesitate, not even for a second. "I'll gather the crew. We'll get there as fast as we can."

"Hawk," Dylan yelled, switching frequencies again. "What's the inventory?"

All the Drifters who'd been packing to leave were suddenly moving for the door, which left Hawk sitting all alone in a corner. He messaged Meredith in the basement, telling her to stay as still as a statue, and began reeling off worthwhile items near Old Park Hill.

"Lots of desks and chairs. You can use those to distract her, but they won't do much damage."

"What do we have that's got some weight?" Dylan asked. He was watching the ground as he flew, searching for heavy objects he could bring with him. There was a limit to what he could carry while he was using so much of his mental energy to fly and talk to Hawk, but he thought he could grab at least one thing.

"Four large trees, but it'll take some work to uproot them," Hawk said. "Wait . . ." He paused, not sure he should mention an idea he had.

"Hawk, if there's something we can use, spill it," Dylan said. "This is no time to play it safe."

Hawk received an incoming message from Meredith as he continued scanning the area around the school for items that could be used as weapons:

Protect her at all cost.

That was all Hawk needed to hear.

"I've located six State vans, all within three miles of the school. Four are idle for the night; the other two are on autopilot."

Dylan was getting close, maybe thirty seconds from Old Park Hill, and Hawk's idea sounded promising but risky.

"All hell is going to break loose if the States find out," Dylan said. They would discover the truth about first and second pulses soon enough, but the longer that could be put off the better.

"I bet I can disable the connection," said Hawk. "They'll look like software rogues that crashed out. It'll raise some eyebrows, but I'm not seeing anything else as good as these vans. They're the perfect weight and size. You can really throw those mothers."

Dylan made up his mind as he landed among the trees at the edge of Old Park Hill. "Tell Clooger to carry them over on his way in. Have him leave them on the football field. One on the fifty-yard line, space the rest ten yards apart, right down the middle of the field. Got it?"

"Yeah, I got it."

Hawk didn't bother to message Clooger about the State vans. If he could disable their monitoring, he'd be able to control them from his Tablet. He could drive them onto the football field with less risk than Clooger and his gang of Drifters could carry them.

As Dylan approached the front doors of Old Park Hill, there was a surprising silence in the air. The whole world had gone quiet. And then, like the crack of a starting gun in the race of his life, he heard the sound of a tree falling.

At least Faith pulled the first punch, as it were. She had leaped to the roof of the school, which was long and flat, walking with purpose and rage. When she reached the edge of the open courtyard, she'd looked down and seen Clara Quinn sitting on a bench, facing the other way as if she didn't have a care in the world. There were three large trees in the courtyard, their canopies higher than the roof, along with some scattered benches and concrete pathways running like an X through the space. The walls of the school rose up around the courtyard, and Faith thought it created the appearance of a giant boxing ring.

Faith knew this would be her only chance to inflict some early damage and hopefully even the odds. She had an idea of how to accomplish this when she took a good look at the largest tree. Its base was four feet wide, plenty of weight to hold down a teenage girl long enough to scream in her face.

Faith thought about the tree and all the unseen roots beneath the ground. She put every ounce of her being into that tree, told it to move much faster than it would if it were simply falling. It would need to move faster than Clara could react to it. There was something like the trigger of a gun in Faith's mind, a method for moving things that Dylan had taught her. She could load up her mind with an idea of what she wanted to do, then hold it there until she pulled the trigger and made it happen.

Bang.

Clara looked up just in time to see the side of a tree hit her in the face. She tried to move out of the way, but natural objects, things that were still alive, had a surprisingly strong effect on her. Faith had chosen her weapon well without even knowing it. The tree wouldn't harm Clara—that was very nearly impossible—but it would present a slight problem. By the time the tree was all the way on the ground, Clara was good and pinned, her top half on one side and her lower on the other. It was gruesome, like everything in between had been crushed into the earth and only the head and feet remained. When she looked up, Faith was standing on the tree, staring down at her.

"Did you kill Liz?" Faith asked. She wanted to hear Clara say it before ripping one of the sharpest limbs from the tree and driving it through her head.

"I never miss what I'm aiming for," Clara said, smiling despite her compromised position. She was not happy about being talked down to, but she was patient. This would be more fun if she drew it out a little bit. "And I was definitely aiming for Liz. You should have seen the blood. Wow."

Faith was so angry it made her head feel dizzy. There was a plateglass window running along the far wall of the courtyard; and thinking it through, Faith cocked the gun once more.

Bang.

The window blew apart, not into small shards but into long, jagged sections of glass. They flew high up in the air, then down in Clara's direction. When they were within a few inches of Clara's face, they stopped. Ten shards of glass, four feet long and as sharp as razors, turned in sideways and pointed at Faith Daniels.

"You really do want to murder me, don't you?" Clara said, a cold calmness in her voice. "The problem with an idea like that is that it's stupid. *You,* Faith, are stupid. You have no idea what you're doing. I could end you right now—does that frighten you?"

Faith didn't know what it would feel like to have shards of glass slice through her body, her face, her legs; but she had a pretty good idea that she would feel the pain before she came to an end. A small piece of her felt like she deserved it; another part was horrified at the idea of dying at the hands of Clara Quinn. She pushed her mind to the outer limits of its strength, trying to force the glass away.

"You're stronger than I expected," Clara said. She'd wriggled free one of her arms, which she held up in the air, letting it sway back and forth. The glass swayed ominously to the rhythm of her movements. "Who showed you how to do these things?"

Faith began to realize something that hadn't occurred to her up until that moment. If Dylan, Meredith, Clooger, and Hawk were on one side, who was on the other side?

"Tell me!" Clara bellowed. She liked to navigate between slippery sweet and raging diva. It tended to disarm her enemies. "Who told you to use the tree?" she said quietly.

Faith had chosen a living thing as a weapon, and it had pinned the most powerful girl on Earth. If she had chosen something else—a giant rock or a pile of desks—Clara would have blown it apart like matchsticks. It had been a complete accident, this choosing of the tree. Or had it? Maybe she had some insight into Clara's mind neither of them yet understood. Maybe the tree had known it could be of use in a world of good and evil unleashed. However, she knew it was true: every second pulse had a weakness in battle. For Clara, it was living things used as weapons against her. It was the same for her twin, Wade. A bullet would do nothing against the Quinns, but a freshly fallen tree, still alive and pulsing water through its knotty veins, had the power to do some damage.

The glass shards began to shake and crack into smaller pieces in the air. Before Clara could grasp what was happening, they were turned to dust particles and blown away like a great wind had swept through and carried them off. Dylan landed on the tree next to Faith, picked her up, and carried her to the roof.

"Stay here; Clooger should arrive anytime."

"NO! I won't just stand by while you save me. I can do this."

Dylan put one hand on each of her shoulders. "No, you can't. Right now our only chance is to get rid of her before she kills you. Just stay here. I mean it."

Dylan took a step backward, then flew off the

PATRICK CARMAN

building and landed where Faith had stood on the tree, over Clara. She smiled sadly.

"So you're one, too," Clara said. She assumed he was a first pulse, a mere nuisance like Faith, and this complicated things. "No wonder I liked you from the start. You put off a certain energy. I should have known."

Dylan was surprised she hadn't moved the tree. It wasn't like her to stay down.

"I've got no reason to fight you," Dylan said. "We'll leave, and we won't come back."

"I think we both know it's too late for that. I wish it didn't have to be this way. I really did like you, Dylan Gilmore."

Clooger landed on the building overhead with nine other Drifters, and they all stood in a circle around Faith, awaiting instructions.

"Faith, just go!" Dylan shouted. "Let us handle this."

But she wouldn't stop making herself stay right where she was.

"I brought backup, too," Clara said. "Mine's better."

In a flash of sound and fury, the tree broke in two, sending shards of wood flying in every direction as Dylan leaped for the ground. Wade Quinn advanced along one of the pathways, lifting the concrete slabs in front of him. Each slab was three feet wide, five feet long, six inches thick. They rose like a snake, chasing

Dylan up in the air and onto the roof as he ducked and dodged for cover.

"It sure is hell finding a man under these circumstances," Clara said, brushing herself off as she walked over to her brother. Wade was looking up on the roof where Clooger was standing with his men.

"Let's kill some Drifters."

Clooger unpinned three grenades and tossed them into the courtyard. The explosions created a diversion he needed, in which Dylan freed himself from the concrete slabs and slammed into Wade's midsection with a brutal kick. Wade sailed through a sheet of plate glass and landed on the floor inside the school. Dylan needed to get Clara and Wade away from Faith, so he picked up Clara before she could wrap her mind around what was happening and threw her into the same corridor with her brother.

"Get down!" Clooger yelled, raising his hands over his head as desks started flying out of the hole where Wade and Clara had entered the school. The Drifters all used their powers to hold off the incoming assault while Faith stood in the middle, wondering what was going on down below. She took a big chance, shooting herself straight up in the air a hundred feet; and when she looked down, she saw headlights on the football field. Six white vans were parking themselves along the center of the field, and she had no idea why. From her vantage point she could see something Clooger and the rest of the Drifters could not: Wade and Clara had picked up the concrete slabs and swung them out like a boomerang. They were making a wide arc, heading straight for the roof of the school.

"Clooger!" she yelled, but there was so much noise and she was so far overhead that he couldn't hear her. She surveyed the ground in the courtyard and decided on a section of the tree she'd already felled. Picking it up with her mind made her fall from the sky in jerks and starts, like the effort was short-circuiting her system.

"Clooger!" she yelled once more, and this time he looked up briefly. "To your left!" Faith yelled. Just as she said it, the first three sections of concrete slammed into the tree she'd moved. The tree fell from the sky and slammed into the side of the school, but three more slabs of concrete were still coming in hot.

"Move!" Clooger commanded, and the group of Drifters dispersed in different directions. The slabs of concrete exploded onto the roof, breaking into brick-sized chunks. One of the pieces careened into a Drifter, and he fell from the sky, landing hard on the grass outside the school. Faith couldn't say whether or not the Drifter was alive or dead, but she watched as Dylan flew out into the open air, followed closely behind by Clara and Wade Quinn.

Dylan knew the risks involved. He had to get Wade and Clara as far away from everyone else as possible. No one else on his side had a second pulse, so he was the only one who could go toe to toe with the Quinns and live to tell about it.

"Clooger, get the hell out of here! Now! Go!"

"We can't find Faith," Clooger responded. "She's gone!"

Dylan hoped against all hope that Faith had been smart enough to run.

"Get your men and go!" Dylan shouted into his Tablet. He wasn't going to have a bloodbath on his hands, even if it meant putting Faith in danger. In a burst of activity, nine Drifters, including Clooger, left the scene and scattered far and wide. If they'd have seen where the one fallen Drifter had landed, they also would have found Faith. She was at his side, holding up his head with one hand.

"It's okay; you're fine," she mumbled. But the man was struggling to catch every breath, blood flowing over his beard from a gash in his temple. "Don't die on me. Don't!" Faith yelled.

The thought of having caused one more person to die was more than Faith could handle. She cried for help, but there was no one.

"They say you're the other one," the man coughed, his voice turning to a papery whisper. "Two by two. That's what they say."

Faith didn't understand. "Just stay alive, please. Don't die on me."

She reached for her Tablet, but it wasn't there. Searching the sky for any sign of help turned up nothing. Not only had she failed to put an end to Clara Quinn, she'd gotten another Drifter in trouble and dragged Dylan into the mess she'd made.

"Look at me," the man said. Faith's eyes were pooled with tears, but she did as she was told. The man had the kindest, gentlest eyes. Surrounded by all that long hair and the beard, they were the most striking thing to look at. He moved his hand to his heart and tapped it, "Your parents loved you," he said. "It broke their hearts, leaving you behind."

"Don't do this!" Faith said, but no amount of wishing was going to change the situation. The man's breathing was getting shorter. Faith could barely hear the words he was saying. He took another gasp of breath, smiled, and said one more thing.

"I'll tell them you were worth it."

He closed his eyes, and he was gone.

Faith hadn't imagined that all this would happen

when she went to confront Clara. She'd imagined a heroic fight to the death, just the two of them. But she'd been deadly wrong. How could things have turned so crazy so fast? She took a breath, wiped her eyes, tried to think.

What can I do?

What the hell can I possibly do?

She touched the tattoo on her neck and wished she could feel the searing pain of the needle.

And then, all at once, she knew the answer.

Dylan stood alone against one of the outside walls of the school, watching. Clara and Wade Quinn both had second pulses, which made them more than just invincible. Together, they were an unstoppable two-person army. Dylan knew how strong their powers of perception were. If anyone inside the mall so much as moved a spoon three inches across a table with their mind, Wade and Clara might feel it. They'd rip the place apart until they found the source.

Dylan knew better than anyone how high the stakes had become. He couldn't save the States alone, and the States had to be protected at all cost. States and locations like them existed around the world for a reason: a fragile planet couldn't sustain humanity without them. There was no going back to people spread out all over kingdom come. The infrastructure wasn't there to sustain that kind of future. And there was another reason the States had to be protected. Ninety percent of humanity resided inside them. A fallen State meant untold millions of casualties. Dylan would need Meredith and the Drifters. But more than that, he would need Hawk and Faith, and both of them were in serious danger. If Clara and Wade discovered the encampment inside the mall, things would take a sharp turn for the worse. He'd be left to navigate the coming wrath all by himself. Not a happy prospect, and not a battle he could win. He had to keep Clara and Wade as far away from the deserted mall as possible, and the best way to do that was to lure them away with a pulse.

He looked in the direction of the football field, then burst up in the air like he'd been shot from a gun. They sensed his presence immediately, taking chase behind him from two different corners of the Old Park Hill campus. He was pretty sure they already knew he had a second pulse, but they were about to discover just how powerful their new enemy was. Dylan lined himself up with the goalpost and stopped, hovering in the air as he turned his back on the field and faced the coming wrath of the Quinns. The field below was dark, so the vans couldn't be seen. His secret was safe as they stopped short, hanging in the air ten feet away from Dylan.

"I'm going to enjoy kicking you through that goal-post," Wade said. He had always felt threatened by Dylan. The fact that he was spending time with Faith Daniels, the only girl Wade had ever truly loved, made him want to tear Dylan limb from limb.

"I hear the games were a real success, only not for you," Dylan said.

Wade laughed. "Those clowns weren't worth my time, and you know it."

"Why don't you join us?" Clara asked. She imagined herself beside Dylan, taking on the world together. It was a far more enjoyable fantasy than doing the same work with her brother. "You don't want to be on the wrong side of what's coming. We could use someone like you."

Dylan half smiled in the darkness. "Killing Drifters is a hobby for you guys. I think we'd have a little conflict of interest there."

Wade could sense Clara's passion for Dylan, and it made him furious. Dylan had taken Faith and sided with the scum of the earth; but Dylan's ability to charm Clara's heart made things even worse for Wade, and that was the situation that pushed Wade into action. The goalpost began to sway behind Dylan, then the pole leading to the ground lurched free and spun up in the air. The end that had once been in the ground faced Dylan's back and fired like an arrow. Dylan somersaulted backward in the air, then steadied himself as he backed up, his long hair tangling into his face as the wind pushed against him.

"Looks like we don't have a future together," he said, lifting the first of six white vans in the air behind him. It was dark, but Clara sensed trouble, turning on the lights around the field with a series of sharp sounds. Dylan ducked, and the first van flew over his right shoulder, slamming dead-on into Clara and catching Wade in the legs as he tried to move. Wade spun wildly out of control, slammed into the ground, and rolled into a standing position.

He was smiling.

"This is going to be fun."

The van crushed Clara into the ground, but she was up and moving in a matter of seconds, feeling her anger start to burn. When she turned, the second van was already airborne, clobbering her to the ground again. They were punishing blows, but Clara seemed to grow stronger with each one.

"Now you're starting to make me mad," she said. It didn't cross her mind that Dylan might have a second pulse. She didn't think it was possible. She'd known about first-pulse Drifters and variants such as Faith— they weren't common, but they were around. A nuisance she took a lot of pleasure in dealing with. They were, at base, incredibly weak. So what if you could pick up a refrigerator and throw it? If you couldn't take a punch, it didn't matter. Eventually, you'd always lose.

Dylan threw two more vans, picking them up and guiding them to their targets. Wade couldn't react fast enough, and this time the van pummeled him into the bleachers. Clara put up a hand and forced the van coming at her to change course. She made it fly straight up in the air and left it hanging there.

"Last chance, Dylan Gilmore. You can come with us; I won't hurt you."

"I think I'll take my chances without you," Dylan responded. Clara was shocked when he took control of the van hanging in the air, dropping it with fantastic speed on her brother, who was barely getting up from the blow he'd just taken.

"Behind you!" Wade screamed, right before the goalpost, which had been lying on the ground behind Clara, slammed into her lower back. It was moving with such speed that it arched her back like a noodle, the two prongs hitting the ground and sliding into the earth until she was pinned against the football field.

Clara hated the taste of earth. She lifted her face, covered in grass and dirt, and felt the stinging sensation that meant her powers had been slightly compromised.

It would take a lot more than a chunk of grass to end Clara Quinn, but she'd played around long enough. If this was how Dylan wanted things to be, then he was about to get his wish.

"You had your chance," she said, blowing the goalpost out of the ground with her mind. It sailed over the school and crashed into a building hidden in the distance. She wiped a smear of what she thought was mud from her forehead, but when she looked at it in the stadium lights, she realized it was dirt mixed with her own blood. No one had ever made Clara Quinn bleed. It scared her, but more than that, it focused her mind on the task at hand. She was smart enough to realize that Dylan was learning her weakness: a hard enough impact into a living thing, such as a field of grass, could do damage.

She pulled one of the tall stadium lights out of the ground with the force of her will, turned the rotted wooden end in Dylan's direction, and fired. The lights sparked and popped on the tail end; and when the weapon hit Dylan in the chest, sending him tumbling end over end, she was surprised by her reaction. She felt her heart turn dry and brittle, like a dead flower on hot pavement. She looked at him lying there on the grass, not moving, and wished he wasn't a weak and useless first pulse.

Her wish, she was surprised to see, came true.

Dylan stood up. Unfazed, he plucked two more stadium lights out of the ground, their wires sparking against the black sky, and hurled them in her direction. She dodged them, but only barely, and realized the incredible truth.

"You're a second pulse?"

"Not possible!" Wade yelled. The idea that someone he hated as much as Dylan could have the same level of power was a reality Wade couldn't deal with. He focused all his energy on one of the smashed vans, picked it up, and hurled it with unprecedented speed. Dylan tried to move to one side, but Wade swerved the flying van in the same direction. The door connected solidly with the top half of Dylan's body, sending him end over end through the air as he tumbled across the field. Dylan was up almost before he was down, shaking the grass out of his thick hair and holding his ground. He had a look of quiet determination on his face as he wiped a smear of dirt and grass off his shoulder.

"I do hate a dirty T-shirt. Makes me crazy."

Clara shook her head slowly, looking across the field at Dylan like he were a ghost she couldn't believe she was seeing.

"I thought we were the only ones."

"Guess you thought wrong," Dylan said.

Clara's emotions, which she had never trusted as much as her intellect, were a tangled mess. She loved the thought of Dylan being like her. His power made him ten times more attractive. He was not her equal, but he was close, and this made him even harder to resist. And yet, this new information made another emotion well up in her chest. Fear. She'd never felt it before, and she didn't like it one bit. Passion was fine, but only if she was alive to enjoy it.

Wade was coming at Dylan at the same moment Clara was, and this was a big problem for Dylan. One of them he could take head-to-head, fighting them at least to a draw. But two was another story. Eventually they would discover his weakness, possibly by accident, and his second pulse would give out. He knew it was a fight he couldn't win, but he was going to throw as many punches as he could before it was too late. He threw the rest of the vans, trying to create a diversion so he could escape, but they picked up every object they could find. Dylan was fending off sections of the bleachers, random van parts that had blown free, entire vehicles, roofing tiles flying like ninja throwing stars—everything that wasn't nailed down tight was heading his way. He was taking hits from all sides as he backed up against the gymnasium wall, pinned down, with an endless array of objects crashing into every part of his body. He took special care to protect himself from flying rocks and boulders, ducking and moving so they wouldn't touch his skin. Everything else was fine; he could take a beating all day. But rock was Dylan's kryptonite. Like living things for Clara and Wade Quinn, a boulder had an especially damaging effect on Dylan Gilmore. A really big one could move past the power of his second pulse. He watched as one of the vans missed its mark by ten feet and blasted a hole through the cinder-block wall. As it did, a slab of cement the size of a car door broke free from the wall, spinning wildly until it struck Dylan square in the chest. His ears rang and his vision blurred as he tumbled head over heels along the cinder-block wall of the gym. When he came to a stop, the door was on top of him, the wide section of cinder block touching skin through his ripped T-shirt. He felt the weight like burning coals, searing the second pulse out of his heart. The cement slab felt like it weighed a million pounds.

"Dylan!"

He knew the voice and was immediately on high alert, looking to the sky for a sign of where she was. Seconds later the block of stone, which sat like granite on Dylan's chest, flew up in the air, turned sharply, and glanced past Clara's head on its way to landing in the bleachers.

"Looks like someone is back," said Clara, following

Dylan's gaze. "And that one, I know, is no second pulse."

She was full of pleasure at the idea of killing Faith Daniels. Nothing she could think of would give her so much pleasure. The problem was, she couldn't see Faith. She was up there, but the floodlights that remained turned everything behind them pitch-black.

"Come out, come out, wherever you are," Clara said teasingly. She'd stopped firing objects at Dylan, but Wade hadn't lost a beat. He continued to pummel Dylan against the cement wall, picking up the heaviest objects he could find and slamming them into Dylan again and again.

"Leave him alone!" Faith howled from the sky above. She'd moved directly over Clara and Wade.

"Faith, no! You can't kill them," Dylan yelled. "Just get out of here. Now!"

A van tire slammed into what remained of the gym wall near Dylan's head, and he dodged pieces of stone as they broke free; but he couldn't avoid them all. The second pulse was weakening. He really felt it, all the way down to his skate shoes.

Clara turned her attention to the stadium lights, turning them slowly in the direction of the sky. Everything on the field turned dark, but the sky above lit up as bright as could be. What she saw confused her; and looking up, it confused Wade as well.

"I said, leave him alone!" Faith screamed. They could only see her in fragments, because a huge swath of something was held skyward between them and Faith. Clara had a strange feeling in her belly, a sense that something wasn't right, and she looked at Wade.

"Go!" she yelled, but Wade just stood there, confused and angry. Clara started to fly as a net bigger than the football field started falling out of the sky. Dylan was far enough to the edge that he could fly up the side of the gymnasium, free of whatever fate awaited Wade and Clara in the center of the field.

Faith had flown back to the old grade school. She'd used every bit of strength she had to uproot the endless, tangled ivy from the walls of the old building. The net that came down on Clara and Wade Quinn was green and full of life. Clara became entangled in it first, feeling her strength fail her like never before. When it reached the ground, Wade tried to run, but it had him, too. Wade's vulnerability was the same as Clara's.

Dylan knew it wouldn't hold them for long, but he hoped it would be long enough. He came up alongside Faith and took her hand, high in the air.

"Not bad," he said, tugging gently. She looked less sad, more herself. The two of them would have been smart to get away from the Quinns as fast as possible, especially given that the floodlights were pointed up.

From her tangled mess on the ground, Clara wasn't trying to break free. She was putting every ounce of energy she had into one task. Her eyes focused on Faith Daniels, whom she could make out in bits and pieces through the vines that held her. She closed her eyes, thinking only of the hammer that lay in the gymnasium. She could feel it beginning to move as Dylan and Faith slowly started to drift away. Soon it would be out of the giant hole in the cinder-block wall and free in the sky.

"We need to move fast," Dylan said. "Everyone else is already gone."

"Gone? Where to?"

She held his hand tighter, felt the power of his presence up her arm and into her neck. When he turned to her, she wanted nothing more than to feel his lips on her own, to fix all the broken pieces of her life.

But that was not to be. She closed her eyes, leaned in as they moved across the sky, and then felt a blow to the back of her head that made her see stars and stars and stars. The pain was deep and sharp and full; but when it was gone, she understood the peace of feeling nothing at all.

Chapter 20

Morning Glory

No one, not even the people from inside the States, had any interest in the California coast. It was a place of extraordinary wreckage and pain. And unless you were an Intel like Hawk, finding a signal for Tablets was impossible. Feral cats and wild dogs roamed the streets of Valencia, a city that had once been fifty miles off the coast. It currently had a marvelous view of the ocean, and no one believed it would last forever. It was only a matter of time before Valencia, too, fell victim to the rising Pacific.

Valencia, California, had been chosen for this very reason. A place that was but might not be for long had a certain appeal for a rebellion. Abandoned buildings lined the streets like empty coffins. Time was what they needed. Time to prepare, to plan, to gain skills they hadn't yet acquired.

"We've got at least four months," Hawk said. He'd calculated the time it would take for the unrelenting ocean to devour their hideaway. "That enough time?"

"Yeah, that should do it," Dylan answered. He'd been quieter than usual during the first two weeks, but now he wondered aloud how Hawk's parents were doing. "I'm glad we could bring them along. They okay today?"

Hawk shrugged. Both of his parents were second-generation Intels, two of the last remaining of their kind. They were part themselves, part Hotspur Chance, and slowly losing their minds.

"I don't think they'll be leaving when we do," he said. After being recruited and talking to Meredith alone, he understood that once the real downward spiral began with his parents, it was only a matter of months, not years, before they'd be gone. He sometimes couldn't believe how recently they'd seemed only book-ish, reading away most of the day in silence. Now they were more like idiot savants, staring at things for hours on end, almost never speaking, typing unintelligible nonsense into their Tablets. The idea that he might end up the same way, if he lived that long, was something he preferred not to think about unless he was forced to.

"I'm sorry to hear that," Dylan said clumsily, not knowing how to comfort his young friend. Hawk was smarter than Dylan could ever hope to be. It was hard to say how he dealt with certain emotional traumas. It had been Dylan who'd taken Hawk's Tablet more than once, each time passing it to Meredith so she could see for sure. Over the course of several different opportunities with Hawk's Tablet she'd come to know for sure that he was an Intel, possibly the youngest of his kind. And she'd known, too, that someone of his intellect would be necessary if they stood a chance in what lay ahead.

Hawk shrugged, a reaction that was becoming more commonplace as the weight on his shoulders grew heavier. He would be counted on for many things in the days to come, tasks no one else could achieve. Sometimes, he knew, saying nothing was the safest response. This was certainly true when it applied to his parents.

"And her?" Dylan asked. He'd spent another night watching Faith sleep. He'd become accustomed to this during the long months of her early training, and he'd enjoyed watching her for as many hours as she would stay in bed. Now he only wished she'd wake up.

"She's not losing brain functions, as far as I can tell,"

Hawk said. He'd been monitoring her vital signs since their arrival ten days earlier. "But she can't stay like that forever. She needs to wake up pretty soon."

"How soon is pretty soon?" Dylan asked. Hawk shrugged. It was one of the few questions he couldn't answer.

Dylan glanced into the corner of the room and felt a wave of regret. The ball and chain lay in a heap on the tile floor. Looking at it reminded him of how he'd failed her. Hawk followed his gaze.

"What a couple of a-holes."

"You said it," Dylan replied, and he couldn't help smiling.

"Let's don't let them win," Hawk said, then he passed through the doorway and left Dylan and Faith alone in the room.

Dylan spent the next hour trying to coax her awake. He did this by concentrating on her, lifting her a foot off the bed with his mind, holding her in his arms in a weightless state of dreaming.

"Come on, Faith. I can't do this without you. I won't make it."

Between himself, Hawk, and Faith, they might stand a chance. Wade was dangerous and unpredictable, and he was a second pulse. It would take everything Dylan had when the time came, and he wasn't near ready yet.

Wade would get stronger, he was sure of that much. Dylan would need to get stronger, too. But Clara was the real problem.

"We won't be able to stop them without her. Not with Clara on their side."

Meredith had come into the room, or almost in. She was standing in the doorway, looking at her son.

"I know," Dylan said. "Clara Quinn, the only one with all three."

Meredith frowned, her papery skin folding into tight wrinkles around the edges of her mouth. "First pulse, second pulse, and Intel, all rolled up into one tidy package. I don't think even Clara knows how powerful she is."

Clara Quinn, the whole deal in one strikingly beautiful girl. She was unstoppable unless they had Hawk's intellect and another second pulse. And the only second pulse they could hope for was Faith. She had the traits; she was young enough; she'd been carefully groomed. Dylan held her in his arms and wished for something that was starting to feel impossible.

"We could hold them back," Dylan said. His mother could be cold; he knew this about her. But she could train them all in ways no one else could. And she loved him more than anyone else, certainly more than his father ever had.

"True," Meredith said. "But eventually they'd pre-vail. It's what Andre wants. It's what *Gretchen* wants. And they generally get what they want unless someone stronger shows up."

"You don't think I can do it?"

"No, I don't. Sorry, champ, there's only one of you. And one's not enough."

It hurt that she didn't believe enough in him to think he could get the job done, but he also knew she spoke the truth. It was simple math that even Wade could figure out. There were two of them and one of him. He could never do it all by himself.

"Training session in an hour," Meredith said. "Bet-ter get something to eat. Clooger is making waffles, and we found a huge stash of coffee at the old Trader Joe's. Who'd of thought something that special would get left behind?"

Coffee and waffles sounded good, but Dylan didn't follow Meredith. He could eat later; there were sure to be leftovers the way Clooger cooked.

"Faith, please."

He didn't know what else to say. He'd brought her into this mess, and now she was practically lifeless in his arms. She'd saved him on the field at Old Park Hill. If it hadn't been for her, he'd still be pinned under a slab of concrete, his second pulse lost forever. The only thing that moved was her chest. In and out. In and out. Slow and steady, like she were resting up for something that would take everything she had.

Dylan let her go, and she floated above the bed. He'd found bright yellow sheets at the deserted Bed Bath & Beyond. He thought they looked happy, like the daisies she drew sometimes, and figured they'd be cool against her skin. He lowered her to the sheets, letting her head rest softly on the pillow. He'd waited all this time to kiss her because he had a feeling about a kiss that scared him half to death. It felt to him that it would either be a kiss good-bye or that it would be the thing that would bring her back. It was stupid, he knew, but that was how he felt about it. Kissing her would be serious business.

He was sixteen, and he'd never been in love. Looking at Faith, he realized how much he needed her, and not just because they had no chance without her. He needed her in order to keep breathing. Every day she was gone was like a death march, walking through the day in a fog, his heart heavy like the hammer.

"I'm going to kiss you now," he said. Enough was enough. At least he could do it while she was alive and in a state in which she couldn't say *Gross! Back off, loser.*

He leaned over her body, touched the soft skin of her arm. His hand drifted down to her hand, which he had kept soft with half-hardened lotion he'd found at the Bath & Body Works. He put his ear to her mouth and felt her soft breath as it escaped from her nose in waves. He could feel the air going in and coming out, like the tides that would soon cover the very room he sat in.

Dylan touched her face with the palm of his hand, turning her slightly in his direction. Her face was incredibly soft, and he wondered if the trembling in his fingers would wake her. He touched his lips to hers and pressed in close. Seconds passed and Faith didn't move. He pulled away, tried again. He wasn't going to stop until she moved or gave him a sign. He would stay right there all day if that's what it took. But this, too, was dumb. It was a sort of final insult that he knew he couldn't sit next to her bed kissing her all day long. Bittersweet. He tingled with excitement because he was kissing the girl he loved. But she didn't move, and that definitely ruined everything.

He pulled back very slowly, letting the full weight of disappointment sink in. But then he realized it was her hand, not his, that was creating a sense of pressure on his palm. She was holding his hand, not the other way around. He watched her face, saw the smallest beginning of a smile, and kissed her again.

Faith was still a moment longer. Was she awake and

enjoying the moment, or had it all been the unconnected movements of a girl in a coma? But then she pushed Dylan away and drew a great, bottomless breath, her eyes wide with a knowing she couldn't express. Her breathing steadied, and she spoke in a leathery whisper.

"I felt it."

"Sorry, I—I'm sorry," Dylan stammered. He was overjoyed that she was awake, embarrassed that he'd kissed her while she was unconscious.

Faith smiled, larger this time, and pulled him close by his white, V-neck T-shirt. This time it was her kissing him. When they parted she said it again.

"I felt it."

"I felt it, too."

Faith shook her head gently. She wasn't talking about the feel of his soft lips against hers. She was talking about something else. All at once Dylan understood what it was.

"You felt a second pulse. Are you sure?"

Faith nodded, smiling, and pulled him into a hug.

"Pick me up again," she said. "I like when you hold me."

Dylan lifted her off the bed and wished she weighed more than she did. She'd need time to gain back her strength.

"My kisses are kind of amazing," Dylan said. "Are

you sure you felt a second pulse? Might have been me."

Faith thought about what a second pulse meant: nothing the world could throw at her could do any damage. She looked into Dylan's eyes and wondered if that included a kiss. She took his hand and placed it on her neck, pressing his fingers firmly into the seam under her chin. And then she thought about her second pulse, which was growing stronger inside her. Dylan felt the first pulse, strong and steady, and right behind it, a shadow pulse, softer but definitely there.

"Meredith is going to be very pleased," he said.

"Let's not tell her just yet. Can we get back in bed?"

Dylan shut the door to the room with his mind and let Faith float free out in front of him, laying her gently on the small bed. He turned and lay down beside her, and Faith placed her fingers on the soft part of his neck, searching for a pulse.

A time of trouble was coming. It would test their devotion and push them to the very limits of their strength. But for the moment it was just the two of them alone, thinking only of each other at the edge of the battered world.

A week later Faith was sitting on the very same cot on a bright, early morning. She was not alone, as the needle stabbed her over and over again. It had run two circles around her forearm already, and now they'd come to the hardest part.

Faith was glad Glory was one of them, glad she'd made the move with the Drifters.

"Come to the end of the chain," Glory said. "Last part's gonna hurt the most."

The needle was busy humming, doing its work on the palm side of Faith's wrist. It was a sensitive area, like the skin on the back side of her legs.

"It all hurts, Glory. That's why I do it."

"You keep talking like that and it'll get under your skin, do some real damage."

Without even realizing it, Faith had discovered her own weakness. The fact that the needle could penetrate her skin at all was a mystery. She had a second pulse. It should have been protecting her from anything that could harm her, but the needle was going in and out; the million little shocks of pain were real. She wondered if, in the end, the sharp tip of a knife would find its way to her heart.

"Those other two, they were for different reasons, weren't they?" Glory asked. It was the first time Glory had tattooed a part of Faith's body that was in full view. A chain wound around Faith's forearm, tangled with ivy. They'd come to the heavy part of the hammer, the metal ball. Glory kept applying the black color, running the needle around in circles and wiping away the excess ink.

"Why didn't you go to the State?" Faith asked, ignoring Glory's question.

Glory had a story of her own, but that was for another time. "They wouldn't know what to do with me in there."

Faith laughed softly, wincing as Glory worked the needle. She stopped for a moment, turned off the machine, stared at Faith.

"You gonna hold this hammer, you better be ready to use it."

"I'm ready," Faith said, extending her arm out and squeezing her hand into a fist, feeling the lingering pain of the needle shoot up and down her skin. "And I know what it's for."

"What's it for?" Glory asked, though she knew the answer.

"It's for killing. The hammer is for killing."

The thought of being able to take as many blows as Clara Quinn could dish out was intoxicating.

They both grew quiet after that, listening to the buzzing sound of the tattoo being applied.

An hour later, Faith's arm was bandaged up and she was walking. The Six Flags wasn't very far, and seeing all the roller coaster tracks saddened her. Water sloshed at her feet until she came to the ride she wanted to find.

It was called Apocalypse, an old wooden relic that had once thrilled teenagers on sunbaked California weekends. Now it was falling apart. One entire section had collapsed, but the highest point of the ride remained intact. She flew up and sat down on the iron track, letting her legs dangle free in the air over the edge.

The thought crossed her mind to simply throw away the letter. What good would it do to dredge up more feelings she didn't want to deal with? She was healing, she was getting stronger. Going backward never struck her as a useful endeavor. But in the end she couldn't do it. She was honor bound to at least read whatever her parents had left behind, no matter how much it might hurt. And so she tore open the envelope, stuffing it into her back pocket and unfolding the paper. She read fast so it would be over quickly.

Faith,

Do you know why we called you that? It was because we believed, against all odds, that you'd be okay. You were our happy accident. We would not have chosen to bring a baby into the world we lived in. But once you arrived, we loved everything about you. We wanted nothing more than to keep you safe and make you happy.

*This was not to be, and for that we're very
sorry. We knew what we were, and we knew what
was coming; and we kept these things from you for
as long as we could. Maybe we shouldn't have, but
we did. It's something we'll have to live with.*

*By now you know most of what we would
have told you if we'd been brave enough to say
the words. But in case you don't know everything,
know this:*

*There is a great evil in the world. It comes to
destroy. We aren't strong enough to stop it. But in
time you will be. Find love, for love in a broken
world will comfort you. Hold on to hope; it will
sustain you. Have faith, for in the end it will save
you. Remember these things, always.*

*With all our love,
Mom and Dad*

Faith folded up the letter and found it a little bit
surprising that she wasn't crying. She'd already cried
so much for so many things, there weren't any tears
left. She looked out over the ocean and thought of her
parents and Liz. She thought of the broken world she'd
been born into and all the mysteries she didn't understand.

And then she let the letter go, watching it bend and flutter on the wind as it was carried out to sea on the power of her own thoughts.

The past was gone, and a new strength welled up inside her. The future would be a fight.

"Bring it on," Faith Daniels said.

And then she flew home.

The Prison

"This isn't going exactly as planned."

Andre had known there would be risks, but he couldn't have imagined his own daughter disobeying him the way she had. He'd let himself believe she was ready when she was not.

"I'll handle Clara," Gretchen said. "You just make sure Wade is ready when we need him."

"I hate having to regroup. It goes against my better judgment."

Gretchen wasn't so sure. "They weren't ready. It would have been a disaster if we'd set things in motion now. Her choice helped us see that."

Andre had to admit that Gretchen was right. Still, he'd never liked hiding out, and there had been far too much of it lately. What he really wanted was to knock down a few buildings, to really wreak some havoc. Inflicting damage on the Western State was high on his priority list. He wanted the world the way it had been before the States, and he understood that this goal would require a certain level of force.

Gretchen touched his hand, looking at the gray coming in around his temples. She understood his motives and the complicated past they shared.

"Patience is a virtue," Gretchen said. "It won't be long now."

Wade and Clara came through a doorway on the far end of the facility. They both had a swagger that told Gretchen everything she needed to know. "At least we understand what they're capable of. That question has been answered."

"Agreed."

Andre tapped a message into his Tablet and waited. He was standing with Gretchen on the concrete floor of an abandoned prison. A long, open hallway with prison cells on each side ran the length of the space.

By the time Wade and Clara were standing in front of him, the catwalk that ran a circle around the space was filled with people. All at once, they jumped over the rail, gliding down to the floor as an army of one. Faith, Dylan, and Hawk had their first-pulse Drifters for some of the help they'd need. But the Quinns would have help in the coming fight, too, and plenty of it.

Andre surveyed his team and smiled, a low growl in his voice.

"Let's get busy."

Many feel the tremor. Few know its power.

Read on for a sneak peek of the second book
in Patrick Carman's **PULSE** series

TREMOR

Chapter 1

Leaving on a Jet Plane

Long before Faith Daniels and Dylan Gilmore found each other on the ragged edges of the broken world outside, a woman was lying on her bed alone, thinking about leaving the one she loved. The thought was like one she'd had a long time before, and it surprised her, because, really, in all the intervening years, the idea had never crossed her mind again.

What would become of me if I left this place and these people behind?

But once the idea was in there, bouncing off the tender walls of her mind like a bee trapped in a cloth sack, she knew her time with these people was coming to an end. She concluded without a hint of emotion that it was the pregnancy. That was the thing that had led her to this bouncing bee of an idea. It was a course of action that would do more than just sting if she followed its pull on her imagination. It would, in due time, spill some serious blood.

Oddly enough, it was the exact same thought some ten years earlier that had led her to Hotspur Chance in the first place. It was during a time in her life when she was two essential things at once: ruthlessly intelligent and disastrously unwise. She did not see eye to eye with her parents about what the future held, not only for them, but for all people. And when she debated with coworkers, she wielded her ideas with cunning and vigor. Eventually, no one wanted to argue with her, and after a time she became something of a loner. Clutching a ticket in her hand, trying to imagine what it would be like to fly through the air, her brilliance and her lack of experience were about to get her into some real trouble.

There were still a small number of airplanes flying between airports in those days, and she had found herself singing a very old, melancholy song as she fled from the place of her birth, away from her parents. The song was about a girl, or so she imagined, who was leaving on a jet plane and was hoping that the one she loved would still be there if she ever returned.

It was a love song, she knew, and not having a person to leave behind had made her feel sorry for herself. For all her intellectual power, she had failed to attract the right person at the right time. Love was like a velvet-lined box locked with an unsolvable combination. It had completely eluded her, this all-important aspect of adult life, producing a sort of simmering sadness she couldn't shake.

She wiped her tears in the nearly empty airport and tried to focus on the fact that in a world gone mad, at least she had been chosen, and not by just anyone, but chosen by the man who had envisioned the States and, by all accounts, was well on his way to saving the planet. He was not waiting at the gate when she arrived, as she'd hoped he would be. Someone else was there. He was about her age, with dark hair and a big, awkward smile.

"I'm so glad you decided to join us, really I am. You're going to be so pleased."

They exchanged pleasantries and names, and he escorted her to a white van, the kind that usually picked up those who wanted to enter the Western State. More and more people were streaming into the States, simply leaving everything behind, not turning back. And there was no room inside the States for a U-Haul full of personal belongings. It was part of the deal with the

States: come as you are, bring your Tablet, leave everything else. Her own parents had talked of leaving, and it struck her as she stood outside on the cracked pavement that she might never see them again. She could return home and find that they, too, had abandoned the outside world without her.

The white van deposited them in the desert, where the young man with the gleaming smile opened her door, touching her elbow softly as he pointed toward a low-slung building sitting all alone. The desert heat took her breath away, like stepping into a sauna, and she hoped the building had air-conditioning. She would never forget how white the van looked against the endless, sandy wasteland as it pulled away and left her behind.

"There are no rules in there. You can't imagine what he's like, what he's accomplished."

"I don't know. My imagination is pretty big," she said.

"Not this big."

And it turned out that he was right. Hotspur Chance, the man who had solved the global climate problem and invented the States, had turned his attention to human biology and the mind. When someone as brilliant as Chance started meddling with DNA, the results were bound to be astounding.

Chance had heard the prevailing idea that humans use only 10 percent of their brains. He knew this claim was patently false, because any part of the brain that isn't used quickly dies. People use only 10 percent of their brain's *potential*. Not so with Hotspur Chance. He used 90 percent of his brain's potential and was said to help others do the same. And it wasn't through mind-enhancing drugs or rewiring or shock therapy. He simply knew how to unlock astounding levels of human potential in certain individuals.

"I was hoping you would take me up on my invitation. I'm very pleased you've decided to join us. Come, sit down."

Those were Hotspur Chance's first words when she arrived. In hindsight, they were eerily similar to the greeting she'd gotten from the man who'd picked her up at the airport. Chance's mention of the invitation reminded her of how she had come to be standing there in the first place. She had taken an unusual test on her Tablet, one that everyone was being asked to take, and apparently her results were promising. The test involved looking at objects on what appeared to be a static picture of a table. There was a green apple, a red ball, a Coin, a knife, a picture. The test had asked her to move those objects with her mind, and while she had assumed it was a trick, she had been successful. She had even sent the knife flying up in the air, turning, and stabbing into the wood of the table.

"How about we see if you can do it for real, shall we?"

Hotspur Chance seemed to read her mind, to understand what she was thinking. Or maybe it was just obvious, given that he was sitting behind the very table from the test and the same objects awaited her. What else would she be thinking about?

"Think about the object you want to move," Hotspur said. "Look at it. Now control it."

Besides his prematurely gray hair cut very close to his head, Hotspur Chance didn't look a day over thirty-five. Everyone knew he was at least sixty, but the skin on his face was tight and crisp, his eyes bright and youthful. He assumed that Meredith was distracted, so he narrowed his instruction.

"Think about the apple," he went on. "Look at it."

It wasn't what she would have called a proper introduction, and looking around the room at the faces staring at her, she began to wonder why she'd come at all. There was another woman in the room. She was tall, with severe, striking eyes that seemed to be saying something.

Why are you looking at me? He told you to look at the apple. Look at it.

She glanced at the young man who had picked her up at the airport, appreciated his warm smile, and turned her attention to the work at hand. It was then that she noticed the one difference about the objects before her: the apple in the test she'd already taken had been green. This one was red.

"Move the apple," Hotspur Chance said. "Bring it under your mind's control."

That was how it had begun, all those years ago, as the apple wobbled and rolled and fell off the table.

"It's too bad," the woman with the severe eyes said. "Not what we hoped for."

"It's enough," said the dark-haired young man with the winning smile.

As time went on the isolation bothered her, but the experiments didn't. In fact, she rather liked the attention as her powers grew more profound. In time she mastered the movement of larger objects with her mind: barrels of water, a motorcycle, even a car. They never spoke of the red apple, and it never really crossed her mind that the only other red objects she ever saw during her time there were attached to Hotspur himself. He wore a red lab coat over a pressed white shirt and red tie, but somehow the color never came up.

The training was enough to distract her from the slow and nearly unnoticeable descent into what could only be described later as worship. She came to see Hotspur Chance as everyone else did, as something more than a man. Nearly a decade later, as the world outside continued to empty into the States, she had the first inkling that she may have stumbled into a cult of the most dangerous kind.

"The States aren't exactly what I imagined them to be," Hotspur confessed. "We may need to make some, how shall we say, *alterations.*"

Hotspur filled their minds with ideas she knew were wrong. But it wasn't long before she had fallen in love with the dark-haired young man, and he was the one to assure her that everything Hotspur was telling them would all make sense in the end. Hotspur Chance had saved the world and given them these remarkable powers. He fed them, clothed them, kept them safe. He knew what was best.

And so she hung on. She grew more powerful in the ways in which she could. She tried to withstand Hotspur's overpowering will. She hoped certain events would never come to pass, terrible things that these people were plotting. Until one day she woke up pregnant and the buzzing bee of an old idea got stuck in her head once more.

What would become of me if I left this place and these people behind?

She had a man to leave now; and kissing him as he slept, she imaged him kissing her back, smiling for her, saying that he'd wait for her. She stepped outside and sang the old song in her head, but she knew there were no more planes to catch. Those days were gone. And this turned out to be all right, because she didn't need an airplane to put some miles behind her. By then she could fly away all by herself.

The man she left behind was Andre Quinn.

The steely-eyed woman who would take her place was Gretchen.

The children who would be born in her absence were the twins, Wade and Clara Quinn.

This woman who flew away was Meredith. Seventeen years later, she would become the rogue leader of a nearly hopeless resistance.

And the baby she was carrying grew into a young man who had not one but two pulses. His name was Dylan Gilmore, and though he asked many times, Meredith never told him who his father was.

A time was coming when Dylan would need to know.

Chapter 2

Bowling Ball Spin Cycle

Faith Daniels was standing in the middle of a large, empty meat locker when the first red bowling ball lifted off the floor and began turning from side to side. The holes where her fingers and thumb would have gone if she were actually bowling looked like a round nose and two vacant eyes boring down on her from thirty feet away. Faith steadied her nerves, shifting her weight from side to side as she focused her mind, and ran her hand through the air in front of her.

"Let's see if a little noise throws you off," she whispered, not loud enough for the five drifters standing behind the floating balls of urethane to hear what she was saying. She hadn't touched all the empty hooks hanging down into the room, but she'd made them dance like chimes in a hot summer wind.

Four more red bowling balls rose up in the air, surrounding her from every side in the soft light and the clanging metal hooks.

Each of the balls weighed ten pounds or more, and they suddenly moved as if they'd been shot from five cannons, fired into the center of the room.

Faith had only recently mastered red objects, a color that presented serious problems for second pulses when they were new to the craft of moving objects with their minds. First pulses, like the drifters in the room with her, didn't have any trouble at all with the color red. It was one of the ways that Meredith, the leader of the drifters rebellion, had known Faith had two pulses even before Faith knew it herself. Meredith had never forgotten how easy it had been to move the red apple so many years ago when she'd first met Hotspur Chance. It had told him Meredith would never have a second pulse. Not so with Faith Daniels. Faith could deflect anything and everything that came her way. She was invincible.

Everything inside Faith screamed *Move!* But she knew moving wouldn't solve anything. These drifters were among the most experienced fighters in the rebellion. They knew how to zero in on a target whether it was moving or not. The best way to deal with red, Faith knew, was to stay still. She closed her eyes, balled up her fists, and held her breath. When the five bowling balls surrounded her in the middle of the meat locker all at once, she felt them nudging her, but only barely. She turned them away like marbles bouncing on pavement, returning fire at twice the speed. The drifters, all of whom were in mortal danger with no second pulse to protect them, dived for the floor as the balls ricocheted off metal walls and slammed into fluorescent lights overhead.

"Take it easy!" one of the drifters yelled.

Faith gathered all the bowling balls and lined them up like train cars, setting them in motion. They moved so fast it was like watching a ring of fire encircling the wide perimeter of the space. The drifters tried to take control of something—anything—but found that Faith was far too powerful to overcome in a confined space. She picked up all of the five drifters, one by one, and hung them on meat hooks by their long trench coats.

"Don't overdo it, Faith. I mean it."

Meredith's voice over the loudspeaker had the tone and quality of a drill sergeant. It was unmistakable.

Faith appeared not to be listening as the bowling balls changed course.

"Faith," Meredith said. "I know red makes you

angry. You have to control your rage. Understand?"

The bowling balls hovered several feet over the heads of the drifters. They were wearing football helmets, which they'd procured from the sporting goods store in a nearby deserted mall. The meat hooks clanged louder and louder as Faith made the balls spin in place and began lowering them toward the people who had thrown them.

"Don't say I didn't warn you," Meredith said.

The doors to the meat locker burst open, a streak of bright light bathing the room. Faith unlatched two of the long hooks, carrying one in each hand as she walked out into the light. As soon as she reached the opening, the real onslaught began. Dylan and a troop of drifters had recently raided a Sears down the street, where thirty or more washers and dryers had been lined up. For a person with the pulse, they were a very nicely sized object for throwing. The appliances were the equivalent of a softball for a normal person and even felt about that big in Dylan's mind as he threw one after another, raining down metal on Faith as she dodged out of the doorway. She used the bowling balls like antiaircraft fire, slamming them into washers and dryers as they came near her. Shards of metal flew past her on all sides, and anything that made it through was slashed and chopped by the meat hooks she carried.

Faith was out of control and loving every second of it, taking everything Dylan threw at her and shoving it right back down his throat.

A drifter was standing off to the side of the training area, and when he decided to pick up a truck tire and throw it in Faith's general direction, Faith turned on him. The tire flipped through the air, and Faith sent a bowling ball through the hole, slamming it into a concrete pillar the drifter was hiding behind. Had it connected with its target, the drifter might not have lived.

"Enough!" Meredith yelled. She was standing on a grated platform overhead, staring down over a paint-chipped rail.

All the washers and dryers and bowling balls fell to the floor at once, and with a brush of her arm, Meredith cleared away the mess. It was as if a giant broom had swept across the floor and pushed everything away.

"Too bad you don't have a second pulse," Faith said, staring up at her as she dropped the metal hooks with a loud clang. "You'd be one badass mother—"

"Let's reset and try the storm simulation," Meredith interrupted. "And this time, how about we dispense with the theatrics?"